Beyond the Third Garden

Iraj Sarfeh

Beyond the Third Garden

By Iraj Sarfeh
© 2016 Iraj Sarfeh

Previously published by Musa Publishing, 2014.

Tell-Tale Publishing Group, LLC

Swartz Creek, MI 48473

Cover design by Clarissa Yeo

Printed in United States of America

Wise Words Publishing   Cosmos Imprint

For my wonderful family.

past as inner demons are released into the light of day. The book also adds a welcome look into traditional, hospitable Iranian culture and the lilt of spoken Farsi to many readers that would otherwise know little of this language or its people, beyond the political headlines. I applaud the author for the raw honesty, emotional pain and clear understanding of the human condition he has fashioned here into beautifully crafted, memorable passages. This was a genre departure for me, but I'm looking forward to the next work author Sarfeh completes, in which ever genre his stories unfold. —Richard Sutton, Five Stars, Goodreads

Foreword

Over the years of our frequent strolls along the lakeshore, Paree and I explored the early days of our relationship, talking about ourselves and each other in the third person, hoping the more dispassionate approach to self-analysis would free us to bare feelings that were far from dispassionate. We vented the crypts of our most painful memories, revealing every minute detail because we knew holding back was the obstacle to recovery. And as we vented, we learned much about ourselves, each other, and the horrific circumstances that brought us together.

Now, gazing over the clear waters of Little Loch Broom, at last I feel strong enough to expose our secrets to all who might benefit from learning of our hazardous journey on the road to health— secrets that threatened our escape from the prison of tormented souls.

Chapter 1

January 7, 1943: Bourton-on-the-Water, England.

Fearing the worst, Paree ran through the pastures and mist-blurred woods, searching for her son. Little John hadn't slept in his bed—another manifestation of his strange behavior since he returned from North Africa. She burst into the gray barn, where a week before, she had found him lying in the hay, staring at nothing. Maybe he was thinking about life before Tobruk, or maybe he was thinking about death in Tobruk. "Come back to the cottage and I'll cook you a nice English breakfast," she had told him, but he kept staring at nothing and muttered, "Just leave me alone, Mother."

She called out his name, but he didn't respond. Hearing a rustling sound from above, she climbed a wobbly ladder to the loft and saw a pair of slate eyes glowing in the dimness. The neighbor's cat hissed at her.

After rushing out of the barn, she ran past the cows and bales of hay and the rusted tractor that hadn't moved in years. Pausing at the edge of a field near her cottage, she looked up toward the crest but couldn't see the chestnut tree for the mist. When Little John was much younger, he loved to climb that tree, hiding there until she came looking for him. The mischievous imp would plop chestnuts on her head, and she would shout, "It's those rascally squirrels again!" He would giggle and shout back, "I was the rascally squirrel, Mummy." It was his ritual for the start of Saturday mornings, and maybe he was hiding in the tree now, reclaiming his better Saturdays.

Trudging through uncut grass, sidestepping cow dung, Paree hurried up the field until the chestnut tree's ghostlike silhouette came into view.

She froze.

* * * *

November 2, 1950: Karaj, Iran.

Just before dawn, Reza startled awake on cold ground, fearing something terrible had happened. A woman was squatting by his side, stroking his head. "Sleep, little boy, sleep. The bad situation is over."

He jumped up and stared toward the shack. It seemed eerie in the moon glow as light rays danced on the walls like giant blue moths. Parked in front of the shack was a police car with spinning blue lights on the roof. Three policemen were pulling Mama to the car. As they were about to push her inside, Reza shouted, "Mama! Mama! Don't let them take you!"

She looked at him over her shoulder and smiled even though her face was bloodied, her nose bent, her teeth broken. "You are a wonderful boy, Reza-*jan*. Don't ever forget that." He ran to the policemen and tried to pull Mama away from them, but they shoved him into the dirt and shoved her into the car. One of them bent over him and fired questions about what had happened in the shack. Despite the stinging slaps to his face, Reza couldn't remember anything. The officer spat at him and left.

Later that morning, Reza found himself at a home for kids without homes, and ten days later, at a home for kids without parents.

Chapter 2

They dumped him in the orphanage as dust and dirt swirled in fierce desert winds howling like jackals. It was a day when hawks flew against the wind without making headway, hovering over him, preparing for the kill. As if he were their helpless prey.

And that was how he felt. Helpless.

Moments after Reza arrived, Agha Mansur, The Principal, summoned him to his office and showed him a newspaper clipping with Mama's grainy photograph to one side. Mansur read the headline aloud: *Husband-killer Dies in Prison.* He said it was a good thing Reza's mother died. Otherwise, she would have been hung as a murderer—probably in Ferdowsi Square, where spectators could watch her dangling off the end of a rope and throw stones at her carcass.

Reza lost control, screaming, kicking, and punching until Mansur clamped him in a headlock, dragged him up two flights of stairs, and threw him into *otagh-e zendan*—the prison room.

Slumped against a wall, Reza closed his eyes and scoured his memory of That Night. But his mind could only summon up terrifying images that flashed on and off like lightning at night, illuminating ghostly shapes for a few heartbeats, long enough to frighten him into fits of violent shivering. Images of waving bottles, groping hands, scarlet eyebrows. He tried to blank them by thinking about the good days, and as long as he held on to the pleasant thoughts, the images didn't reappear.

The only way to cope was by living in the pleasant side of his imagination.

* * * *

For Reza, three months of hell at the orphanage crawled by at an old donkey's pace.

On a cold winter morning, the children stood in line behind the serving counter to collect their breakfasts: moldy naan, smelly cheese, watery tea. They sat on benches alongside plastic-covered tables—nine tables, Reza had counted, each with six kids. His multiplication wasn't very good, so one night in bed, he finger-counted nine six times and come up with fifty-four. Fifty-four kids without parents.

Most of them were nasty kids, except Fereshteh, which means "angel" in Farsi. He thought it was the perfect name for her. She didn't mind if he was quiet and distant, if he looked angry, sad, or empty. She would sit by his side during recess and stare at nothing, like he did.

Every so often, they would talk in a near whisper, as though the words passing between them couldn't be shared with anyone else. Their secret little garden of unspoken feelings and whispered words. There, he imagined walking hand in hand with her, stopping to pick fruits, smell the *yasmin*, and listen to bluebirds warbling in the pomegranate trees of the gardens where he lived before That Night.

That day was no different. Nine a.m. class came and went, and Agha Mansur scolded him for staring out into the courtyard, watching a hawk feather fluttering about at the mercy of the desert gusts—just as Reza was at the mercy of Agha Mansur and The Proctor. If only he could fly like a hawk… If only…

"Reza, if I catch you daydreaming again, you'll get six strokes in front of the class."

Six swishes from the stick to his palms. They didn't hurt much though, because he had grown calluses from when he labored in the gardens and from the two- or three-times-a-week beatings. "I'll tame you yet," Mansur kept telling him, but the more beatings he got, the less they hurt. Besides, for some reason, pain had become like any other unpleasant feeling: no better, no worse. Like hunger or thirst. Since That Night, feelings had become strangely dulled. Everything had become strangely dulled except Reza's imagination, where he lived while in bed, in the prison room, or during daydream moments.

At midmorning recess, he went into the courtyard, a walled-off cement block strewn with wastepaper, dirt, and bird droppings. Weeds sprouted between the cracks, somehow surviving in the dryness of the desert known as *Dasht-e* Kavir. Every Saturday after morning class, Agha Mansur gave one of the kids a broom to sweep up the place, and often he picked on Reza. Reza didn't mind though, because he could busy himself, no one would bother him, and he could daydream undisturbed.

Bolted into cement in the middle of the yard was an old swing set, the seats gone and ropes fraying. Some of the boys would hang onto the ends of the ropes, swing around in circles, and shout, "Look at me, I'm Tarzan!"

A few days earlier, Fereshteh had caught Reza gazing at the swing set and told him no one should play with ropes. "They're bad things," she said, "because the police hang people from them." Distressed at hearing about ropes and hangings, he covered his ears, and she stopped talking.

Leaning against a wall now, he thought about life outside the orphanage. Abdullah, who was at least two years older, stepped in front of him.

"Did you wet your mattress again last night, little boy?"

The words hurt, and Reza started to walk away, but Abdullah kicked him hard in the rear and yelled, *"Pedar-sag-e kassif!"* Dirty son of a dog!

The fog of rage suddenly clouding his mind, Reza dove at him. They rolled to the ground, dust, dirt, and fists flying. Abdullah was bigger and he landed more blows, bloodying his opponent's nose, but Reza fought back like a crazed animal, clawing, kicking, head butting. A dozen boys formed a circle around them and shouted, "Kill him, Abdullah! Kill him!" Within moments, Agha Mansur stepped in, grabbed the fighters by the collars, and jerked them up. He dismissed Abdullah and stood before Reza, towering over him like an angry giant.

"This is the third time in a week I've caught you fighting," he growled. "What's your excuse now?"

"Nothing, sir."

"You have a bad temper. I'll tame it, along with all your other repulsive traits."

"What are repulsive traits, sir?"

Three swishes of the stick to each palm. Mansur was big, and everyone at the orphanage was afraid of him. He had a scar on the right side of his forehead, and someone started the rumor that the scar was the result of a scimitar fight, which he won by cutting off his enemy's head. But Reza didn't care about the scar or how it got there. He only cared about escaping from *jahanam*—hell.

After the beating, he strolled past the main entrance's double gates, hands tucked under his armpits. His eyes were fixed on the enormous padlock that kept him out of Freedom-land, away from the shores of a blue lake surrounded by white-topped mountains.

A beautiful, peaceful place without other people. Just Reza and Mama—and maybe Fereshteh.

Chapter 3

As the last of the sun hovered over the horizon, Paree Windom stood on the edge of the terrace, gazing about the garden of cypress trees and privet hedges, reminiscing about the distant past when her life was full of joy, meaning, and purpose. Her gaze settled on a gray pigeon preening by the reflecting pool, and she found herself envying the creature because it could fly whenever and wherever, free from guilt, free from torments of the soul.

Paree was on her third Smirnoff-on-ice. There would be a few more until the terrace started spinning, after which she would share a light supper with her husband, Mike, listen to his complaints about her drinking, and stagger off to bed. Around two a.m., she would bolt upright, pulse racing, heart hammering after the usual nightmare. Stumbling into the living room, she would pace about for a while then flop down on the sofa and doze restlessly until dawn to face another grim day. Another day of dark thoughts bouncing around in her head like fleas on a dog, hopping from place to place, but always ending up at the same spot.

A lone chestnut tree at the crest of a lonely field.

Mike walked onto the terrace just as Paree finished her third drink. She turned to face him, impressed he still had a spring in his step, still had the boyish features despite his age: sixty. He was well over six feet tall, with broad shoulders, unruly hair, and a lump on the bridge of his nose—the memento of a long-ago fracture as a rugby player at Cheltenham College. Eight years younger than Mike, Paree didn't think she was aging as gracefully. Strands of gray streaked her black hair, and although faint, crow's feet radiated from the corners of her brown eyes that were once enormous and exuded hope. Now, they drooped and exuded despair. Every few months, a new wrinkle would appear, as if to warn her that heavy drinking accelerates aging.

But as long as it accelerates dying, so much the better.

"You could have at least waited for me," Mike snapped, staring at her drink.

"I only had one," she said, her face suddenly feeling on fire because she wasn't a good liar.

"Oh, really? Why is the vodka bottle half empty? It was full yesterday morning. Looks like between then and now, some pretty stiff drinks came out of it."

"Maybe the alcohol evaporated?"

He rolled his cobalt eyes, shook his head sadly. "Please let go, Paree. For God's sake, let go. Haven't you punished yourself enough? Haven't all these years of guilt been enough? Come back to me, Paree. Come back to reality."

Of course Mike despised her excessive drinking, but she sensed that to some extent he tolerated it because of her ongoing torment—as long as she drank only during cocktail hour, which started promptly at five p.m. "If you insist on drinking alcohol any other time, I'll take you back to England and put you in an institution for hardened alcoholics," he had threatened a year after they returned to Iran.

To which she had retorted, "How will you take me back? In chains?" But despite the defiant response, she decided it would be more prudent to stay away from Smirnoff outside the allotted time because he would break the bottles—another past threat.

"And if you hide them, by Jove I'll find them," he had added as if he could read her mind.

To avoid the constant allure of vodka, with Mike's encouragement she kept herself busy. On weekdays, she volunteered at a government-run hospital for the poor in southern Tehran—years earlier, an accidental trip through the city's most wretched ghetto had left her with such a woeful impression that she vowed to involve herself in charitable causes.

She helped the hospital staff with clean-up chores, changing bed linens, pushing stretchers, and talking with the many patients who had no visitors. The work was rewarding, especially the times she spent with the friendless impoverished sick, to whom she brought a daily bouquet of flowers to cheer up their dreary wards stinking of waste, disinfectant, disease. It was time well spent, time that somehow lessened the emptiness within her.

Throughout the previous two weeks, she had been particularly drawn to an elderly patient, a street vendor of sundries like postcards, pencils, and fly swatters. Nurses had told Paree he wouldn't leave the hospital alive because he suffered from advanced leukemia. So, along with the flowers, she brought him rosewater ice cream and sat at his bedside while he chatted about the years he had spent on the streets of Tehran or inside a makeshift tent in an abandoned bazaar of the slums.

Not once did she hear him complain about his lot in life. On his last day on earth, he grasped her hand and in a weak, quivering voice thanked her for making his final days so pleasant. When she leaned over to kiss his forehead, she wept her tears on him and he whispered, "It's raining in heaven."

Mike now paced about the terrace, a stein of imported Guinness ale in hand. "I have news, my dear. Mosaddeq won, we lost, and it's only a matter of months before we lose control of the AIOC."

Paree had been aware of this possibility, the subject of Mike's daily grumbling. Thanks to an ambitious politician by the name of Mohammed Mosaddeq, the Anglo-Iranian Oil Company would soon fall into Iranian hands. At his urging, the masses demanded it, mobbing the streets and shouting death to the English, while thugs and criminals took advantage of the bedlam, looting homes and stores that were not defended or barricaded. Unrest was rampant, and the Shah's seat on the Peacock Throne was threatened. But Paree didn't care what happened to the Shah or to the AIOC as long as she could live on in Iran, far removed from the village of Bourton-on-the-Water, Gloucestershire, England.

"How will the change affect your work?" she asked Mike.

"The AIOC board plans to send many executives back to England. I could be one of them." He grinned. "Just think, Paree. We may go back. Back to England and to civility."

And back to the scenes of my torment. She shuddered as the ghastly images threatened to materialize in her mind. Closing her eyes, she conjured up images of better yesteryears, of breastfeeding her infant son, humming lullabies to him as he gazed at her from his crib, taming his hair so he wouldn't look like Mr. Turnip.

"Please stop this infernal daydreaming," Mike pleaded, standing before her. She opened her eyes and stared at him blankly. He snapped his fingers. "For goodness sake, Paree, wake up!"

"Sorry, Mike. What were we talking about?"

"The prospect of us returning to England."

"Oh, yes. Why don't you retire and stay in Iran? We'll live out our lives together, right here in our beautiful home."

"It won't work. Because of Mosaddeq and his patriotic rubbish, the British are now the most despised people in this country. I don't wish to live where I'm not wanted. If they transfer me, I'll welcome it."

"When will you know for sure?"

"In the next two or three months, I should think."

"I can't go back to England, Mike. Just can't."

He stared at her, wide-eyed. "Why not?"

"You know very well why not. It's the…"

"Memories?"

"Exactly."

"Don't worry. We won't live in our old cottage."

"It doesn't matter. England is England, and that's where *it* happened."

"What do you suggest we do, then?"

"If you insist on going back, there's only one answer, isn't there?"

He shook his head as if to clear it. "Do I understand you correctly? Do you honestly want us to separate?"

"Not really, Mike, but it seems we have no other choice."

He clicked his tongue, which was his way of signaling his frustration with her. "That will be wonderful for you, won't it, Paree? You can mope around and drink yourself into stupor whenever you want. With no husband around to keep you from sinking to the depths of alcoholism." He locked eyes with her. "If you think I'll aid and abet you in your habit, think again."

"What are you telling me?"

"I'm telling you I hope you enjoy your life in Iran—without my financial support."

The haze of vodka quickly scattered as Paree realized the threat, albeit an empty one. Although his usually suppressed fascistic trait had surfaced, she knew he would never leave her destitute. All the same, she was the one who was forcing the separation, so he had no obligation to support her.

She contemplated life without Mike and his income, acknowledging that she still had deep, fond feelings for him, even though they had blunted since she stepped onto that field on that misty, gray morning in the winter of '43. In his absence, she would somehow survive on her own, assert her independence, and show him—and herself—that she could overcome the weakness that had engulfed her existence ever since that fateful winter. The weakness of not coping, of failing to confront her pain, of depending on Smirnoff for strength.

He draped an arm around her shoulders. "Please be reasonable, Paree. Come with me to England. I'll have a psychiatrist treat you, and you'll be your old self before you can finish decorating our new home."

Paree shook her head. "Sorry, Mike, I'm not going. I'll find a job and I'll manage. Iran is where I was born and raised, and Iran is where I belong."

"You're not thinking rationally, Paree. Who in this damned country would hire a fifty-two-year-old woman for a decent job? Except as a street sweeper or charwoman, of course, and I'd hardly consider those decent jobs."

All at once, she realized he had a point, and the doubts flowed in—gushed in. Despite the tide of doubts, however, of one thing she remained certain. She must avoid living in England at all cost.

She dashed inside the house—to the liquor cabinet.

Chapter 4

Winter passed, spring arrived, hope faded.

Reza finally came around to believing that Mama was dead. His grief surrendered to anger, and much of the anger surrendered to guilt—the constant feeling that he was somehow responsible for her death.

He had been at the orphanage for five months now. Five months of being almost alone. He had one friend, many haters—an outcast in a hideous place inside four walls. He knew the kids hated him for not talking to them or joining in their games, and he did nothing to win them over. All he wanted was to be left alone to roam about in the pleasant side of his imagination, to avoid distractions that would draw him back into the reality of a life without his mother, of a life plagued by recurring, terrifying snapshots of an event repressed in his mind. Fereshteh was the only person at the orphanage whom he liked, because she didn't bother him when he daydreamed, and because she treated him kindly.

On the first Thursday of spring, Reza stood trembling in Agha Mansur's office, dreading another blistering tirade from The Principal. Glaring at him through horn-rimmed glasses and a cloud of cigarette smoke, Mansur slammed a fist on his mahogany desk. "You're an uncommunicative, volatile little boy."

"But, sir, I don't understand what those words mean."

"It doesn't matter, because I'll beat them out of you, and then you won't need to understand what they mean."

The threat cemented Reza's will to escape, which became an obsession, despite knowing the awful consequences of capture, and having no plans of how to survive in Freedom-land without money, food, or shelter.

* * * *

As the dim oil lamp flickered in a corner of the second sleep room, which like the first was for boys only, he rolled to his side and stared at the cold stone floor. He rubbed a hand over it, wishing it was the wooden floor of the shack that was their home at the gardens, wishing Mama lay beside him. At the earliest light of dawn, he sat up and looked around.

The other boys were asleep, which was a relief. He could go to the outhouse without anyone calling him bed-wetter. The previous Monday at morning recess, The Proctor had shouted at him, humiliating him in front of all the other children for wetting his mattress. Reza had never wet himself before That Night—at least not that he could remember.

Crawling past the dozen mattresses, he snaked his way outside into the cool desert air, the wind whistling through cracks in the wooden gates, the dawn glowing orange over the horizon. The outhouse was a roofless mud-and-straw hut near a corner of the courtyard, and only the boys could use it—the girls shared two toilets on the ground floor of the building. As he stepped into the smelly enclosure buzzing with flies, he wondered if flies ever slept. He wondered if he'd ever sleep without the terrifying images popping in and out of his nightmares; images that would still be there when he woke up, and to get rid of them, he'd have to concentrate on happy times at the gardens.

"Flies are lucky," he whispered to himself, "because they probably never sleep, and so they never have nightmares."

After relieving himself in one of the two holes-in-the-ground, he walked past the double gates at the far end of the courtyard and noticed the padlock was still there, still secured. Over the months, he had waited patiently, hoping someone would forget to lock the gates, but no one had forgotten. Now, he must find another route of escape from the *jahanam* known as the Mansur Orphanage.

During recess later that morning, he strolled to the far end of the yard and sat alone next to the woodshed, where Agha Mansur kept the cleaning tools. Slumped against the shed, he gazed at the baked clay walls that surrounded the courtyard and were over twice his height.

"I could easily make a hole in the clay if I had a pickaxe," he muttered. "A hole big enough to escape."

He would escape to the Kavir Desert beyond the orphanage then to the mountains beyond the desert. He had often seen them in full view from the window of the prison room, where the kids were locked up because they misbehaved or because Mansur simply felt like locking them up—he called it a preventive measure, the meaning of which no one understood and no one bothered to ask. Alborz was the name of the mountains, and on clear days, Reza had seen them from afar when he lived in *Bagh-e Sevom*—the Third Garden.

Fereshteh told him she had also seen those mountains from the prison room. After spending a night there, the next day during recess she pulled Reza to a corner of the courtyard and they talked in their usual whispers.

She said, "Mountains are near the sky. Close to heaven."

He remembered Mama telling him almost the same thing: "Mountains are ladders to heaven."

"Have you ever been to the mountains?" he asked Fereshteh.

"No," she replied, "but I once saw close-up pictures of one. You should have seen the pictures, Reza. They were *so* beautiful. Snow covered the top of the mountain like a white hat, and mist wrapped around the middle of it like a gray, wooly shawl. You could see everything floating upside down on a lake below. The water was blue, as clear as the glass windows in Agha Mansur's office."

He promised himself that someday he would live in those mountains with the white hats and the gray shawls, where he would be near the sky and near heaven. At the time though, as he thought more about it, he wasn't so sure he would be allowed into heaven.

Baba had often told him that *behesht*—heaven—was a place for *good* boys, obedient boys. The other place, *jahanam*, was where rotten boys belonged. When he was angry at Reza, which was often and for no apparent reason, he called him a rotten bastard from *jahanam*—he defined bastards as kids who didn't look like their fathers—and then whipped him with his leather belt. The name-calling and beatings only happened on Baba's bad days. On his occasional good days, he could be quite pleasant. Even to Mama.

"Can I say something, Reza?"

Startled, Reza turned to face Fereshteh, who had quietly settled next to him by the woodshed, and he hadn't noticed because his mind was roaming the distant mountains. She was pretty, like Mama was pretty before the broken nose and broken teeth. Fereshteh's black hair fell like a waterfall over her shoulders, and her chocolate brown eyes were enormous—enormous but sad. She was quite frail, with bony arms and legs. And with a constant cough.

One time during lunch, Reza saw her cough out a ball of spit streaked with crimson. In a near whisper, he asked her, "Do you cough up blood a lot?"

She made a face. "Mind your own business."

He pushed his plastic plate of naan and cheese in front of her. "Eat for both of us, Fereshteh, and then you won't get sick."

She pushed back the plate. "Take care of yourself and stop trying to act like a nanny," she said in a joking sort of way.

She never ate much of her food, sometimes none of it, but the kids didn't get much to eat at the orphanage anyway. Agha Mansur said the authorities didn't provide enough money to buy the orphans more food or to buy them secondhand clothes and shoes without gashes or holes. "We need a better government," he was fond of saying. "A government that knows how to manage our economy." One of the girls asked him what economy meant, and he told her to look it up in the dictionary he kept in the *Otagh-e Ketab*—Book Room, which was a closet of bookshelves crammed with books no one read and a dictionary no one looked up.

"You can say whatever you want, Fereshteh," Reza now told her. "I won't stop you."

"I think you're planning to run away from here."

He stared at her in disbelief. "Can you see inside my head or something?"

"No, I can just *feel* what's inside it. Was I right?"

He shrugged.

Fereshteh twirled a lock of hair around her finger. "If you run away, they'll catch you and punish you worse than ever. Lots of strokes with the stick, lots of cleaning chores, lots of nights in the prison room. Oh, and no Friday treats." Friday treats were usually watermelon slices. Occasionally half-apples or half-persimmons.

"I don't care. Anyway, I didn't say I was running away, did I?"

"You *will* run. I just know it."

He searched her eyes. "Want to come with me?"

She shook her head, which made her hair wave about and he imagined stroking it or burying his face in it like he used to do with Mama's hair.

"If you come, I'll help you get well and then we'll adventure in the mountains. What do you say, Fereshteh?"

"No."

"Why not?"

"Because I'm going someplace else."

"Where?"

"*Behesht*." Heaven.

Chapter 5

Perched on a wooden crate in the living room, the Seth Thomas clock chimed five times. Paree smiled to herself. Cocktail hour had arrived at last. The magical hour would anesthetize the remains of the day and grant her a while of relief from dark thoughts, from gruesome images.

The Administration Board had announced its decision, and Mike was one of thirty British executives reassigned to their homeland. He would assume his former position of supervising the Oil Company's dealerships in western England. Now a month after the announcement, their house and much of the furnishings minus some essentials for Paree were sold.

As she predicted, Mike had retreated from his threat of withdrawing financial support. He repeatedly tried convincing her to let him provide a modest stipend for her living expenses, but she steadfastly refused. Living alone, after all, promised to restore her independence and a modicum of self-respect. She was damned if she would relinquish those by accepting the easy way out.

Tomorrow, she and Mike would vacate their home.

And the day after tomorrow, he would vacate her life.

Sarvar, the middle-aged, overly devout Muslim housekeeper and the most punctual person Paree had ever known, opened the living room door a few seconds after the fifth chime of the clock. She maneuvered her way around the packing crates and cardboard boxes, placed a bowl of cracked ice on the counter of the liquor cabinet, and cast Paree a disapproving glance. Paree understood the meaning of that glance. *You're a drunkard, a disgrace to Islam and the Holy Koran.*

"This is my last evening here, *Khanom* Windom. With all due respect, I hesitate to say this, but—"

"Then with all due respect don't say it."

Sarvar walked out.

After pouring a glass of Smirnoff-on-ice, Paree reclined on the leather sofa. For the umpteenth time, she wondered if she had tried hard enough to convince Mike to retire and live in Tehran, to live in the home that had provided all the comfort and seclusion she needed. It wasn't far from the peaceful surroundings of Mount Damavand, which she visited three or four times a month to escape, to reminisce about happier times.

She was born into a middle-class Iranian family in Tehran. Her father, an army captain, died of fulminant hepatitis when Paree was four years old. Her mother never remarried, living with her daughter off a modest pension in a modest apartment at the western end of the city. She once told Paree that she never remarried because she was fed up with Iranian men's attitude of their God-given superiority over women—thanks to their cynical interpretation of the Koran, which she was convinced had been doctored by the mullahs over the centuries to espouse male dominance. She constantly urged that when Paree became of age, she should seek out European men because of their more liberal attitude toward women.

That notion, Paree thought, was based on her mother's friendship with an English couple, the Harringtons, who moved next door when Paree was ten years old. The husband, a fledgling executive at the then-fledgling Anglo-Persian Oil Company, rarely interfered with his wife's activities that often flouted traditional Iranian views of feminine decorum in public—activities such as no smoking, no riding bicycles, no speaking unless spoken to, no wearing clothes much more revealing than the chador. The childless couple doted on Paree, taught her how to speak English fluently, and often raved about the wonders and beauty of their homeland, which she soon dreamed of visiting someday.

Despite the absence of a father figure, Paree led a pleasant childhood and spent much of her teenage years with her best friend, Minu. They talked about faraway places and boys and their bodies, and about which one of them would end up with the bigger breasts. "Boys just *love* big breasts," Minu used to say, "and mine will be much bigger than yours." A prediction that proved not quite correct because they didn't get *that* much bigger.

During the final year of high school, Paree thought much about her future, which from her perspective seemed neither exciting nor promising. At the time in Iran, mostly wealthy, upper-class women could attain higher education; the rest were expected to marry, bear children, and keep house. If marriage wasn't a possibility, they were expected to work in trades such as carpet-weaving, tailoring, pottery, or embroidery, all of which Paree found objectionable.

Determined to be self-sufficient and earn enough to travel abroad, she finally decided on a career with the Anglo-Persian Oil Company, a firm that—according to Mr. Harrington—paid its employees far more than typical Iranian businesses paid. She would start at the bottom rung as secretary and ascend the ladder as far as possible, resolving to overcome the era's resistance to women's ascendancy in the corporate world. Therefore, after graduating from high school, she spent a year studying how to read and write English and how to type—all of it thanks to Mrs. Harrington, who was more than willing to act as her tutor, at least forty hours a week.

A few days before Paree's English and typing lessons were set to end, her mother succumbed to heart failure. After two weeks of mourning, Paree applied for a position at the Anglo-Persian Oil

Company's Tehran headquarters. Because of Mr. Harrington's influence, she was hired as secretary to an ambitious junior executive, an Englishman by the name of Mike Windom. Keenly aware of Iranian traditions and sensibilities, Mike was politely reserved in her presence, and he made no advances, even though she obviously captivated him.

On the first Wednesday of June 1920, however, he about-faced. In the early evening, they were heading out of his office lobby when he suddenly folded her into his arms and asked her to marry him. Stunned at the abruptness of the proposal, she consented without giving it much thought—after a brief debate about religious issues, which didn't last long because neither of them was overly religious. Although at the time she wasn't *passionately* in love with Mike, she very much liked him, enjoyed his company, and looked forward to traveling to the faraway places—especially England—that she had for so long yearned to visit.

Two months later, she and Mike were wedded in a civil ceremony at the British embassy. Afterwards, they held a reception at *Bashkah-e Naft*—the Oil Club, the Company's lavish resort in northern Tehran with all the amenities the British expatriates enjoyed, including a restaurant/night club, swimming pool, tennis courts, gymnasium, and performing arts auditorium. The newlyweds then spent their honeymoon at another lavish resort on the Caspian seashore.

In the summer of 1921, as automobile sales soared throughout America and Europe, the Oil Company transferred Mike to Gloucestershire, England, to oversee the firm's petrol distributorships in the region. He and Paree soon settled into a peaceful, pleasant country life around the Cotswold Hills, where she assimilated into the British culture while her love of Mike blossomed.

Their son was born on April 1, 1922, seven months after they arrived in England. Mike wanted to name him Jonathan, Paree wanted Jahan. After a lengthy discussion, they compromised with John—Little John, they both called him. The joy of their lives. He grew up to become a sociable young man, gifted athlete, and a leader among his peers at Cheltenham College, the same school Mike had attended.

And then on a winter's night of 1943, Little John wandered off.

The same year in spring, Mike chopped down the chestnut tree that he blamed for their misfortune, and as it crashed to the ground, so did his anguish. "Enough is bloody well enough," he said to Paree through gritted teeth, his brow glistening with sweat. "I'll look for another position in Tehran. You'll be much happier there, and that'll make me much happier."

Later that year, they relocated to Tehran, where his career with the Anglo-Iranian—now changed from Anglo-Persian—Oil Company had begun. Paree welcomed returning to her country of birth. At least Iran brought her some pleasant memories of her formative years. They were uncomplicated years of growing up with Minu and wondering which one of them would develop the bigger breasts.

Mike and Paree had now lived in Iran for eight consecutive years, but every other summer he had vacationed in England to visit friends and relatives—without Paree because she refused returning to the land where her blissful memories would be squashed under the weight of painful ones.

* * * *

Looking grim, Mike marched into the living room, muttered a hello to Paree, and poured himself a glass of sherry. He paced around between the boxes and crates without speaking, and Paree left him alone. She was used to his ritual of silent pacing while

23

drinking sherry and looking grim, because that was his leave-me-alone time. Talking to him during the ritual only annoyed him, and she tried not to be the annoying sort.

When his glass of sherry was empty, the ritual ended. He refilled the glass and settled in the leather armchair opposite the sofa, a worried look now replacing the grim one. "I'm concerned, Paree."

"About what?"

"About you living alone."

She stared at him. "Why are you concerned? Because I'm a woman? Don't you think I can take care of myself?"

"You can, but you won't be able to live the luxurious lifestyle I've given you—not without my income. I'm afraid you'll be miserable."

She cast him a wisp of a smile. "Luxury is relative, my dear husband. For the Shah of Iran, luxury is a palace in Tehran, another at the Caspian Sea, and another in the Alborz Mountains. For the homeless beggar, luxury is a tin shack in the Kavir Desert."

"You're being bloody illogical, Paree. Why don't you at least accept my offer of a monthly allowance?"

"Like some child gets? That's so demeaning, Mike. Besides, I don't need your money. I'll survive quite well without it, thank you. Wait and see."

"Yes, I'm sure you'll survive, but I'm afraid…"

"Afraid of what?"

"Living alone will give you too much time to ruminate about Little John."

She grimaced. "I suppose you've put him completely out of your mind, haven't you? You and your British stiff upper lip."

His cheeks reddened. Looking away, he mumbled, "You'll never know, Paree."

"What did you say?" she asked, knowing exactly what he had said.

"Nothing." He blew his nose into a handkerchief then locked eyes with her. "Have you honestly thought what your life without me and my support will be like?"

Paree had given life without Mike much more thought since the possibility became actuality, enough to realize that living in England and surrounded by reminders of her darkest hours might push her over the brink of sanity. Living in Iran with or without Mike would at least keep her away from that brink, although not far away. She had already contacted Roger Holmes, a senior executive and her once not-so-secret admirer at the Anglo-Iranian Oil Company, who promised he would find her a job at the firm's Tehran headquarters. So financially, she would be all right. Not well-off, just all right.

In two days, life without Mike would begin—without responsibilities except at work. And outside of work? Living alone to go wherever she pleased, grieve whenever she chose, drink whatever she desired. She would spend much of her spare, sober time volunteering at the hospital for the poor, absorbing the misery of the impoverished sick as if to dilute the misery within her, as if to convince herself that human suffering is a shared burden.

She raised her glass. "Won't you at least wish me luck in my new life, Mike?"

He raised his glass. "Yes, I'll wish you luck, my dear, but I know you'll soon regret your choice."

Chapter 6

Everyone was asleep except Reza. In the dim light of the oil lamp, he dressed quietly and crawled out of the second sleep room. He stepped into the courtyard that was faintly lit under the half-moon. He would inspect the padlock at the double gates, and if it was as usual secured, he would search the kitchen for a sharp instrument.

As he headed toward the gates, a heavy thud on the shoulder jolted him. He spun around to face The Proctor, a surly, nasty man with ugly, thick eyebrows twisted to sharp points at the outer ends, which made them look like little black horns. His neck was as thick as his head, and he was even bigger than Agha Mansur and handier with a stick.

Before becoming Mansur's assistant, he had been in the Iranian army, and he often reminded the kids of it. "I was a very important sergeant, so you brats had better behave around me."

So the kids behaved around him—all except Fereshteh, who often stuck her tongue out or made a face at him. The Proctor now shook a finger in front of Reza's nose. "What are you doing out of bed, boy?"

"I need to piss, sir."

He pointed to the outhouse. "There's the piss hole. You're going in the wrong direction, boy."

"Yes sir, sorry."

"You're not sorry at all. What are you up to?"

"Nothing sir. I just wasn't thinking."

"You *can't* think, boy. That's your problem."

"Yes sir."

"*Pessar-e ahmagh*—stupid boy," The Proctor muttered, stomping away.

Over time, the deluge of epithets flung Reza's way had pecked away at his self-esteem, which had plunged to an all-time low. He generally felt unwanted now, and he stayed away from people—except from Fereshteh, who somehow managed to restore his self-esteem whenever he was with her. It was the reason why he wished she would join him in his escape, why he wished she would stop spitting blood and become healthy so they could enjoy their lives together in the mountains of Freedom-land.

He slunk into the outhouse, did his business, and returned to the cold mattress on the cold floor, thinking about his escape. At recess that morning, he had lingered in a corner of the courtyard, and when no one was looking, he had used his uncut thumbnail to scrape the clay wall. To his delight, the baked mud had scraped off easily, but soon his thumb grew tired and sore. All he needed was a sharp instrument, like the knife in the sheath that usually dangled from Baba's belt. Baba used the knife for slicing watermelons and cantaloupes and cucumbers… and sometimes for threatening his wife and son.

Although Reza hadn't been in the orphanage kitchen before, he imagined there must be a knife there for cutting up the almost-once-a-week watermelon and the once-a-week boiled chicken. The only utensils offered at mealtimes were plastic spoons for the soup, which most of the kids didn't use because they drank straight from the bowls. They ate the once-a-week boiled chicken with their fingers.

A long while later, when he thought The Proctor would be in bed asleep, Reza again crawled out of the sleep room and tiptoed down the corridor to the kitchen at the far end. He tried opening the door, but it was locked. There was no point in going outside to try climbing through the window, because it was too high for him to climb and he didn't have a ladder. Besides, all the ground floor windows of the orphanage were locked after dark—they didn't have bars like the windows of the upper stories.

One day in class, Fereshteh asked The Proctor why the higher-up windows were barred. "To stop you brats from falling out," he snapped.

She made a face. "Do you mean jumping out, agha?"

He glared at her. "That too, brat."

She made another face. "We're children, not brats, agha."

The Proctor smacked his stick on the floor in front of her and yelled, "Don't you dare disagree with me, *brat!*"

Reza tiptoed back to his mattress and lay awake, wondering whether there were any sharp objects tucked among the brooms and mops and buckets inside the courtyard woodshed, which didn't have a lock on its door. Something to check the following night.

He fell asleep and dreamed of Baba and Mama inside a shed, Baba waving a bottle, Mama trembling and bent over in a corner, covering her head with her hands. Reza ran to her, but a hole opened in the floor of the shed and he fell inside. He kept falling until he suddenly stopped in midair and a strange, warm feeling engulfed him. An angel in a white dress held him, a thin angel with soft black hair and enormous chocolate brown eyes. She kissed him on the cheek and said, "We'll see each other again in heaven."

He opened his eyes. A warm breath brushed his cheek like a soft summer breeze, and he didn't know if this was more of the dream. He lay there for a while, enjoying the moment until a muffled cough startled him and he sat up. In the dimness, he saw Fereshteh lying next to him on the mattress, smiling at him, her face as white as her dress, flickering in the dim light of the oil lamp.

"Be quiet, Reza," she whispered, pulling him down.

"Fereshteh, what—"

"We're both leaving this *jahanam* soon. But before then, I wanted to be alone with you for a little bit."

"We could leave together."

"No, you have your way of leaving, and I have mine. But someday, we'll meet in heaven. I just know it." She put a bony arm across his chest, nestled into him, and rested her head on his shoulder, her soft hair flowing over him like the gentle waters of a stream. "I love you, Reza-*jan*," she murmured.

"I love you too, Fereshteh."

They lay nestled against each other for a long time until she started coughing and buried her face in the mattress. When the coughing stopped, she turned back to him, her lips brushed against his ear, and goose bumps sprouted all over him.

"I bet you really miss your parents," she whispered.

"I miss Mama. What about you?"

She gave him a little squeeze. "I miss them both."

"How did they die?"

"In a fire. It burned our apartment in the poor part of Tehran. I was sleeping on the roof, and I couldn't help them."

"How did you get away from there?"

"People in helmets climbed a ladder and carried me down. After they put out the fire, they told me my mama and baba were dead. I couldn't help them, Reza—couldn't help my mama and baba. So I lived and they died and they went to heaven."

As her warm tears soaked his face, he knew she was crying because she felt just as he did. He couldn't help his mother, and Fereshteh couldn't help her mother and father. He was certain that neither Fereshteh nor he would ever understand why they lived when the people they cherished most died.

Gliding her fingers over his face, Fereshteh traced his brow, nose, lips, and the cleft in his chin. "I must leave now, Reza-*jan*. God will look after us. He'll look after *both* of us." She kissed him softly on the cheek and he returned the kiss, stroking her hair, letting her warmth pass into him, feeling as one with her.

"Why are you so nice to me, Fereshteh?" he whispered. "I mean, all the other kids hate me."

"Because you're just like me—you hurt and you never complain. And like me, you're full of love and have no one to share it with."

He hugged her. "But I have someone now."

She hugged him back. "Me too."

She left quietly while he still wondered if he was dreaming.

* * * *

The next morning at recess, he looked for Fereshteh and found her sitting beside the woodshed.

He whispered, "I dreamed you came to see me last night."

"Was it a nice dream?"

"It was the nicest one I've ever had."

"Maybe it was real then," she said and smiled knowingly and coughed.

Once the coughing spell was over, she asked him, "When will you leave here?"

"In the next few days, I hope, and I still wish you'd come with me."

"No, I'll leave in my own way," she replied and coughed out a ball of spit streaked with crimson.

He wanted to hold her against him, to again enjoy the feel of her hair on his face, her body nestled against him. After glancing around to make sure no one was watching, he took her hand and squeezed it into his side.

Iraj Sarfeh

I love you Fereshteh.
I love you too, Reza.

Chapter 7

On that sunny morning, Mehrabad Airport was crowded and noisy, passengers jostling for position behind the departure gate. Mike seems quite unhappy, Paree thought standing next to him in the disorderly queue, which was more like a column of flying elbows.

"You're as stubborn as a bloody mule," he told her for the third time since they awakened at dawn. "Are you sure you won't change your mind and come to England with me?"

"I'm positive."

He shook his head dejectedly, turned his eyes to the vaulted ceiling. "God knows, how I wish I could force out your bloody demons."

"They're not demons, Mike. They're frightful memories."

"Can't you just order your brain to squeeze them out?"

"Is that what you've done? Squeezed them out?"

"I did whatever it took to move on with our lives, Paree—which is far more than you've done."

"I'm not like you, Mike. I can't get rid of my feelings so easily. They run deep."

"And mine are shallow?"

"They're…stilted."

He threw his hands in the air. "Is that what you think of me after thirty years of marriage? After all the affection I've poured over you?"

Paree felt her face burning. She was being damned unfair, and she couldn't help it. If only just once she could see Mike weeping for their son…

The melee began inching past the departure gate. He engulfed her in his arms and kissed her lightly on the lips. "You know how to find me, my dear. And I'm sure you'll join me once you realize the sheer misery of living alone."

"Misery or not, I could never step foot on British soil again."

Paree looked away, realizing she had blurted those words without conviction. The remains of a lone chestnut tree on the crest of a lonely field constantly beckoned, and she constantly resisted. She had done her best not to be lured back to the scene, hoping that time, the supposed healer of all miseries of the soul, would suppress the nightmares that awakened her in a state of panic. But time had failed her, failed her after eight years and still counting.

The chestnut tree was an imposing feature of the nightmares, sometimes black and satanic under dark clouds, sometimes silvery and ghostlike under the moon's glow. In the twilight of her sleep, it would die, shedding its leaves and transforming into an eerie skeleton of itself, only to rise again from the dead at the dawn of her awakening, when it would become indistinguishable from reality.

All the same, she knew that by not confronting the scene, she would always harbor the guilt that *she* should have been the one at that tree in that field on that misty morning. Paree Windom, *not* Little John Windom. The same guilt pained her with incessant reminders that she should have done much more as a mother, as a protector. Mike had chopped down the tree as if to chop down his own guilt, but perhaps she should have carried out the deed herself, and afterwards she might have felt whole again—as he now did, acting like his old self before Little John's solution.

Mike was strong and resilient, having survived the trenches of World War I and come away from them unscathed, his mind unscarred by the wretchedness that must have abounded. If only she were endowed with his strength. If only their son had been endowed with his strength. Then the chestnut tree would have remained the Happiness Tree from which they gathered chestnuts for Little John to become the Conkers Champion of Bourton-on-the-Water.

As the jostling mass now moved on to the tarmac, Mike turned and waved. Paree waved back, feeling lonelier, gloomier, emptier than usual, hoping he would admit defeat, come back to Iran, and assume a life in retirement with her. That, she imagined, would be the best outcome of all. Much better than utterly alone.

She left the marble terminal and glanced at her watch. Still a long time before cocktail hour at her new apartment. She'd have to crack the ice herself because she no longer had a housekeeper, which was fine because she could do without Sarvar's angry looks disapproving of her anti-Islam, anti-Koran habit. In any case, Paree was certain that neither Mr. Smirnoff nor vodka were around when Mohammed conceived the Koran, so how could drinking the stuff be anti-Islam and anti-Koran?

She arrived at the apartment and retrieved the almost full bottle of Smirnoff from a kitchen cabinet. After emptying the ice tray from the refrigerator and cracking out the cubes, she was about to fill a glass when a wave of anxiety surged through her. She realized that without Mike, alcohol would dominate and consume whatever remained of her life. Was she ready to concede defeat? Ready to drown?

Bottle in hand, she dashed to the sink, poised to pour the vodka down the drain.

But she didn't.

Chapter 8

Reza waited not only until the other children were asleep, but until he heard the midnight train waking up and puffing up its engine, fast at first, then slow, steady puffs like a donkey's breaths as it trudges along carrying a load of watermelons.

He knew it was the midnight freight train from Karaj to Tehran, because Agha Mansur had talked about it in one of his classes. He said most trains run by steam, and if the kids were to stay awake until midnight, they would hear the Karaj-Tehran train's engine bellowing steam into the air. Reza wondered if the train would go beyond Tehran, head north to the mountains, and take him with it.

To mountains of cotton wool, feathery and soft as the clouds.

He rolled off his mattress, crawled out into the courtyard, and tiptoed to the woodshed. The door was as always unlocked, and he inched it open. The hinges squeaked and he froze, dreading The Proctor would appear out of nowhere. He didn't. Reza jerked open the door—one long squeak was better than many short ones. Inside was dark. He fell to his hands and knees and worked his way around the brooms, buckets, and mops that were strewn everywhere and used once a week.

He froze again at hearing a tapping noise, but he relaxed when a high-pitched squeal came after the taps. A rat squeal, which he knew well because rats occasionally came out after dark into the family shack at the Third Garden. He groped around on the floor, feeling for anything with a sharp edge. At the far corner of the shed was a wooden crate without the lid. He rummaged inside. A few rags, a brush, a dustpan, and…

A hammer! One side of its head was rounded and the other was forked with sharp tips.

After tucking the hammer under his shirt, he crawled out, shut the shed door to more squeaks, and stood by the nearest wall, his heart pounding at the thrill of his discovery. He prepared to start working on his escape hole, but just then, an amber light turned on in a second-story window, which he knew faced out of The Proctor's bedroom.

He waited there for a long time as the light stayed on, and now he could see The Proctor pacing up and down, thrashing his arms about like he was arguing. A tall woman paced up and down in the opposite direction, thrashing her arms about like she was arguing too. He recognized the cook because of the hair. When she wasn't wearing a chador, her hair was rolled into a bun at the top of her head with a green ribbon tied around the base.

Along with the housekeeper/matron, who didn't do much housekeeping or matroning that Reza had ever noticed, the cook came and went six days a week to prepare vegetable soups, lamb-bone soups, and once-a-week boiled chickens. On Fridays, the cook's day off, The Proctor had the older girls—the twelve-year-olds—make everyone naan sandwiches for breakfast, lunch, and supper. Sometimes cucumber sandwiches, sometimes cheese, sometimes honey.

With no signs that The Proctor or the cook would soon quit arguing, Reza tiptoed back to the sleep room and hid the hammer under the head of his mattress. He tried to sleep, but the excitement of his find kept him awake until dawn, which he didn't mind because he preferred exciting thoughts to frightening nightmares. Exciting thoughts of his adventures in Freedom-land. It occurred to him that he would have no money to buy food, but that really didn't matter. As long as he was in Freedom-land, nothing else mattered.

He fell asleep before dawn and had two wonderful dreams in a row instead of the usual nightmares. One of the dreams was about Fereshteh and him dipping their bare feet in a mountain stream and wiggling their toes while Mama sang a children's song, as she often did when she tucked him in bed.

I ran and ran and I came to a mountain. I saw two women. Once of them gave me bread, the other gave me water.

* * * *

That morning during recess, Reza and Fereshteh sat leaning against the woodshed. She said he had on a bit of a happy face, not his typical angry face or blank face.

He shrugged and she whispered, "You'll run away tonight, won't you Reza?"

He nodded. "Are you *sure* you don't want to come with me?"

"Positively sure."

"So I'll go alone."

"You'll be caught, and they'll beat you then throw you in the prison room—and they'll do that over and over again for days."

"I don't care because I'll keep trying until I get out of here."

"You're as stubborn as a donkey, Reza Ahmadi."

"What about you? You refuse to eat, and you're looking sick."

"That's because I'm running away too—floating away, actually."

"How can you *float* away?"

"Don't you know? There are two parts to each person, the part that *can't* float, and the part that *can* float."

"So how do you get into the part that *can* float?"

"By getting away from the part that *can't*, silly. And you do that by dying."

"Where do you hear all this stuff, Fereshteh?"

"From my mother, long before she died in the fire and floated away."

"Did your father float away too after he died in the fire?"

"Of course he did. *Everyone* floats away after they die."

Fereshteh asked him how he planned to escape. He told her about the hammer and its claw that could dig a hole in the wall, big enough to let him climb out.

Staring at him wide-eyed, she gripped him arm. "Where's the hammer now, Reza?"

"I hid it under my mattress."

"*Oh Khodah-e man*!" Oh my God!

"What's the matter?"

"Someone told me The Proctor and matron are searching all the sleep rooms, looking for hidden stuff."

He ran to sleep room two. The Proctor was there, on his knees, searching under a blanket. Not knowing what else to do, Reza dove on top of his mattress.

The Proctor jumped up, marched over, glared at him.

"What are you up to, boy?"

Chapter 9

Paree awakened at dawn, her head pounding like a jackhammer. She stumbled into the checkerboard-tiled bathroom and groped around the medicine cabinet until she found her relief of countless mornings after. Bayer Aspirin. She swallowed three of them, climbed back into bed, and waited for the drug to do its work.

Drunken night, pounding headache, aspirin. Drunken night, pounding headache, aspirin. An eternity of misery. Like the gods' punishment of Sisyphus, the devious prince in Greek mythology whom they forced to push an enormous rock up a steep hill, caused the rock to tumble down, and forced him to start all over again for an eternity.

Once the aspirin took over, her head felt better, but not the misery. She bathed, dressed, and applied a touch of makeup to her cheeks and eyes, which she thought did little to camouflage her prematurely aging features.

And should I care?

Her appointment at the Anglo-Iranian Oil Company headquarters was two hours away. After pouring herself a cup of tea, she went into the living room, turned on the Philips radio, and tuned it to the BBC Overseas station. An announcer solemnly introduced the London Philharmonic Orchestra's rendition of Mozart's *Requiem.* She listened for a few seconds to the hauntingly depressing music then switched it off.

Reclined on the sofa, she gazed around the apartment and was surprised to notice how cold it looked, with its barren blue walls, uncarpeted wooden floor, and no decorative touches to add warmth. A month before departing, Mike had engaged a real estate agent and sold their northern Tehran house and most of its furnishings except the items Paree wanted—the bare necessities for apartment living.

Before the close of escrow, he helped her find an apartment in an upper middleclass neighborhood on *Takht*-e Jamshid Avenue. Although she didn't accept a regular stipend from him, she acquiesced to his offer of leaving the equivalent of five hundred British pounds—around eight thousand Iranian tomans—in *Bank-e Melli*, their Tehran bank. The money would be plenty to keep her in the apartment until she was on the payroll of the Oil Company. She was certain of being hired there because of her past friendship with Roger Holmes, Director of Personnel, Tehran Headquarters.

Mike also left her the one-year-old Chevy coupe, which she loved to drive through Tehran, flouting the pervasive Iranian attitude that driving a vehicle was the sole province of the male.

* * * *

At eleven a.m., she walked into the lobby of Roger Holmes's office. Paree had first met him when she applied for work soon after her mother died. Born and bred in London, educated at Harrow and Cambridge, Roger had been in Iran and with the Company since 1913, five years after it was founded and a year before the outbreak of WWI, about which he was fond of saying, "I discovered the perfect way to avoid that bloody war, eh what?" Now in his early sixties, he would never leave Iran.

"I feel as if I'm more Iranian than most Iranians," he once told Paree at a party, during which he tried flirting with her but she managed to stave him off without hurting his feelings. At the same party, he said to her, "I love Tehran and I love the Persian people, whose hospitality is unparalleled. *Khuneh-e ma khuneh-e shoma*— our house is your house. Maybe the adage is now a cliché all over the world, but it originated right here, in Iran. So you should be dashed proud of your heritage, Paree."

She liked Roger mainly because he didn't belittle Iranians, like a few of the British expatriates did, snobs who had nothing to be snobbish about. Wogs, those few called Middle-Easterners behind their backs. Wogs as in Golliwogs, the black rag dolls that could be bent into every conceivable shape.

Roger's attractive secretary knocked softly on the office door, opened it, and announced, "Mr. Holmes is most happy to meet with you now, Mrs. Windom."

Paree stepped inside the spacious, carpeted room, the walnut-paneled walls busy with framed photographs of the Alborz Mountains, the Caspian seashore, and an oil tanker.

Beaming as soon as he saw her, Roger leapt off his swivel chair. "I'm so glad you didn't go back to England, Paree. With Mike now away, I'll have you all to myself."

She grinned. "Don't you wish, you old married so and so."

He laughed, which reddened his puffy cheeks and quivered his second chin—Paree thought he had doubled in weight and girth since she saw him last.

"I'm absolutely *dee*-lighted you applied to work for us again," he said. "I remember you as one of our most efficient secretaries until Mike kidnapped you."

"I think I left voluntarily, but that was a long time ago."

Roger waved her to a chair in front of his rosewood desk and settled into the swivel chair. "I'm sure you're aware that the AIOC will soon be transformed into the NIOC, National Iranian Oil Company. And when that happens…"

"You may be forced to leave the company, but not me—that is, if you decide to hire me. I'm Irani."

"Right you are. Mr. Parviz Shappour, our Assistant Director of Regional Distributions, needs a secretary. Do you know him?"

"Yes."

She had met Shappour a few times through his association with Mike. The same age and with the same length of service at AIOC as Mike, Shappour was a mid-level Iranian administrator with a sour disposition who would never climb higher than Assistant This and Assistant That—at least not until Iran ruled the Company and he sweetened his disposition.

Roger continued. "He's on leave for a few days, but he trusted me to make the right choice of secretary for him. If I didn't have one already, I'd insist you work with me, eh what?"

Paree smiled. "And spend most of my time fending you off, eh what?"

"But you do that, oh so pleasantly."

"Because you flirt, oh so pleasantly."

He chuckled. "Mr. Shappour doesn't flirt—at least not that I'm aware. Do you foresee any problems with him as your boss?"

"I can't think of any."

"Consider yourself hired, then."

She would start work the following Saturday, equivalent to Monday in western nations, because in Iran *Jomeh*—Friday—is a day of prayers, peace, and rest.

Roger leaned forward, cast her a penetrating gaze. "I'm worried about you, Paree. I usually don't make personal comments, but please forgive me for making one now. You look depressed to me. Your eyes, they've lost the luster I once saw in them. They've become sort of…far away. You know, cold. Cold with more than a touch of sadness. Does Little John still weigh heavily on your mind?"

She abruptly stood, her upbeat mood suddenly barreling downhill, out of control. "I'm so sorry, Roger, but I must dash off to another appointment. I'm sure we'll have many pleasant chats once I start working here."

She hurried off before the tears would give her away. Before she would break down and sob hysterically and make a fool of herself in front of the man who had just provided her with a livelihood.

Once outside, she dried her eyes and climbed into the Chevy. She had five days left before starting work at the Oil Company. Five days of solitude in the Alborz Mountains.

Chapter 10

Reza had lain on the mattress, trembling, feeling certain that The Proctor would discover the hammer, the key to Freedom-land.

The Proctor now stood over him, pointing a finger and glaring at him. "What are you up to, boy?"

"I-I was…"

"Answer me, boy!"

"I-I was tired and…"

"Are you sick?"

"Yes…yes sir, *very* sick, and I think I'm going to throw up." He rolled to his side and pretend-retched a few times.

The Proctor eyed him for a moment. "Clean up your mess when you're done, boy." He marched out.

Reza took the hammer from under the mattress and tucked it behind the nearest metal locker.

* * * *

At the first puffs of the midnight train, he put on his shirt, shalvar, windbreaker with the gaping hole at a shoulder seam, and secondhand shoes with rigid tips and holes in the soles. After removing the hammer from behind the locker, he crawled out of sleep room two and into the moonlit courtyard.

He looked up at The Proctor's bedroom window, and no lights were on. Tiptoeing past the double gate, he checked the padlock. As usual, secured. He wondered if he could break it open with the hammer, but decided not to—the lock was made of thick metal, and hammering away at it would make too much noise.

He crept to the back of the woodshed, which was a few paces away from the nearest wall, where he wouldn't be seen from the orphanage building. Kneeling down, he started carving out his escape hole two feet above the ground—the wall was thinner there than at the bottom. He used the hammer's claw, scraping away the baked mud gently to keep the noise down.

He worked for three straight hours on one spot, and the deeper the hole became, the easier the baked mud crumbled. Just when he could feel a light breeze wafting in through the hole, a muffled cough startled him. On his knees, he peered around a corner of the shed and saw a girl's outline in the moon glow. Barefooted and wearing a white dress torn along one side, she tiptoed toward him, and for a moment he thought she was a barefooted white angel until he saw her face. Fereshteh's face, pale with hollow cheeks and dark shadows under her enormous eyes.

She squatted down beside him and whispered, "I brought you a going away present, Reza."

"Go back, Fereshteh, or we'll both get caught."

She pressed something soft into his hand, and he stared at it. A ball of cotton wool the size of a persimmon.

"Well, aren't you going to look for the present inside?"

Carefully, he teased apart the wool until in the middle he found a glittering object. A thin, plain golden ring.

"Where did you get this?"

"It was my mother's. A man in a white jacket took it off her finger and gave it to me just before they took her body away. But I can't wear it because it's too big, so I've kept it hidden inside my mattress." She rested a hand on his arm. "Reza, this ring is the most precious thing I've ever owned. Now, I'm giving it to you because I don't want you to forget me."

"I won't forget you Fereshteh, I promise."

"Then put it on."

He slipped the ring onto his fourth finger, but it was too big. He tried his index finger, and now the ring fit without feeling too loose.

"I'll wear this forever."

"And that means you'll have a little part of me forever."

She kissed him on the cheek, stood up—a little unsteadily, he thought—and tiptoed away, leaving him to wonder if he would see her again, if she would float over him once she left that part of her body that she said *can't* float.

As soon as Fereshteh was out of sight, he looked up at the window of The Proctor's room. Inside was dark, quiet. Under the moonlight, he worked on the hole again. Now, the baked mud fell away almost as easily as autumn leaves off a tree. At the first glimmer of dawn, the hole was large enough for him to crawl through. He glanced at the windows one last time, especially at the window of sleep room three, where he knew Fereshteh slept. All he saw was the flickering light of an oil lamp. He wished she were standing at the window so he could catch one last glimpse of the girl who was forever a part of him because he would wear her ring on his finger for the rest of his life.

Goodbye, Fereshteh.

* * * *

After crawling out of the hole headfirst, he landed on the rocky desert soil in Freedom-land. His mind was chaotic with the excitement of beginning his journey to snow-topped mountains wrapped in misty shawls, their upside-down images reflected on the lake waters below. He broke into a run, sprinting for as long as he could and then slowing down to a fast pace. He could see the faraway peaks now, faintly shimmering in the glow of early dawn. Constantly keeping the peaks in sight, he stayed along the dirt road that had brought him to the orphanage in a police car with a rifle in the front seat between two policemen. One of them kept exchanging glances between the rifle, the rear doors, and Reza, as if daring him to jump out of the car, his expression radiating hatred and brutality. He was the same officer who had repeatedly slapped him on That Night.

As the first of the sun's rays lit the horizon and turned the distant mountaintops white, Reza reached the railroad tracks, which would lead him toward Tehran if he headed east. From there, he would head to the mountains north of the city. He heard a distant rumble and wondered if it was a Karaj-Tehran train. Crouching behind a large boulder, he waited. Minutes later, he saw puffs of steam and the nose of a train engine coming fast toward him. In a flash, the engine and the string of carriages in tow flew by at a dizzying speed, and he knew he had no chance of hopping aboard.

Once the train passed, he continued the journey east as jagged desert stones stung his feet through the holes in the soles of his shoes. Every so often, he had to stop and take out the pebbles that were jammed inside. He didn't mind the pain that much though, because it was only pain—and because he was free.

Walking between the rails, he could clearly see the Karaj Highway a hundred paces to the north. Soon, traffic was coming and going at a steady rate, so he walked along the far side of the track, which was on lower ground and would keep him hidden from view of the highway and Agha Mansur and The Proctor. He was certain that by now, the two of them were driving around, looking for him.

He was thirsty, and his empty stomach growled like Agha Mansur, as if it were angry at him for not putting food in it. Another hour brought him opposite a *caravansara*—roadside inn—on the near side of the highway. He clambered over the tracks and walked to the inn, hoping someone would see him and offer him a drink of water and maybe a little food, like a piece of naan or a slice of cantaloupe. Although several cars were parked outside the wood and plaster building, he saw no people. Now too tired to keep going, he rested cross-legged in the shade of a shiny black car.

Hunger, thirst, and fatigue had slowed him down, and he had made no plans for dealing with them. Now, he wished he would have at least eaten Fereshteh's food at supper, which lately she didn't even touch. Leaning back against the car door, he closed his eyes. A few minutes of sleep might bring back his energy.

The orange of sunglow behind his eyelids gradually faded as he drifted to sleep and dreamed the same dream about the same shed and the same hole that swallowed him down into darkness when he tried running to Mama.

But this time no angel stopped his fall.

Chapter 11

Paree returned to the apartment at one p.m., lay on the sofa, and thought about the next five days of freedom alone before starting work. She had already decided to forgo volunteering at the hospital for the poor on those days, to forgo sharing the despair of the diseased, forsaken souls of Tehran.

A respite from misery.

She had spent the morning at the bedside of Habib, a young man born with a spinal deformity. He was abandoned as a child in the streets to beg for baksheesh and somehow to survive off the charity of those who pitied the wretched poor of their city. Paree had spoken to him almost daily during his hospital stay. He didn't have a last name, didn't know his age, didn't remember much about his parents or his childhood. He remembered a stray dog though, who shared the little food Habib bought from his beggar's takings and who kept him warm on cold nights. The dog must have run off after Habib lay down to sleep at a cul-de-sac off Khayyam Street, where in the morning, people found him blue in the face and frothing at the mouth. They called for an ambulance, which rushed him to the hospital for the poor so he could die in bed instead of on cement in a pool of urine.

At seven minutes past eleven on that morning, which was a week after he was hospitalized, Habib gave up the fight for survival and died with his cracked lips shaped in a peaceful sort of smile. Paree laid a bouquet of red roses over his chest and stared teary-eyed at his smile, recalling that in the winter of '43, Little John had worn a similar smile as he gazed up at the chestnut tree and…

The telephone ringing interrupted her thoughts.

"My dear, I thought you'd be interested I arrived safely," Mike said, his long-distance voice echoing over the crackles and buzzes and hisses.

"That's wonderful, Mike."

"Is that all you have to say?"

"What else would you like me to say?"

"That you miss me."

"I miss you."

"Your tone sounds so cold, so bloody distant. For heaven's sake, can't you be a little more affectionate?"

She hesitated. Yes, she was sounding cold and distant, but she wasn't sure why. Maybe she was still angry at him for leaving her and Iran. Or she was still thinking about Habib and all the sufferers at the hospital for the poor. Or maybe she envied—resented? — Mike's strength that let him live in England without being constantly reminded of the winter of '43.

"Sorry Mike, I'm tired."

He sighed. "Come to your senses, Paree. Come and join me and stop tormenting yourself." He cleared his throat noisily. "How much vodka have you consumed since I left?"

"Have a pleasant life in England, Mike."

She slammed down the receiver. It was time to clear her head—clear it of Mike and the hospital and the confines of her apartment. The canyons and streams of Mount Damavand beckoned. She would stay at Hotel Damavand, which was thirty kilometers north of Tehran and was her and Mike's favorite resort. They had stayed there on many weekends in their first year of marriage, heavenly weekends in another lifetime.

After a light lunch of naan and cottage cheese, she was ready to start packing, now feeling quite remorseful for talking so indifferently to Mike. When the telephone rang again, she picked up the receiver right away, hoping it was him, in which case she would do her best to act more affectionately.

Parviz Shappour, her future boss at AIOC, was on the line. "Paree, I'm very pleased you'll be working for me."

How about working with *you*? "Thank you, Parviz."

"Paree, it's all right for you to call me by my first name when we're not at the office. I mean, we've known each other for a long time, but…"

"But at work you would like me to call you Mr. Shappour."

"Yes. The same applies to formal occasions outside the office, as when we entertain Oil Company guests. In fact, I don't believe secretaries should ever address bosses by their first names. There's an old English expression, something like familiarity breeds… How does it go? Breeds…"

"Contempt?"

"Exactly. Could we meet for dinner? We should discuss your duties."

"I'd love to meet with you, Mr. Shappour, but I'm about to leave town for a few days before starting work."

"Where are you going without Mike?"

"To Hotel Damavand."

"By yourself?"

"Of course."

Pause. "That is not… How should I say? It's not entirely proper, is it?"

"Why not?"

"Because this is Iran, not England. Women should not go on vacations alone, even if only for a few days." Another pause. "How will you travel to Damavand?"

"I'll drive, of course."

Another pause, longer this time, during which Paree had a good notion of what was going through Shappour's mind. *Proper Iranian women do not drive cars.*

"I certainly hope you enjoy yourself," he said—rather sarcastically, she thought.

Dial tone.

As soon as she hung up, Paree wondered how long she would last with *Mister* Shappour, who sounded like the traditional Iranian man asserting his dominance over the Iranian woman. But she needed the income and he needed a secretary, so she would stay and act as his humble inferior for as long as pride would allow her. After which she would look for another job, and another and another.

It was time to rethink her not-so-promising future at the Anglo-Iranian Oil Company while she roamed the foothills of Mount Damavand.

Chapter 12

"What are you doing, boy?"

As the words seeped into him, Reza opened his eyes and squinted at the silhouette blocking the sun's rays. He struggled to his feet and stood before a big man wearing a white shirt with rolled up sleeves and gray trousers with creases as sharp as Baba's knife.

The man sucked on a long black stem with a lit cigarette at the end. After blowing out the smoke, he snapped, "I asked what you're doing, boy."

"Nothing, sir."

"Do you live here, at the *caravansara*?"

"Y-yes, sir."

"Then get away from my car. Go to your room and sleep there. You're dirtying my Mercedes."

"Your what, sir?"

"Go away, boy!"

Reza walked away dejectedly, feeling as if hatred had followed him from the orphanage into Freedom-land, wondering if hatred had become his constant, unwanted companion.

Standing before the polished wooden door of the inn, he glanced over his shoulder. The big man still stood there, staring at him, the gold buckle of his black belt glinting in the sun, cigarette smoke bellowing out of his nostrils. Fereshteh once said Agha Mansur looked like a dragon monster when he smoked, and then she talked more about dragon monsters because she thought Reza might see them while he was in Freedom-land. "You should stay away from them because they gobble up children—especially orphans." He was sure Fereshteh made up some of the stuff she told him, but he didn't say so because he didn't want to hurt her feelings.

The inn's door was heavy, but after a few heaves he managed to open it and walk inside. The place was dimly lit and reeked of onions and grilled meat. A dozen customers sat at small round tables, too busy eating or talking to notice him. A waiter, wearing a red vest and black shalvar held to his waist by a silken drawstring, saw him and raced over. "Get out of here! We don't allow beggars."

"But sir, I—"

"Get out or I'll throw you out!"

Reza gazed at the waiter's tray holding four glasses of water. His mouth dry, throat parched, he reached out a hand. "May I please have some water? That's all I want."

The waiter eyed Reza's hand. "Is that a *real* gold ring on your finger?"

"I don't know whether it's real or not, sir."

"If you give it to me, I'll give you water *and* a skewer of kebab."

Reza flung his hand behind him. "No thank you, sir. I'll never part with my ring. But I'll work very hard for some water and food."

"Get out."

He started walking away, but the waiter told him to stop. His expression was much softer now as he handed over a glass, which Reza emptied in a few gulps. At once feeling relieved, he gave the glass back, thanked the waiter, and stepped outside.

The big man had hardly moved, still standing beside his black car, arms crossed, enormous muscles bulging under his shirt with the rolled up sleeves.

He removed the cigarette holder clenched between his teeth. "So, you don't live here after all, eh?"

"No, sir."

"Where *do* you live?"

Reza shrugged.

"A vagrant, eh?"

"No, sir."

"Then what are you? A runaway?"

He shrugged again.

"You must be hungry."

"Y-yes, sir. Very hungry."

The man grinned to show two perfect rows of teeth. They were much different from Baba's teeth that were uneven and covered with brown streaks. One of the top ones was missing, and he would whistle through the gap when he was happy, which wasn't very often. But this man's eyes were like Baba's eyes, lurking in the shadows under his brow. Now, the way they stared from behind half-closed lids brought Reza the uneasy feeling that he had seen the same stare before, after which something horrible had happened. He couldn't remember what.

"Come, let me feed you," the man said. "My home is only a few kilometers away." He opened the passenger door. "Get in. What's your name, boy?"

"Reza, sir."

"You may call me Agha Tabrizi. I'll give you a nice meal of *chellow kebab*. Would you like that?"

Reza nodded, his mouth watering at the thought, the pangs of hunger overcoming his uneasiness. Once a month, the owner of the gardens would put on a feast of *chellow kebob*—grilled minced-lamb-on-skewers served over rice—for the workers and their families. His servant would serve the meal on three enormous silver trays, which Baba said must have cost over a thousand tomans. At the end of the meal, the owner, who had the biggest belly Reza had ever seen, would tell everyone there that they should be thankful he was so generous. But Reza never heard anyone saying they were thankful the owner was so generous.

"Be careful of generous people," Mama whispered to Reza during one of the feasts. "They want something in return."

One time, when Baba was in Tehran with Agha Akbar to pick up gardening supplies, Reza saw the owner walking into their shack, carrying a shank of lamb. Curious about the visit, he stood by a window and listened, occasionally peeking inside. The owner gave Mama the shank of lamb and asked her to accompany him to his house because his wife was visiting her mother in Isfahan, and he felt *kheili, kheili tanha*—very, very alone. Mama politely declined. The owner said it would be a pity for her to give up such a wonderful piece of meat. She said, "Yes it would, but no thank you all the same." So he took back the shank of lamb and left— very, very alone.

Reza now wondered if he should be careful of Agha Tabrizi because he seemed like a generous person.

After pulling the cigarette off its holder, Tabrizi flicked it away, deep breathed a few times, then ushered Reza into the passenger seat. He shut the door and used a key to lock it from the outside. Inside the car smelled of rosewater. The seats were leather, the dashboard polished wood. Reza had never sat inside a car as luxurious as this one, with music and fresh air seeping through the dashboard and with floor mats as soft as Mama's hair.

He and Mama had ridden a few times inside the ancient car of Agha Akbar, the head gardener of *Baghah-e Sabz*. The car was faded blue, full of dents, and smelled of stale smoke mixed with farts, which Agha Akbar was fond of exploding after telling his passengers to roll up the windows because he was cold. He then laughed while his passengers made faces and held their noses. The cloth seats had holes in them, and he often said the holes were there to let in the fresh air and let out the farts.

Driving eastward on the Karaj Highway now, Tabrizi said nothing but occasionally glanced at his passenger through shadowy eyes. The glances again set off an uneasy feeling, and a voice inside Reza cried danger, but hunger made him ignore it.

* * * *

They were still on the Tehran-Karaj highway when Tabrizi suddenly put a massive hand on Reza's thigh.

Reza was panic-stricken. A vague memory of That Night sprang into his head. He wanted to vomit, open the car door, and jump out. He didn't care if he would be injured or killed. Anything was better than the massive hand, now groping higher and higher toward his private parts. He grabbed the door handle and turned it, but the door wouldn't open. Tabrizi smacked him with the back of the same groping hand. "Leave that handle alone, or I'll hit you much harder."

Reza sat still. The hand crept back onto his thigh; the fingers crept upward, slowly, like a spider creeping up a web. He screamed. The car swerved, almost off the road. It pulled to the shoulder and skidded to a stop. Tabrizi gripped Reza's arm. "Either sit quietly or I will beat you mercilessly."

"Please don't touch me again, sir."

Tabrizi grinned, and his teeth glinted. "I was simply showing my affection for you, Reza-*jan*. Relax and I will take good care of you. I'll take you to my house, feed you, clothe you, and protect you. You'll never want for anything again—as long as you're nice to me. Doesn't that sound like your dreams come true?"

Reza thought it sounded like his nightmares come true. He sensed the intent of Tabrizi's hand, and what it liked to touch. He sensed the shame, the fear that it would bring, and now he was riding in a plush car in his nightmare, about to relive the shame and fear he had felt during That Night. He couldn't remember why he had felt that way. Only that it had to do with a certain hand and a certain touch.

He decided that when Tabrizi wasn't looking, he would pull up the knob on the window ledge. The knob was like the one in Agha Akbar's car, and he knew it was there for locking and unlocking the door. He would fling the door open and leap out, even if Tabrizi was still driving at a high speed. To die in a shack or at an orphanage or on a highway were all the same. He would join Mama in heaven where there were no men with bulging muscles and roving hands. Then Fereshteh would join them, and the three of them would adventure together in the mountains of heaven.

They drove on in silence, and he noticed Tabrizi's narrowed eyes shifting between him and the road, narrowed eyes that warned Reza not to try escaping again. Near Ferdowsi Square, the traffic stopped as a mob marched down the highway, waving fists, shouting *Marg bar Englisee*! Death to the English!

Reza knew it was Ferdowsi Square because of the enormous stone statue Agha Mansur once talked about. "The statue is in honor of Ferdowsi, the man most responsible for saving the Persian language," he said. "But you children don't care about our language, so why am I telling you this?

Reza now saw his chance to flee. "I have to piss, sir."

Tabrizi scowled. "We'll be at my home in fifteen minutes. You can wait."

"But I'll wet my shalvar and your lovely car, sir."

"Very well."

After pulling the car to the curb past a group of onlookers shouting death chants in rhythm with the marchers, Tabrizi said, "Stay seated until I open your door from outside."

Reza nodded. As soon as Tabrizi had one foot out of the car, Reza pulled up the knob on the window ledge, flung open the door, and leapt onto the pavement. As he sprinted away, over the crowd noise he could hear Tabrizi shouting after him. "*Bia injah, pessar-cheh!*" Come here, little boy!

Reza had run no more than twenty paces when a tall, thin man stepped in front of him and grasped him by the collar. "Your father is calling you, boy."

"He isn't my father, sir."

"Who is he then?"

"I don't know, sir."

"We'll soon find out." The man dragged him back to Tabrizi. "Does this filthy boy belong to you?"

"Yes, he does. Thank you for bringing him to me. He's a servant boy, constantly running away. Now I'll teach him a lesson."

The man left as Tabrizi wrapped his enormous hand around Reza's thin forearm, fingers digging into flesh, almost into bone. "Get back inside the car," he said in a low, angry tone.

"I will not, sir."

The fingers dug in harder, and a shock of pain shot down to Reza's fingertips. "You will obey me, filthy child."

"I will not, sir."

"In which case, I'll hand you over to the police. They'll throw you in prison for vagrants and runaways, and that'll be the end of you."

Horrific memories of the police sprang into Reza's head: uniformed men with clubs, gripping Mama's arms, dragging her out of the shack. And memories of a fog of rage all at once blurring everything, of him running in the fog, kicking, punching, screaming. They shoved him to the ground and shoved Mama into their car with bright headlights that lit up the night. It was a car with circling blue lights on the roof, their rays dancing around the shack's walls like giant blue moths. The police questioned him, slapped him, but he didn't have the answers. So they took Mama away. Forever.

Now Tabrizi was the police, and Reza's arm was Mama's arm, fingers digging into it like the iron jaws of traps the gardeners used to capture jackals straying into *Baghah-e Sabz*. Reza's fog of rage suddenly returned, engulfing him, pumping him with strength, blanking his mind to the consequences of his actions.

Reaching back with his right foot, he slammed the rigid toe of his shoe into Tabrizi's shin. The steely grip all at once slackened, and he wrenched his forearm away.

He ran, weaving between the blurs of people, bumping into them, hearing them curse at him. He kept running until his legs grew weak and he gasped for air. Collapsing onto stone steps that led into a tall building, he leaned against the railing and waited for his legs to strengthen, breath to return, mind to clear. When his mind cleared, he thought about the terrifying start to his journey, and he thought about his destiny.

On a Thursday evening while Baba was in Karaj, Mama had talked about *taghdeer*—destiny. She said, "People believe your future is in the hands of Allah, but I think you can sometimes change Allah's mind by trying very hard to change direction. Then maybe He will take pity and grant you a new future—far away from a place like this shack, which seems to be *my* destiny, *my* hell." Reza asked her if she had ever tried changing Allah's mind.

She frowned, and her eyes drifted to the sky. "I'm trying, Reza-*jan*. Always trying."

In the end, she had managed to change Allah's mind, because now she was dead and far away from her hell, the shack at the far end of the Third Garden. Reza thought if he tried hard too, he might end up far away from *his* hell, the Mansur Orphanage. So he must keep going in the new direction he had chosen, and fight to overcome all obstacles along the way. The Agha Mansurs, The Proctors, the Tabrizis, the police. Once Allah saw how hard he was trying to change his destiny, He would take pity and let Reza journey on.

To the mountains, to heaven.

* * * *

He wandered along the pavements of Ferdowsi Square, dismayed by the hate pouring out of the demonstrators—not very different from what he had experienced at the orphanage.

Up to that point, Freedom-land seemed as lonely a place as the orphanage.

Shops lining the square were open, many of the shopkeepers standing at the doorways, some of them holding sticks or clubs, looking fierce like Baba first thing in the morning—and on and off throughout the rest of the day, depending on whether it was a bad day or a good day. Walking by a copperware store, Reza heard a passerby ask the shopkeeper why he was holding a club. The shopkeeper told him it kept the looters away. The passerby said looters usually came at nights, to which the shopkeeper retorted he didn't care because he'd be ready for them. "And if they dare to attack me, I'll use my gun too," he added, patting a bulge under his vest. Reza ran off in a near panic.

Guns frightened him—something to do with That Night.

The aroma of *naan-e sangak*, flatbread baked in a clay oven over fire-heated pebbles, lured him to stop in front of a café. His mouth watering, stomach growling louder than ever, he watched as a middle-aged couple at a window table devoured the freshly baked flatbread in between mouthfuls of omelet and sips of tea. They were oblivious to the mob outside shouting death slogans, oblivious to Reza standing at the window and constantly swallowing his spit. He walked away before a beggar-hater could scare him off.

His brief stay in Ferdowsi Square had taught him there were quite a few beggar-haters around, especially among the merchants who obviously mistook him for one. A shopkeeper had cleared his throat and fired a spitball at him. Four others had waved their sticks or clubs at him, and others had shooed him away after cursing him. He passed a grocery store with a rainbow of fruits stacked neatly in a pyramid behind the display window. The manager glared at him as he hurried by.

He passed a woman in a black chador standing behind the crowd, a wad of leaflets in one hand, a partly eaten, bright red apple in the other. He waited and watched her for a few moments, hoping she would throw the rest of the apple on the pavement, but she munched away until the fruit looked like a thin yellow bone with brown seeds stuck in the middle.

Farther down the square, he saw a man in a khaki uniform walking ahead, a boy Reza's age skipping alongside. Something dropped on the pavement by the boy's side, but he didn't notice and went on skipping. Reza picked up the object. It was a wristwatch, the leather strap unfastened. The face was black, the hands luminous green, just like the watch Agha Akbar always wore and said it cost him almost as much as all the watermelons and cantaloupes in the Third Garden.

At first, Reza was tempted to keep the watch and exchange it for food at a grocery store. But then, he thought the boy might get into terrible trouble because he had lost such a valuable object, which must have been a gift from the man in the khaki uniform, probably his father. Reza still cringed every time he recalled losing his New Year's gift, a *jigh-jigheh*—squeaker toy. He lost it a day after his father gave it to him. As punishment for losing it, he received several whacks of Baba's belt to the back of the thighs until Mama screamed, stood in the way, and deflected the blows.

Reza caught up with the boy and gave him the watch. The boy took it without even a thank you, and the man in the khaki uniform, who must have thought Reza was trying to steal it, yelled, "*Gom-sho, dozd!*" Get lost, thief!

At the eastern end of the square, Reza lost sight of the mountains behind the tall buildings and trees, and he needed to know the quickest way to go there. An old man shaped like a sickle was standing in front of a pottery store, gazing through the window. Reza came to his side and tugged at his sleeve.

The old man turned and stared at him. "Go away, boy. I don't have any money on me."

"I'm not a beggar, sir. Could you please tell me the way to the mountain?"

"What mountain are you talking about?"

"The one with snow at the top."

"Many mountains have snow on top, little boy."

"Isn't there one near Tehran?"

"You mean Mount Damavand?"

"Yes, that's it."

The old man frowned, and his wrinkles doubled. "How do you plan on getting there? It's too far to walk."

After hesitating for a moment, Reza replied, "My father will drive me, sir. H-he's shopping right now."

The old man eyed him and the ragged clothes as if he didn't believe him, clucked his tongue, and waved a hand covered with brown spots toward a highway across the square. "That is *Jadeh-e* Pahlavi. Stay on it all the way to Shemiran. Once you're there, you'll have a clear view of the mount."

Reza thanked him and walked on. He dodged his way around the demonstrators, a few of whom cursed him because he wasn't screaming Death-to-the-English, and he again wondered why the demonstrators were as full of hate as the kids at the orphanage—except Fereshteh, of course. He crossed Ferdowsi Square and headed up Pahlavi Highway that would lead him to his mountain, where he would live out his life, away from hate.

Touching the sky.

For an hour, he walked uphill along the tree-lined pavement, and as he walked, he kept his eyes to the ground, hoping to find a discarded piece of naan or fruit. He found neither. Soon his legs grew rubbery, his stomach ached, his head spun. He flopped down under the shade of an elm and closed his eyes. Within minutes, a wonderful calm settled into him. It was as if his muscles had all at once relaxed, yielding to the weakness of hunger. Perhaps, he thought, going hungry like Fereshteh was the quickest way to finding peace, peace that had left him That Night and never returned. He smiled to himself and fell asleep. A brief, restful sleep with only one dream, in which he was floating above his body, looking down at it and feeling a calmness he had never felt while he was still in the other part of his body that Fereshteh said *can't* float.

A dog sniffing his face jolted him awake. He sat up and patted the thin, black-and-white mutt dotted with bald patches. It panted and looked at him with sad hazel eyes. "I wish I had food to give you," Reza said, and the dog scampered away. He looked about him, feeling a little confused. Where was he? Oh yes, on the way to Mount—what was the name? Oh yes, Mount Damavand. He tried to stand, but his legs wouldn't obey, so he curled himself into a ball because his stomachache was much worse than before, and somehow curling up into a ball lessened the pain. He fell back to sleep, deaf to the blaring car horns, screeching tires, barking dogs.

And deaf to his own wretched sounds in nightmare-filled sleep that periodically awakened him drenched in sweat.

* * * *

"Child, are you not well? Why are you crying?"

He opened his eyes, and through tears he saw a young man in a short-sleeved shirt standing over him. The man had red hair, green eyes, and freckly arms.

Reza said nothing.

The man bent down and shook him by the shoulders. "Talk to me, child. What is the matter with you?" He spoke with a funny accent.

Reza wiped his eyes. "Nothing, sir. I was sleeping."

"Where do you live?"

"Up the road, sir."

He studied Reza. "Your clothes are filthy, and you are filthy. Are you a beggar?"

"No, sir."

He grasped Reza's wrist and pulled him up. Reza stood for a moment, but his vision misted and the ground spun about him. He collapsed onto his knees.

The man knelt down next to him. "You belong in a hospital, child."

"Some food and water is all I need, sir."

"So you *are* a beggar."

"No, not a beggar."

"Wait here."

He ran to his long black car parked along the curb, a red flag with a white cross in the middle fluttering on the side of the hood. He talked to someone through the window, who handed him a paper cup and a silver ball the size of a walnut. He brought them to where Reza had collapsed and gave him the paper cup first, which was filled with cherry soda. Reza drank it all. The man took the empty cup and gave him the silver ball.

"This is all the food I have in the car," he said. Reza looked at the silver ball, puzzled. The man laughed. "It is Swiss chocolate, but first you must remove the tin foil." Reza removed the foil and ate the chocolate ball in one mouthful. It tasted of creamy strawberries and was delicious. He wished he had another.

"Do you want anything else?" the man asked him. "A few rials, maybe?"

"I don't want your money, sir. I'm not a beggar."

"All right, you are not. Now get up and I will take you home."

Reza didn't understand why the man was so kind to him. Was he like Agha Tabrizi? Did he want something in return? Did he want to grope?

Reza stood up and shuffled away. "I'd rather walk home. Thank you, sir."

The man rolled his eyes. *"Khodah hafez*—goodbye." He strolled away.

Reza watched him climb into the car and drive off. He still didn't understand the kindness. Only mothers were supposed to be kind. Not strangers. Unless they wanted something, and then they became generous. That was what Mama said.

He started walking, and his legs didn't feel quite as rubbery. His stomach pain was gone, as was the dizziness, but he was still hungry. He continued his journey up the highway, toward the mountains and the sky.

Chapter 13

As soon as awakening from a nap, Paree glanced at the Seth Thomas clock on the coffee table: two p.m., which meant she would have a late start for her journey to Hotel Damavand. After bathing, she stood before the full-length mirror, studying her naked body that she thought was aging quite gracefully compared to her face. She noticed an egg-shaped bruise on her left thigh but wasn't sure of the cause. Possibly a dresser drawer was the culprit, since one was partly open when she had risen at dawn, and she vaguely recalled staggering to the bathroom in the middle of the night for aspirin to relieve her vodka headache.

She put on her yellow dress, which was Mike's favorite because he said she didn't look so gloomy in it—she was sure he meant she didn't look so *old* in it. From the partly open dresser drawer, she removed a wad of cash she kept under a folded blouse. The money would be plenty for three days and two nights at Hotel Damavand. At the bottom of the same drawer lay a faded photograph that she had found while emptying the boxes and crates after moving into her apartment.

The black-and-white photograph was of her posing with Minu, which Mike had snapped seven years earlier while Minu and her family had dropped in for a visit. It was the last time Paree had seen her best friend of adolescent years, when she realized that their friendship had cooled because happiness had come between them—Minu's happiness shared with her happy husband and three happy children. For some reason, Paree found herself increasingly ill at ease in the company of happy people.

Looking at the snapshot now, she smiled thinking of their long-ago close friendship, when she and Minu were inseparable, when they withheld few secrets from one another. Except one little secret. At the age of eleven, Paree experienced her first menstrual period. She grew frightened and thought she had done something terribly wrong, so she told no one about it, not even Minu.

Days after the event, Paree's mother found the soiled underwear hidden under a mattress. She lectured her daughter all about how nature had decided that women should menstruate because the blood would cleanse their womanly insides in preparation for receiving a baby, and therefore Paree had nothing to be frightened or ashamed of. "But how will the baby get inside me, Mama?" Paree asked.

Her mother smiled and replied, "You're too young to understand, my dear daughter."

It seemed she would always be too young to understand, because her mother never talked of sex. Paree later learned a little about it from a female classmate, who had learned a little from an older sister, who had learned a little from a contraband booklet. Informing the offspring about sex was simply not the Iranian parental thing to do. That was what husbands were for, supposedly.

"Most husbands probably learn of sex on their wedding nights," eighteen-year-old Minu said two weeks after marrying thirty-four-year-old Hormoz the *akhoun*—preacher—and spending their honeymoon in the holy city of Qom, which Paree didn't think was such a terrific place for a honeymoon. "The husbands fumble about in the wedding bed until they figure out the penis is almost in the same spot as the vagina. So they figure it must belong in there like a key inside a lock, and the rest is easy—at least for the husbands. They pound away, and before you realize what's happening, they roll over and fall asleep and snore. Then they wake you up in the middle of the night and at dawn and do the same thing. And after being pummeled for all that time, you still don't understand why you thought sex would be great. You'd think sex is meant to be great only for the husbands."

So Minu said, and so the mullahs and *akhouns* said the Prophet Mohammed said.

Paree learned all she needed to know about sex during her honeymoon at a Caspian Sea resort, Hotel Romsar. Mike taught her. She learned that women could actually enjoy sex if the husband wasn't in too much of a hurry and prepared his wife with sensuous stuff like gentle kissing and touching—she learned all that once Mike taught her the English word, foreplay, and showed her how it was done. And sometimes he wasn't in too much of a hurry to foreplay.

After packing a few necessities for her trip to Damavand, Paree headed out of the bedroom, reflected for a moment, turned around. She retrieved the snapshot, tore it into shreds, and threw the shreds in the wastebasket.

She was done with memories of Minu and foreplay and happy times that she didn't think would ever return.

* * * *

She drove to Pahlavi Highway, one of the two main thoroughfares heading north to Shemiran, from where she would drive on to the mountains. As she turned onto the tree-lined highway, the skies were gray and darkening. By the time she was a few kilometers away from Shemiran, the torrential downpour began. Within minutes, the visibility became near zero, heavy winds pounding the rain into her windshield, the wipers not up to the task of keeping it clear.

Cursing her bad luck, she pulled the Chevy to the curb as others had done and waited for the rain to abate, but fifteen minutes passed and it still came down in torrents. To her left on higher elevation, she saw the outline of an enormous white billboard, which she couldn't read through the sheets of rain but was sure it was the Hotel Alborz billboard. In happier times, she and Mike had often driven past the hotel, and each time they had vowed to stay there someday—the reputation of its spacious rooms and international cuisine was outstanding.

"Why not now?" she muttered.

A room with a view at a famed hotel—and a bottle of Mr. Smirnoff's best.

Chapter 14

The steady uphill walk had drained him, and within four hours, his walking pace had slowed to a crawl. As the afternoon skies darkened and threatened rain, his stomach again groaned in hunger, his legs protested the fatigue. To the left was a paved lane, leading up toward a tall white mansion nestled among trees at the side of a steep incline. Mounted on a wall just below the roof was an enormous poster inscribed with two words. Thanks to Agha Mansur's three-times-a-week writing lessons at the orphanage— taught with threats of the stick and prison room, Reza managed to spell out the two words and pronounce them: *HOTEL ALBORZ.*

Gazing at the poster, he thought maybe there would be a woodshed on the grounds of the hotel, where he could shelter and rest. Even find some food, because Mama once told him good hotels have great kitchens and wonderful food, but not the hotels in southern Tehran. "Those are for the slum people," she said, "and they don't even come with beds. Just bare rooms with cracked walls and broken windows."

Mama said she and Baba had grown up in a Tehran slum. "We lived in a crumbling apartment building they called a hotel. It was full of flies and rats and cockroaches. Most of the men and women there begged for money on the street corners. The others worked as servants or gardeners for people who were less poor than us."

Reza asked her if she was a gardener or a servant. She shook her head. "No, and I didn't beg either. You should *never* beg, Reza, because it's so…so shameful." He wondered what she did to earn money. She squeezed her eyes shut as if she were in pain.

After a while, she opened them and said, "I was with many men, and they…they took care of me."

He asked her if Baba was one of those men. She replied, "Yes. One day, the head gardener from *Baghah-e Sabz* came to the slums, looking to hire laborers. Your father was lucky enough to be the first person he talked to, so he eagerly took the job. He begged me to go with him, because he was in love with me and wanted to marry and take care of me. But at the time, he didn't know…" Her voice tailed off.

Reza tugged at her sleeve. "He didn't know what, Mama?"

Her gaze drifted to the sky. "Your father didn't know you were a tiny seedling in my tummy."

Reza would never find out if the seedling was there because of Baba or because of some unknown man. But after That Night, he would always wish for the unknown man.

As he walked up the lane now, between the trees on his right he saw a stream, which was a little wider and deeper than the creek at the Third Garden. He lay down by the stream's edge, dipped his head in, and drank enough of the cold water to quench his thirst. Feeling refreshed, he sat up, finger-combed the water out of his hair, and looked around. He was in a forest of trees that he hadn't seen before—trees with green needles for leaves and a pleasant scent.

"Maybe those are pine trees," he muttered to himself.

One of the gardeners once spoke of trees with needles and scents like the eucalyptus shrubs that were scattered about in *Baghah-e Sabz*. He said pine tree forests in Iran grow on higher ground like the foothills of the Alborz Mountains, so Reza now supposed he must be nearing Mount Damavand. He picked up a sticky, prickly pinecone and sniffed it, and the scent reminded him of the chewing gum Mama once bought him in Karaj. She never bought it for him again, because the constant chewing annoyed Baba on a Thursday night when he came home with a bottle.

Reza headed toward the hotel and was soon standing on the edge of a circular roadway paved with pinkish cobblestones, a few polished cars parked along the sides. At the other end of the circle was the enormous white hotel with too many windows to count and a stone archway in front. The building dwarfed a small white house on the left, a house with three chimneys belching smoke. He was gazing at the chimneys when a waft of smoke breezed past, bringing with it the odors of grilled meat and saffron and freshly baked naan. Maybe the small white house was the kitchen for the hotel, and maybe someone inside would give him a taste of meat or naan.

He started walking toward it, but halfway around the circle, a gravelly voice shouted, "What businesses do you have here, dirty boy?" Reza peered in the direction of the voice. Looking ferocious, a wide man in a green uniform and gold buttons stood at the end of the archway, waving a fist.

Reza ran into the forest until he reached the edge of the stream. He stopped there and waited, hoping the uniformed man hadn't followed. He hadn't.

Thunder rumbled in the distance, and the skies darkened even more as Reza decided to explore the forest on the other side of the little white house, wishing he could find food and shelter there, but doubting he would succeed.

His empty stomach in knots, legs weakened, feet sore, he suddenly felt as alone and helpless as ever. Yes, he had managed to escape from the orphanage, but he had made no plans for supporting himself once he was out. With despair threatening to overwhelm him now, he feared that Allah may have already decided his destiny: death because of no food and no shelter. What would happen to him after his body died? Where would he float to? *Jahanam*? He shuddered at the thought, hoping that hunger and weakness had brought on the gloomy attitude. All he needed was a meal and a good night's rest, and in the morning, the dark thoughts would be gone and he would resume his journey to the mountains.

While walking on beside the stream, he spotted a crumpled pile of cloth ahead of him. It was a dirty towel, but it looked dry. A blanket or pillow for the night, he thought while picking it up. He was about to continue when thunder rumbled louder and nearer, and the rain started. It was only a few splatters at first, and then torrents. He lay down under a pine tree. After rolling up the towel, he tucked it under his head and closed his eyes, worried about his destiny, wondering if Allah was watching over him, pitying him.

He fell asleep and the nightmares began.

Chapter 15

The rain-soaked Chevy engine groaned to life after a few attempts, and Paree drove up the lane toward the hotel. A moment after she reached the cobblestone driveway, the rain stopped as abruptly as it had started. She considered pressing on with her journey to Mount Damavand, but decided this was as good a time as any to try the famed hotel, at least for one night. She parked in front of the archway entrance, where an oversized, uniformed doorman picked up her suitcase and ushered her to the registration desk.

Potted palms were spaced along the walls of the red marble lobby, a fountain in the middle, a stone model of Mount Damavand spouting blue water out of its dome. The place was sedate, a dozen fashionably dressed guests sitting about and chatting in low tones while soft western music, mostly strings, wafted from overhead speakers.

The receptionist, a young man in a charcoal gray suit and green tie, was courteous and said, "May I suggest our top story suite? It has a magnificent view of Tehran." Then he added with reverence, "Princess Ashraf once honored us by staying in that suite."

Paree was a fan of the princess, the Shah's twin sister who was strong-willed and the antithesis of the submissive Iranian woman intimidated by the domineering Iranian man. Ashraf was renowned internationally for advocating women's rights, which angered the mullahs to the point of spreading ugly rumors about her sexuality, none of which were based on fact, and none of which the princess dignified with denials.

Paree asked the price of staying one night at the suite, the receptionist told her, and she sighed and started walking away. He called her back. "Perhaps *khanom* might prefer a single room on the third floor at half the price? It also has a very nice view of the city." The price was still too high, but Paree decided to take the room. After all, soon she would have a steady income, and her personal expenses were modest enough that she could afford the occasional splurge.

A parking valet took her car keys, and a bellhop picked up her suitcase and led her to the single room on the third floor. Inside was quite luxurious. The curtains were white lace, the bed an old-fashioned four-poster with a colorful quilt cover. A vase of pink tulips was atop a glass coffee table with cedar legs carved in the shape of a large animal's paws. The bellhop opened the French doors to the balcony, allowing in a breeze that floated the lace curtains about like fine mist.

After tipping him, Paree stepped onto the balcony now bathed in sunshine, and she inhaled the panorama of Tehran, beautiful from this vantage point, its ugliness completely camouflaged in the distance. The ugliness of angry mobs, limbless beggars, homeless vagrants, and Death-to-the-English chanters. And the worst eyesore of all: the slums in the southern parts of the city.

During their first year of marriage, she and Mike had lost their way and driven through those slums. The poverty and misery sickened Paree, filling her with guilt of her own charmed life with Mike in their beautiful home, and of their evenings spent at the lavish Oil Club restaurant/night club. There, wine flowed in ornate crystal glasses, delicacies tantalized palates, and couples danced to western music while wearing the latest fashions and glittering jewels and diamond-studded watches. After seeing the dismal conditions under which the impoverished people lived, she made a practice of donating generously to charities for the poor—which would have to be far less now that Mike and his income had departed for England.

Thinking of the slums now reminded her of the wretchedness that the soldiers of WWII must have seen and experienced. The wretchedness that her son, Little John, must have seen and experienced and couldn't blot out of his mind, even after leaving Tobruk and North Africa.

It was time for some amnesia-inducing liquid. She called room service and ordered a bottle of Smirnoff and bucket of ice. The order arrived twenty minutes later, and she embarked on her usual evening of drinking herself into oblivion.

After dragging a chair to the balcony, she sat down and relished the smooth taste of the Russian vodka, eagerly looking forward to the mind-numbing effects that would dissolve her dark memories into the alcohol and replace them with trivial thoughts about matters that really didn't matter. Was it time to get rid of the gray in her hair? Change the color of her eye shadow? Buy dresses meant for twenty-year-olds? Perhaps even a touch of plastic surgery to get rid of the age about her eyes. Impulsive, silly thoughts that were respites from the darkness.

She was still on her first drink when she heard the sobs. Peering down from the balcony, she could see the circular driveway, now steaming under sunshine. Beyond loomed a forest of pine trees that swayed gently to the cool breezes like Fred Astaire to soft music. She stood, leaned over the railing, listened. More sobs, and then *"Mama, kojah hasti?"* Mother, where are you?

Obviously, it was the voice of a child in a room below, a child whose mother had left alone and gone to the lobby, socializing, parading her latest creation from Paris.

Paree sat back down and sipped more vodka, hoping the mother would return soon and the pitiful sobs would yield to cries of delight. They didn't, and she grew concerned enough to investigate. She hurried out of the room and rode the guest elevator down to the lobby, which was busy now with a cocktail party for the Swiss ambassador and his entourage. Feeling appallingly out of place, she rushed past the bustling gowns, starchy tuxedos, and excessive perfumes. She stepped outside into the cool, clear air, which she inhaled several times to rid her senses of the perfumery odors.

Standing a few paces away from the hotel building and looking up at the windows and balconies, she at once realized that the sobs came from behind her, not from one of the rooms. She hurried to the edge of the driveway along the forest of pines and stopped. The sobs stopped too. She stood motionless for a long moment and listened, but she heard only a chirping bird, wind in the pines, and flowing water.

She walked into the forest, her footsteps crunching the blanket of fallen pine needles and twigs, her heels now and then sinking into patches of mud that threatened to swallow her feet along with her shoes. A creek appeared ahead under a shroud of mist rising from its waters. Paree stopped in front of it, slowly turned a full circle, and scoured the forest.

She spotted the shoes. Filthy shoes with holes in the soles, sticking out from behind a tree to her right. She tiptoed toward them, which did little to dampen the sound of crunching pine needles and twigs. Peering around the tree, she saw a sleeping boy, at most ten years old, his clothes as filthy as his shoes, his windbreaker caked with mud and torn along the seam of one of the shoulders. He breathed heavily, and his face was contorted in a grimace as if reacting to a painful dream. His hands twitched, as did his feet and sometimes his whole body.

He suddenly let out a mournful cry, and Paree was overwhelmed with pity for the wretched child. Kneeling next to him, she tapped his shoulder.

He opened his eyes, and after seeming confused for a moment, he broke out in a broad smile. "Salaam, Mama."

Chapter 16

At first, he thought the woman kneeling over him was Mama, but then he realized she was someone else. Someone who *looked* like Mama but was much older. Perhaps twenty years older. She had the same sad, kind eyes, the same comforting smile, and the same long black hair, although it was streaked with gray strands.

"I am not your mother, child," the woman said. "Did you lose your parents? Are you lost? Are you all right?"

He looked at her blankly and started shivering. He wasn't cold. Just shivering. He ran a hand over his windbreaker. It was wet and gritty. Rays of the sun filtered through the pine trees, and a single ray was focused in the middle of his jacket. That spot was warm, and perhaps the warmth would stop him from shivering. Absently, he placed a hand over the spot and wondered who this woman was, squinting at him now, her head cocked to the side as if waiting for answers to her questions.

"Are you all right, child?" she asked again.

"Yes, *khanom*."

"Are you lost?"

"No, *khanom*."

He struggled to his feet, picked up the rolled-up towel, and headed out of the shade toward the lane, toward the sun.

She walked alongside, steadying his gait with an arm linked around his. He pulled his arm away. "Please don't touch me, *khanom*."

But she held onto him again, softly like Mama did when they strolled around the Third Garden, searching for the ripest watermelon or cantaloupe or pomegranate.

At last, they were on the edge of the lane and in warmth of the sun hovering over the horizon; but he still shivered. This woman, this older likeness of his mother felt warm too. He could feel it in her arm linked around his, and he could sense it in her smile and in her sad-and-kind eyes.

He must pull away from her, because this was surely another sick dream that started in joy and ended in fright. A dream in which they were strolling along a stream when she would gradually transform into a monster with a bottle or into a policeman with a club. He would stop, but she would keep walking until her transformation was complete. Then, she'd turn around slowly and come at him one deliberate footstep at a time, and his legs would turn to stone. She would keep coming, waving the bottle or the club over her head, her face turning uglier with each footstep, stubbles growing on her chin, a big mustache drooping down, foamy spit oozing from the corners of her mouth.

He jerked his arm away and backed toward the forest.

"Don't go," the woman said, walking toward him, not transforming, not waving anything, still looking as pretty as Mama looked before That Night.

He stumbled into the forest and fell down a few paces later, the pine needles pricking him all over. She knelt down next to him. "*Now* will you come with me?" She grasped his arm and helped him stand as he still held on to the rolled-up towel. She guided him onto the lane and steered him toward the hotel. He didn't resist because he had little strength left, and because he no longer thought this was a sick dream.

Maybe it was a *good* dream, and those came once in a while— like the two that had come one after the other a day before he fled the orphanage. They were so vivid that it took him a long time to realize they had been dreams, and not very complicated ones.

The first was about him and Fereshteh dipping their feet in a mountain stream and wiggling their toes. The second was about him and Mama walking along the creek at the Third Garden, holding hands, humming her favorite song, *Yad-e Koodaki—Childhood Memory*. In a nearby pomegranate tree, a bluebird on a branch, looking at them sideways before flying onto his shoulder. Then the three of them singing by the creek.

"Where are you taking me?" he asked the woman.

"To the hotel, where you'll get dry and then I'll take you home. You do have a home, don't you?"

He looked into the distance. "Yes, *khanom*."

"Would you mind dropping that filthy towel? There are plenty of clean ones in the hotel."

He dropped it.

They climbed the steps to the archway entrance of the hotel. The broad-shouldered doorman opened one of the double glass doors and stood before the woman. After glaring at Reza, he said to her, "He's that beggar child I saw earlier. This is no place to bring him, *khanom*."

"He is ill."

"Then he belongs in a hospital. Not here."

"I'll clean him up and feed him, and he'll feel much better. Afterwards, I'll drive him to his home."

"I can't let you inside the hotel with him, *khanom*."

Reza noticed her eyes narrowing in anger. "How will you stop me? By force?"

The wide man leaned toward her. "If necessary, yes, but…" He glanced around and said in a lowered tone, "But of course, I could always make an exception in your case." He grinned, winked, and stroked the palm of his hand.

She took some paper money out of her purse and put it in the doorman's palm. He nodded and pocketed the money. Keeping them close to the wall, he ushered them to an alcove in the far corner of the lobby. As they walked, Reza could feel the people's eyes boring into him, the same looks he had received at the orphanage when he first arrived there, the kids pointing at him, whispering amongst themselves.

The men in the lobby had shiny hair and wore shiny black suits with tails on the jackets. Their *kravats*—neckties—were shaped like butterflies in flight. The women wore dresses that showed off the tops of their breasts and necklaces that glittered like dewdrops in the sun. The lobby smelled of springtime in the gardens, a blend of rose blossoms, lilacs, and lavenders, but Reza didn't notice any flowers around the place. He wondered what he smelled like. He couldn't remember the last time he had bathed or washed his clothes. Once every two weeks at the orphanage, each kid was forced to bathe in one of the rusty tubs and wash his or her clothes in the rusty water, but occasionally Agha Mansur and The Proctor forgot about some of the kids. It had been over a month since Reza had bathed in a rusty tub with rusty water and a rough piece of soap that didn't smell of anything.

The uniformed man led them to the front of an open metal cubicle, touched the visor of his green cap, and said to the woman, "Please use this service elevator when you bring the boy down. And please try to stay out of sight." He walked away. The woman and her sad, kind eyes led Reza into the cubicle with buttons mounted on a wall.

She asked him if he had ever been in an elevator, and he shook his head. She closed the gate that folded into itself and she pushed one of the buttons. Miraculously, the elevator started moving up, whirring quietly, climbing steadily. He didn't understand this new world that was so different from *Baghah-e Sabz*—the Green Gardens. Nor did he understand its people, who looked so much more elegant than the gardeners with their muddy, floppy clothes and their hats that looked like upside down bowls, some black, some brown, some with jagged holes, some with sewn-on patches.

The elevator finally stopped, and the woman opened the folding gate and steered him out. They stepped onto the red-carpeted floor and walked down a long corridor, toward the end of which they stood before a polished wooden door. The woman unlocked it and led him inside a room with see-through white curtains, framed pictures of mountains on the walls, and an enormous bed on legs with a canopy suspended on four wooden columns rising high from each corner of the bed. Covering the mattress was a thick quilt with green, gold, and red leaves printed all over it, reminding him of the colors of autumn in the Third Garden. She told him the bed was called a four-poster. Reza had never slept on anything but a floor mattress or bare ground.

"Take your wet clothes off," she said.

He felt panicky. "No, *khanom*."

"Don't worry. I'll give you something to wear while they're drying."

She smiled a genuine smile, not like Agha Mansur's pasted-on smile when he greeted grownups. More like Mama's smile when they were in their shack and playing find-the-handkerchief, a game which one of them would hide a handkerchief and the other would have to find it before the count of twenty. It was a game that Reza almost always won because Mama couldn't find the handkerchief before time ran out. He sometimes wondered if she let him win because she was Mama and wanted him to feel good.

Every time he won, she would smile her genuine smile and tell him, "You're such a clever boy, Reza-*jan*, and I'm so proud of you." He once asked her why she was so good to him, and she replied, "Because it makes *me* feel good."

So he tried to feel good too, by helping others with their chores, like he often helped his father and the gardeners at *Baghah-e Sabz*. The gardeners appreciated his efforts, and once or twice a week, they would reward him with treats such as roasted sunflower or watermelon seeds and *gaz*—nougats filled with pistachio kernels.

The woman opened a closet filled with shelves, hanging clothes, and shoes neatly arranged on the floor. From one of the shelves, she removed a shirt and shalvar, both with vertical pink and white stripes.

"You can wear my pajamas," she said.

He looked at her puzzled, because he didn't know what pajamas were.

"Clothes to rest or sleep in," she explained and pointed to a white door. "But first, you must take a warm bath to heat you up."

He was still shivering.

She opened the door and beckoned him inside a white room with white tiles and a white tub with gold handles and no rust. She turned the handles and kept adjusting them, all the while finger-testing water that wasn't rusty. She plugged the hole in the tub, which soon filled with steaming liquid.

"Your bath is ready," she said. "Take your clothes off and step in."

"I will not, *khanom*."

"If I leave, will you do as I asked?"

He shrugged.

"The hot water will stop you shivering. Or do you *like* to shiver?"

"I'll go in the water when you leave."

She took a thick blue towel off a rack and placed it on a wooden stand next to the tub. "When you feel clean and warm enough, dry yourself with this." She hung the pajamas on the towel rack, headed to the door, and turned around. "Don't forget to use soap to wash off all that dirt. Afterwards, put on the pajamas and hang your wet clothes on the rack."

When she left, he knelt next to the tub and dipped his hand in the steaming water. It felt soothingly warm, so he dipped in both hands. He splashed them about until he heard a knock on the door. "Did you get in the tub yet?"

"No, *khanom*."

"Please get in. I'll have wonderful food for you when you're done."

Food! The shivering and all the excitement of being in this place, which he was sure was meant only for rich people and not for slum and gardening people, had made him forget his hunger. Reeking of bodily stench, blended with the scent of the trees he had just slept under, he quickly took off his clothes. He stepped into the water, sat down, and slowly sank in his body, relishing the heat, the return of feeling to his numb skin. Seconds later, the shivering stopped.

Lying there, he closed his eyes and imagined floating down the creek next to the shack that was once home. Within moments though, the dark thoughts started creeping in, as they often did without warning. He sat up, splashed water all over him, and imagined he and Mama were playing hide-the-handkerchief. When the dark thoughts scattered, he sniffed the bar of green soap in a receptacle at the side of the tub. The soap smelled of springtime. He washed himself all over; his behind too, because it stank and itched.

In a corner of the bathroom was a strange looking white bowl with a black cover. He wondered what it was for. He needed to piss, and there was no hole-in-the-floor that he could see. After removing the tub's plug, he stood up and pissed in the draining water that swirled like the creek water going down a tunnel at the end of the Third Garden.

"That's why there's a metal grate there," Mama once told him. "Otherwise, you'd be sucked down into that tunnel." But he didn't think being sucked down would be so bad, because he was sure he would end up in a lake surrounded by mountains—Agha Akbar said most lakes are land basins filled with water from snow melting off the mountains.

After stepping out of the tub, he dried himself, and put on the pajamas. He had to roll up the pants-legs so they wouldn't drag on the floor, and roll up the sleeves so he could see his hands. The pajamas felt soft as Mama's hair, and he suddenly had the urge to feel the woman's hair, because if it was like Mama's, maybe he could trust her more than he did at that moment. But then, maybe he could never trust anyone else again. Anyone except Fereshteh, who was a part of him now just as her ring was a part of him. Someday when he was grown up, he would find her, they would be wedded, and they would live in their own heaven. The last time he saw her though, she looked pale and sick, and her cough was much worse. And she wasn't eating.

Oh God, please don't let Fereshteh die.

Chapter 17

Paree had seen the same look before. It was a faraway look that tried hard to hide pain but couldn't do so completely. It was Little John's look when he returned from North Africa, and now the vagrant boy, unkempt that he was, reminded her of her son. The proudly sloping brow, the flared nostrils, the chin with a deep cleft, the high cheekbones. And the eyes. Big, unblinking, slightly curved up at the outer corners. The coloring was different of course. Little John had Mike's cobalt eyes. This boy's eyes were brown with amber speckles that glittered in sunlight, and his skin was tan, not lily-white like Little John's. His body was entirely different, sort of like the stick figures Little John had once carved on their pinewood kitchen table in Bourton-on-the-Water.

Realizing that the child shouldn't see her drinking vodka, she capped the bottle and tucked it inside her suitcase. From room service, she ordered one serving of *badenjooni pelow*—eggplant pilaf—and a roast beef sandwich. A moment after the food arrived, the bathroom door opened to reveal a clean-looking boy with damp, wavy hair and wearing pink-and-white striped pajamas that hung on him like an oversized sack. She motioned him to an armchair in front of the coffee table, opposite where she was sitting.

Pointing to the rice dish on the table, she said, "There's your supper, child. What's your name?"

"Reza."

"Reza what?"

"Ahmadi."

"My name is Paree. That's what I want you to call me. Now eat, and once your tummy is full, tell me where you live."

He scooped up the rice in his fingers and dipped it in the eggplant sauce.

"You may use a fork if you like," she said, pointing to the silver fork next to his dish.

"Yes, *khanom*."

"Paree."

"Yes, Paree."

He stuffed the food already in his fingers into his mouth, licked them methodically, and picked up the fork as if it were a garden spade. Paree watched him eat like a ravenous animal, and within a few minutes, the dish was empty. After downing the glass of water next to it, he cast her a faint smile.

"*Mamnoon, khanom.*" Thank you, lady.

"Paree."

"Thank you, Paree." Reza eyed her untouched roast beef sandwich, which was sliced in half. "Aren't you going to eat, Paree?"

"I'm not very hungry right now."

"You should eat, otherwise you'll get sick."

What a considerate child. She took half the sandwich for herself and pushed the other half in front of him. "This is yours. I'll have the rest. "

He ate the portion as ravenously as the rice dish. Hours, even days of hunger to make up for, Paree imagined.

When he was done, he leaned back, grimaced in pain, and put a hand over his stomach.

"What's the matter, Reza?"

Without answering, he rubbed his stomach. She understood. "Go to the bathroom. It will ease the stomachache."

He seemed confused, and she understood because she suspected he had never used a western style commode. She took his hand, led him into the bathroom, and raised the lid of the commode. "This is a modern toilet, Reza. You sit down, do your business, and afterwards wipe your bottom with this." She handed him a roll of toilet paper from a receptacle next to the commode. "When you're finished wiping thoroughly and have put all the soiled paper into the toilet bowl, you flush everything down."

"Flush?"

She grasped the handle of a chain dangling from the overhead tank. "You pull this and water pours into the toilet bowl and washes away all the waste."

He stared inside the bowl, a third of which was filled with water. "But there isn't a hole in there, Paree. Otherwise, the water would go down it."

"Don't worry. The hole will open up when you flush. And don't forget to wash your hands in the sink when you're finished."

Paree left and closed the door behind her. Feeling oddly content, she sat before the coffee table, thinking how she would relish a few drinks of vodka over ice, but she quickly dismissed the notion. For obvious reasons, getting drunk was out of the question while Reza was with her. For the time being, she was responsible for a child, as she had been in her former life as Mrs. Paree Windom, mother of Little John Windom. In those days, she drank infrequently except on an occasional Friday evening with Mike at the nearby Sword and Hammer Tavern, when she drank not to anesthetize her mind but to enjoy an evening out with her husband.

It felt good to be responsible for someone again, even though it would be for only a short while. And what would she do after returning Reza to wherever he came from? She'd return to her routine, the unending cycle of gloom, vodka, oblivion…gloom, vodka, oblivion…

* * * *

She heard the toilet flush, water run in the sink, and then nothing. After waiting for a while, she was about to check what he was doing when he walked out of the bathroom, no longer seeming in pain. To her dismay, she noticed he was dressed in his still wet clothes.

"I'll leave, Paree," he said. "Thank you very much for the food."

"Where's your home?"

That faraway look crept into his eyes. "In the mountains," he muttered.

"How did you get down here?"

"I walked."

"That's quite a long walk. Do your parents know you left?"

"I…my parents went away for a few days."

"They left you at home all by yourself?"

"Yes."

"Where did they go?"

He fidgeted, and his cheeks flushed. "T-they went to…" He walked to the door and grasped the handle. "I must leave now, Paree. Thank you."

She gazed at the child standing at the door, a hand resting on the handle. An unsure, trembling hand. Of course he wasn't telling the truth. Secrets were buried deep in his soul, and he could not, would not, reveal them. A runaway perhaps, escaping a turbulent home or a turbulent scene, wandering aimlessly alone, searching for…what? A mountain that would swallow him and his secrets, relieve him of his tormented thoughts.

A mountain or a chestnut tree?

She would not, *must* not let him wander off alone. "Leave him in his shell for now," she told herself. She would protect him until finding out the truth behind his anguish, until finding out if he actually had a home.

Paree approached him. "I'm going to the mountains in the morning, Reza. Would you like me to drive you there?"

His face brightened. "To the mountains? Do you like the mountains, *khanom*?"

"Paree."

"Do you like the mountains, Paree?"

"I adore them, and I'll drive you to them tomorrow if you wish. Are you *sure* that's where your home is?"

"Yes, Paree."

She had him return to the bathroom and put on the pajamas again. When he came out, she led him to the four-poster. "Now you must get some sleep."

He looked at her for a long moment, a worry frown crossing his brow. "Do you want me to sleep in *that* bed, Paree?"

"Yes, Reza. Climb in."

"But where will *you* sleep?"

"On the far side of the bed, if that's all right with you."

"You won't..."

"What?"

His face paled, and Paree glimpsed a trace of fear in his eyes. "The bed is huge, and you won't even know I'm in it," she said. "But if it worries you to sleep next to someone you hardly know, I'll have room service bring a floor mattress and I'll sleep on it."

He seemed to relax. "It's all right, Paree."

He lay down on the very edge of the bed. After covering him with the thick quilt that smelled of roses, she went into the bathroom and closed the door behind her. She soaped, scrubbed, and rinsed his clothes in the tub, draped them across the tub's edge to dry, and returned to the bedside. The boy was curled up in the fetal position. He was asleep, but with frequent grimaces and body twitches.

From her suitcase, she retrieved *Moving the Mountain*, Charlotte Gilman's novel about creating a utopian society. She read until her eyes tired, until her mind drifted to her former life with Mike and Little John in their utopian cottage in the utopian village of Bourton-on-the-Water. Quietly, she took off her dress and slipped on a blouse over her underwear. Mindful that Reza seemed to shun physical contact, she climbed onto the opposite edge of the bed, leaving a wide space between them. After switching off the bedside lamp, she lay awake for a long time, again wondering about the boy in her bed, wondering about his story.

A frightened, lost child like the Charles Dickens waifs barely surviving alone in an unfriendly world. Her imagination soon took over, conjuring up various scenarios that could have led to Reza's predicament, mostly to do with parental abuse. She dozed off.

Waking up in the darkness, she felt a warm breath caressing her cheek, a thin arm draped across her chest. She put her arm around Reza's bony shoulders, gently pulled him into her, and fell back to sleep.

A dreamless, restful sleep.

* * * *

He was falling down the dark hole again, and an angel stopped his fall. She looked like Mama at first, but then her face became Fereshteh's face, and then the face of the woman whose bed he was sharing. He opened his eyes, and the woman was still there and he was nestled against her. So he quietly rolled away from her, closed his eyes, and fell back to sleep.

A dreamless, restful sleep.

Chapter 18

Reza awakened to the sun's rays seeping through the window shutters. The woman—Paree was her name, he remembered—stood at the foot of the bed, gazing at him. She didn't have as much sadness in her eyes just then, which made her look a lot more like Mama before That Night, when the sadness was always there but not quite as noticeable.

Feeling surprisingly refreshed, he sat up in bed and smiled at Paree. "Salaam, *khanom*."

She smiled the same smile that seemed so comforting when they had first met. "My name is Paree, and salaam to you, Reza." She reached out a hand. "You've slept for over half a day. Time to get up, eat an early lunch, and head to the mountains."

He didn't take her hand but climbed out of bed, his legs feeling as strong as they did before his escape from hell, the Agha Mansur Orphanage. On the round glass table were two plates with skewers of kebab and naan, a glass of tomato juice, and a cup of coffee that reminded him of Baba in the mornings. Baba and his coffee and his cigarettes and his foul moods. And on Thursday nights, Baba and his bottles and his even fouler moods.

After doing his business—Reza figured out the toilet bowl was meant for pissing too, he found his dried clothes neatly folded on the wooden stand next to the bathtub. He put them on, and they smelled of springtime like the soap he had used the night before.

Sitting on the floor at each side of the coffee table, they ate in silence. He appreciated that she didn't press him to talk. Glancing at her occasionally, he imagined she was someone's mother, someone who would sacrifice everything for her child. Like

Mama. Someone who caressed her child while he slept. Like Mama. Like last night, when he had awakened to find himself nestled against Paree until he realized she wasn't Mama or Fereshteh. He had pulled away of course, but not in fear or disgust. Although Paree was a stranger and he wasn't her child, he had felt oddly close to her.

But not close enough.

How wonderful it would be if he could find closeness again, the kind he shared with Mama at the Third Garden and with Fereshteh just before he escaped from the orphanage. Perhaps if he could spend more time with Paree, if they could…

His warm thoughts quickly scattered as uncertainties of the moment again weighed on his mind. Uncertainties about another stranger showing him kindness. Unlike Agha Tabrizi though, Paree had done nothing to make Reza suspicious and she had asked for nothing in return. Not up to that point, anyway. Surely she wanted *something* from him, but gazing at Paree now, he couldn't think of what that might be.

The uncertainties remained. They were hard to get rid of.

* * * *

They drove through a town called Shemiran and another town called Tajrish, at the center of which was an enormous traffic circle with a fountain in the middle. Shops lined the circle, and Paree stopped the car on the curb opposite a shop with a mounted picture that stuck out from above the doorway and swayed in the breeze. The picture was of a cone with swirls of yellow cream on top. She told him to wait in the car, climbed out, and disappeared inside the shop. A moment later, she walked out holding two cones filled with swirls of yellow cream. *"Bastani—*ice cream—for our desserts," she said.

It was the most delicious dessert he had ever tasted. Roses and honey. He had eaten ice cream a few times before, when Mama would buy it for him from a street vendor in Karaj. It came in a paper cup with a wooden spoon and tasted of sour strawberries in crushed ice.

They drove on, past the main street teeming with people and onto a highway that pointed toward a snowcapped peak in the distance. "Mount Damavand," Paree said. "Is that where you live?"

Reza nodded, and she smiled and drove on. The road soon turned to gravel, twisting and turning upwards around steep cliffs, which made him dizzy when he looked down, so he stopped looking down. They drove for another half hour, when the air turned so cold that she pulled out a knob and heat spewed out from under the dashboard, making his feet hot and sweaty. Now he could see snow blanketing the ground, which reminded him of what Baba once said on one of his good days: "Snow is amazing, because it melts into sweet-tasting water and runs down the mountains to nourish the trees and gardens." Reza wished Paree would stop soon so he could get out and feel and taste the snow.

Five minutes later, she pulled the car off the road and onto a lot where another car was parked. A young man and woman stood at the edge of the lot, looking up at the mount in the distance, their arms around each other's waists, swaying gently like elms in the wind. Reza thought there was something special in how they swayed together. Two people in one. Mama and Baba were never two people in one. Most of the time, they were two people far apart, and Reza often wondered if he was to blame for keeping them apart.

"From now, we must walk to go any higher," Paree said. "Are you sure that's what you want to do, Reza?"

He nodded. "Yes, please. I want to go all the way to the top of the mount and see what's on the other side."

"But I thought you live in these mountains, so you should know what's on the other side."

"I-I never saw it."

"We're not mountain climbers, Reza. We can only walk up another one or two kilometers. Do you *really* live up there?"

He didn't respond.

They stepped out into the cold air, his breath steaming, and he noticed her breath was steaming too. He ran to the edge of the lot where there was a snow bank, and he dipped a finger in the snow. It felt soft as cotton wool and cold as ice cream. He tasted the snow stuck to his finger, but it didn't taste sweet like Baba said it did.

Paree came to his side and pointed to a path, which was more like a long, winding dip in the snow that headed uphill and vanished. She said they should put on a warm cover before walking up, and led him back to the car. After opening the trunk, she took out two green blankets and wrapped one of them around him. Instantly feeling warmer, he thanked her, again questioning why she was so kind to him.

They started the climb up the path, and soon his feet were cold and wet from the snow seeping into his shoes. Gasping for air, he glanced at her, and she was gasping too.

"It's very high around here, and the air is thin," she said. "So you have to breathe harder."

"Yes, *khanom*."

"Paree."

"Yes, Paree."

"Do you want to turn around and go back now?"

"No, Paree."

He was determined to press on, to reach the top of the mount and touch the sky, to look at the world from above and look at the world on the other side. Maybe it would be a different world, without orphanages and anger and hate.

But what would he tell her once she realized his home wasn't there? He didn't know.

They trudged on for another kilometer, the snow deepening, the path now almost invisible, the air even thinner.

Paree stopped to scoop a handful of snow into her mouth. "Are you thirsty, Reza?" she asked.

He nodded and did as she did. The snow melted in his mouth, wetted his parched throat, and this time, it tasted a little sweeter. He imagined what it would be like to have all the snow taste like the ice cream she bought him in Tajrish. He would never go hungry or thirsty, his mouth would always taste of honey, and the fruits of the gardens below the mountains would be sweeter because of the honey nourishing them.

They continued the trek for another few minutes until she stopped and squatted down, panting. "I can't go any farther, Reza. The air is too thin, my feet are ice, and my legs are tired. Are we near your home yet?"

"I'll go on by myself, Paree. Thank you for everything."

She squinted at him, her head cocked to the side, and he wondered what he would do in the mountain wilderness without her. Where would he sleep? On the cold snow, like the cold ground on which he had awakened the morning after That Night? But anything would be better than going back to Agha Mansur's orphanage, which was where she would take him if he admitted he didn't have a home in the mountains.

"Can you see your home from here?" she asked.

He shook his head. "I can't see it, Paree. Not yet." Maybe there was a shed or bushes that would shelter him at the top or over the other side.

She smiled. "You don't really have a home, do you Reza?" She stood up, stepped in front of him, and wrapped her blanket and arms around him. "Tell me the truth, Reza, I won't let anything happen to you."

He felt comfortable under the two blankets and in her arms. Like his last *Now-Ruz*—New Year—at the Third Garden, when Mama crept onto his mattress, kissed him, covered him in a blanket, and wrapped her arms around him. "I'll be here for you always," she said, "and I won't let anything happen to you." It was the last time he had felt such comfort. She couldn't keep her promise though, because the policemen took her away and he couldn't stop them. He wished he knew what he had done wrong for them to take her away. He wished he could remember That Night.

Paree squeezed him against her. "Answer me, Reza. Where is your home?"

He pulled back from her and waved toward the mount. "It's up there. Goodbye, Paree."

He slipped off the blankets, handed them to her, and walked away, frightened about the loneliness, the cold, the white wilderness facing him. If only he could reach the top of the mount, then everything would be all right again. Mama would be there, waiting for him with another blanket, and someday Fereshteh would join them. He squinted at the summit, but all he saw was whiteness, a filmy mist creeping down one side of the peak. What if Mama and Fereshteh were wrong and mountains were nothing more than freezing wastelands? What if mountains were anything but heaven? Then he'd have nothing left to reach for, and without a reachable dream, there would be no purpose to living.

He trudged on, the clouds of doubt growing darker with each footstep.

Paree called after him. "Reza, please don't go. I can't leave you here alone."

He kept going.

"Reza, I will not let you wander about alone and unprotected. If you don't stop, I'll have to send the police after you."

He froze. "Please don't, Paree. Please don't get the police."

Panting, she came to his side. "I won't send for them if you tell me where your home is."

"I-I don't have one."

"Where have you been sleeping, then? Who clothes you? Who feeds you? Come on, Reza, tell me the truth."

He buried his face in his hands. "I live at Agha Mansur's orphanage, and I don't want to go back there."

She gently pulled his hands away, brushed the hair out of his eyes. "I won't let you roam the mountains by yourself. I must first take you to Mansur's orphanage. But if I think it's bad, I'll find you a far better place, where you'll be much happier and won't need to run away."

Staring at the ground, Reza thought about Paree's offer.

What if she doesn't think the orphanage is bad? He shuddered at picturing the scene after she delivered him there and left. Agha Mansur's eyeballs and scar would turn fiery red, he would thrash him mercilessly for running away, and then he would grab him by the collar, drag him up to the prison room, and lock him inside for the evening and night. He would repeat the punishments for another three days, because he once said running away was the worst crime of all, and whoever tried running away would be caught and punished four times the usual amount.

But what if she does *think the orphanage is bad?* In which case, she would take him to "a far better place." He imagined, though, that any other orphanage might be not much different. There'd be another Agha Mansur who would pat Reza's head and smile and tell him nice things—until Paree left. Then he would become the second Agha Mansur. Mean, always ready to use the stick.

And Reza again planning his escape. To the mountains.

As they walked down the snow-covered path, he realized that he had no choice except to give Paree a chance to see the orphanage. If she decided to leave him there, he would run away and never trust anyone again—except Fereshteh.

Chapter 19

They were headed downhill, away from Mount Damavand. Paree looked at Reza walking beside her, and all she could see was Little John. Post-Tobruk Little John: distant, into himself, seemingly oblivious to others, even to his mummy and daddy. Somehow she must salvage Reza, this confused, frightened little boy with the enormous sad eyes like those of an abandoned puppy. She had to prevent him from falling into an abyss as the one Little John had created for himself. A freefall she had failed to avert, for which she had felt responsible and always would.

Perhaps she should have Reza live with her as her ward, show him the kindness and warmth that no orphanage could ever provide.

Paree would be a mother again.

But was it logical to shelter a boy of dubious origins and character? Maybe he was a thief or a child with a dreadful mental disorder. She couldn't possibly handle such a child, especially since in a few days her fulltime job at the Anglo-Iranian Oil Company would begin. If she were to take him on, she'd be a part-time mother at best.

After more thought, she decided it would be wise to return him to the orphanage and pay Mansur a monthly stipend to take good care of Reza and treat him kindly. She'd visit the boy often, bringing him presents and clothes and honeyed ice cream. On weekends, she would take him to Tehran's parks, bazaars, cinemas, and dine him at first-rate restaurants like Shamshiri. But once the weekend was over, she would have to suffer his forlorn expression while hugging him goodbye then abandoning him to dissolve back into his little world of hell.

All the same, it was the best solution. Take him back to the orphanage, pay Mansur treat-the-boy-kindly money, and visit Reza often.

They walked on in silence to the car and climbed in. She glanced at her watch. It was almost 4 p.m., enough time to drive him to the orphanage—it couldn't be too far away since he had walked—and then head back to the mountains, to Hotel Damavand, which had been her original plan before the detour to Hotel Alborz.

Driving away from the parking lot, she turned the heat on maximum and asked Reza, "Where is Agha Mansur's orphanage?"

He looked into the distance. "I-I don't know, *khanom*."

"My name is Paree. If you don't know where the orphanage is, I'll stop at a police station and ask."

His face suddenly telegraphed fear, and he cowered like a frightened puppy. "No, not the police, *khanom*. Please not them. They came and took…"

"Took what?"

Without responding, he pulled his skinny knees into his chest and buried his head in between.

"Are you more afraid of the police than the orphanage?"

He remained silent.

"Reza, you leave me no other choice but to find the nearest police station."

"Please, *khanom*, don't. I'll show you the way to the orphanage. But after you see it, will you leave me behind if you think it isn't so bad?"

She hesitated. Did she have the willpower to leave this cowering, frightened little boy there? "I'll talk to Agha Mansur and persuade him to take good care of you. If I feel he won't do so, I won't leave you behind."

He raised his head. "How will you know if he would take good care of me or not? He'll be nice when you're there, and he'll turn mean as soon as you're gone. Then he'll beat me because I ran away."

"Mansur beats you? With a stick?"

"Yes." He showed her the palms of his hands, the calluses, the scars.

Paree shook her head in disgust. This was 1951, a millennium removed from the Dark Ages and a century removed from the Charles Dickens era. Yet, physical punishment of children seemed the norm throughout Iran and perhaps throughout the world. It was no different in England's schools, which were ruled by the cane, often the bamboo cane. Depending on the infraction, six or twelve swishes to the bared bottom of children who dared talk during study hour or didn't remember when the Magna Carta was issued or couldn't parse a Latin sentence. Inhuman treatment doled out by inhuman adults. She recalled a time when her son had been punished at elementary school because he smeared paper glue on the history teacher's chair. Little John came home that evening looking a little pale, but he said nothing about the punishment until suppertime, when she noticed him grimacing as he sat down at the dining table. She asked him why he looked pained, and he told her. That night, as she watched him climbing into the bathtub, she saw in dismay the massive welts and bruises on his buttocks.

She at once summoned Mike, who glanced at the damage, shrugged, and said, "I was raised by the cane too, and that's the way it bloody well is." Undeterred, the next morning Paree made an appointment to meet with the headmaster. That afternoon, she sat before his enormous oak desk in his enormous oak-paneled office and politely asked him about the school's policies of physical punishment. She received a response not unlike Mike's. "The cane is how we discipline the children, madam. It is the way of most schools, but if you disapprove, you're more than welcome to remove your son from here."

She did exactly that and transferred Little John to another private school just outside Cheltenham—Ullenwood Manor Preparatory School for Boys. Despite the headmaster assuring her that the school made minimum use of physical punishment, a month after Little John was enrolled there, she saw the same welts and bruises and cruelty.

Blinking away a tear, she said to Reza, "I will judge Agha Mansur, and then I'll decide what to do with you."

* * * *

They were stopped for a traffic signal in downtown Shemiran. Paree noticed Reza groping for the lock button on the window ledge of the passenger door, which she had pressed down after he was seated. He would jump out, possibly be run over, or disappear among the throng on the sidewalks and head back to the mountains. After which, she would have to add him to her guilt list of failures as mother and as protector.

"Reza, please don't unlock the door. Just trust me to do right by you."

He pulled his hand away.

Although he knew none of the roads by name, he seemed to have a good sense of direction. At the southern end of Pahlavi Highway, he pointed to the west, and she drove them past Ferdowsi Square, past Cinema Homah where she and Mike had watched countless movies. Paree had seen *The Best Years of Our Lives* four times, three of them without him, and each time she had cried. Cried for the man who lost his hands and for the men and women who lost their lives or their souls to WWII.

And she cried for Little John.

Twenty kilometers past Mehrabad Airport on the highway to Karaj, Reza pointed to an unpaved road disappearing south behind the desert hillocks. She drove onto the road, which crossed railroad tracks and soon tapered down to a single lane. Within five or so kilometers, it ended at double wooden gates interrupting a tall clay wall. She parked the car to the side and glanced at her watch: a quarter to five.

After eyeing the bleak surroundings, she patted Reza on the head, climbed out of the car, and approached the double gates. She peered through an eye-level, grated opening at a square courtyard, the asphalt cracked, weeds sprouting between the cracks. Beyond was a sprawling, three-level plaster house with chipped white paint and a flat roof. All the windows of the upper stories were barred— probably to prevent the children from trying to kill themselves, she thought. The place looked like a wilderness prison. A cold, isolated compound, keeping orphans away from the outside world as if they were criminals or diseased and must be quarantined like lepers.

No one was in sight. She pressed the doorbell mounted below the grated opening, stepped away, and waited. Moments later, one of the gates creaked open and a big man stepped out—in his mid forties, she guessed. His hair was cropped military style, the ends of his eyebrows were curled up like little horns, and his black eyes were disinterested yet surly. He wore a starched white shirt, khaki slacks held up by khaki suspenders, and spit-and-polish army boots.

He studied her for a few seconds and asked, "Are you with Children's Welfare Administration?"

"No. I wish to speak with Mr. Mansur."

"What's your business with him?"

"Personal. Are you a teacher here?"

"The children's proctor." He squinted at the Chevy. "Who's with you?"

"A friend."

"A very young friend by the looks of him."

He cast Paree a surly glance and marched to the passenger side of the car. After peering inside, he flung the door open, gripped Reza's arm, and jerked him out.

"You'll soon pay the price of running away, boy," the proctor growled.

She watched in dismay as Reza kicked him in the shin and ran off, but the proctor was too quick for him. He caught up with Reza in a few long strides and grasped him by the scruff of the neck.

"The price of running away just doubled, boy."

Chapter 20

Paree stood cross-armed before Reza's surly captor. "Take your hands off the boy or I'll summon the police."

"He's our charge, and we'll deal with him as we see fit. Where did you find him?"

"I'll discuss all that with Mr. Mansur. If you refuse to let me see him, I'll return here with the Children's Welfare authorities."

After glaring at her for a moment, the proctor led them into the compound. As they walked across the courtyard, he steered her to the back of the woodshed and pointed out a patch of fresh-looking clay on the wall. "The boy dug a hole there. That's how he escaped."

"Is this a prison?"

"An orphanage. If you're here to make trouble, you can leave this instant—but without the boy."

"I will not leave until I've spoken with Mansur."

She felt Reza's trembling, sweaty hand grip hers. She glanced at him and his pale face, beads of sweat gleaming on his brow. She bent down and whispered to him, "Remember I'm with you." He didn't respond. Just held on to her tighter.

They climbed the front steps into the house and entered a lobby. The floor was stone, the walls plaster, the atmosphere cold. The proctor ushered them down a corridor and past a room with not much in it except a chalkboard and a map of Iran tacked on a wall. Paree also noticed a thick stick, which looked like a trimmed tree branch, leaning in a corner of the room. They walked on as she shook her head in disgust. They passed another more spacious room that hissed with whispered chatter. Inside were young boys and girls—ten to twelve years old, she guessed, sitting on benches at two sides of linoleum-covered tables. In front of each child was a bowl of watery yellow soup and a plate with a slice of naan and white cheese.

The proctor stopped at the doorway and yelled, "Suppertime. You may start eating."

Paree looked with dismay at the children. Most of them wore clothes that were torn or patched in various places, many oversized and hanging over their wearers like banana peels without the fruit. The children were filthy, their hands grimy, their gaunt faces streaked in shades of gray. No one was smiling. They just looked sullen or aloof. The room reeked of stale cheese and misery, and her heart cried out for the children.

The proctor led her and Reza up a flight of stairs to the first story. Near the end of a corridor, he stopped in front of an oak door.

He knocked, opened the door, and stuck his head inside. "We have our runaway back, sir."

"Bring him in."

"There's someone with him."

"Who?"

"A woman."

"Bring them both in."

Grasping Reza's hand, Paree followed the proctor into the office that was hazy with cigarette smoke and seemed luxurious compared to the rest of the place. A Kashan carpet centered the polished wood floor, and the walls were freshly painted in beige, decorated with numerous framed photographs of the Caspian seascape. A life-sized portrait of the Shah of Iran in royal regalia hung to one side of the bay window that overlooked the desert and mountains beyond.

The man behind the cedar desk stood up as Paree and Reza walked in. About the same age and almost as big as the proctor, Mansur was overweight, wore a gray suit, white shirt, blue tie, and horn-rimmed glasses. His shiny black hair was plastered down, his smile pasted on. A linear scar streaked across the right side of his forehead—like the scar of a knife slash. Paree studied his dark eyes that were fixed on her intently. She didn't see coldness or anger in them. Just suspicion.

He waved her to a chair and said to the proctor, "Take the boy to the dining room. I'll talk to him later."

Paree looked at Reza, whose eyes were wide in fear, whose body trembled in fear. "Don't worry, Reza, because I won't let anything happen to you," she whispered to him.

His fear didn't seem to abate.

Once Reza and the proctor left, she sat on a wooden chair before the desk. Mansur sat on a leather swivel chair behind the desk. He asked for her full name, and she obliged. He took out a silver case from his jacket, removed an oval cigarette, and tapped one end on the desktop. After lighting the cigarette and inhaling deeply, he asked, "Where did you find Reza, *khanom*?"

"On the road to Shemiran. I fed him and provided him with a good night's rest."

"How kind of you. Did he talk much about our orphanage?"

"Enough to let me know he's very unhappy here. Please tell me about him and his background."

"I'm sorry, *khanom*, but that's confidential information."

"Why do you think he's so unhappy here?"

"Because he is unruly and antisocial. In a word, he is *vahshee*—wild."

"What does he do to merit such a label?"

"He doesn't obey the rules. Constantly daydreams in class, fights the other children, and shows utter contempt for our system."

"Is it because you make him feel like a caged animal?"

The pasted-on smile all at once vanished. "Respectfully, *khanom*, I'm busy and must ask you to leave—the children's proctor will let you out. Thank you for returning Reza."

Furious at Mansur and the proctor and the prison-like environment, Paree tried to keep her tone calm. "After all the trouble I took to bring him back, don't you think I deserve a few more answers about him and about this place that's supposed to be his home?"

He tapped his cigarette ash into a brass ashtray and stood up. "I don't have the time. You may leave now."

Unable to control her temper, Paree leapt off the chair. "Then I will discuss Reza and this orphanage with the government authorities. I'll tell them about the appalling conditions and what the children are given for their suppers. A piece of dry-looking naan with stale cheese and watered down soup." She bore her eyes into him. "And furthermore, I'm taking Reza out of here with me."

"He is our ward and you can't take him away. That would be tantamount to kidnapping."

"And who'll stop me? You or your surly assistant? And *how* will you stop me? Beat me like you beat those unfortunate children?" She found herself shouting now, her face and back of her neck on fire, her body shaking in rage.

Seemingly stunned by her fury, Mansur inhaled another lungful of smoke and settled back into his swivel chair. "Please calm yourself, *khanom*. Sit down and I'll tell you about him."

Paree sat, still furious, but her rage now blunted by a measure of satisfaction that she had managed to intimidate an Iranian male—a sadistic one at that.

He stubbed out the cigarette, leaned back, and clasped his hands behind his neck. "Almost five months ago, Reza was brought here after a terrible crime took place in his shack of a home at a fruit and vegetable farm east of Karaj. His father, Abbas Ahmadi, was shot to death. His mother, Khatimeh, confessed to shooting him during a violent argument and was thrown in prison. And before you ask, I don't have any of the gruesome details."

"Did Reza witness the crime?"

"I was told he slept through it all, but that doesn't seem very likely. I doubt he could have slept through all the ruckus going on."

"What happened to the mother?"

"She died in prison."

Paree flinched. "Died of what?"

"After spending a week behind bars while awaiting trial, she died of a seizure. That's all I know."

As Paree digested the tragic facts, Reza's face materialized in her mind's eye. No wonder it was the face of wretchedness, of isolation. No wonder he was running to the mountains to let the cold, thin air and hunger deaden his sorrow. She was now certain the child was on a self-destructive path, and understandably so.

Somehow, someone must step in his way and redirect him onto another path that would take him to warmth. Take him to a friendly place where time would glue his shattered soul back together firmly enough so that the pieces wouldn't fall apart again at the first setback, the first jolt of a repressed memory springing out of its hiding place. Like her own repressed memories that would spring forth every time she saw a young soldier or a khaki kitbag or a chestnut tree.

Mansur lit another cigarette. "Reza requires strict discipline, *khanom*, and we shall tame him."

"Tame him? How?"

"With time-tested methods."

Paree had seen and heard enough. The place depressed her, Mansur depressed her, and the children of misery depressed her. "What happens to the children after they leave here?"

"They're sent to another government-managed orphanage for older boys and girls. When they turn sixteen, they're sent to work until they can take care of themselves. Then they're on their own."

"What's their ultimate fate? Do most of them become decent, productive citizens? Or do they end up in the slums as beggars and vagrants?"

He shrugged. "Who knows?"

Paree blazed her eyes into him. "You mean, who cares?"

"I didn't say that, did I?"

She bolted off the chair and stomped to the door. As she gripped the handle, she realized that if she walked out of the office, she would walk out of Reza's life. She paused, took three deep breaths, and faced Mansur. "What must I do to get Reza out of here and take care of him myself?"

He squinted at her. "Do you have a criminal record?"

"Of course not!"

"In which case, the process is quite simple. For purely economic reasons, the government is always anxious, always more than willing to give up the children to individuals who would care for them." He opened a desk drawer, pulled out a multi-paged form, and waved it at her. "You can either adopt the child or become his legal guardian. Just fill out all the pages on this form, and then we'll clear it with the authorities in Tehran. If they find you acceptable, he's yours."

Paree walked to the table. "I'll fill out the form. How long will the process take?"

"For legal guardianship, six to twelve weeks. For adoption, six to twelve months."

She reflected for a moment. Adoption was out of the question for now. She was too consumed with her own problems to be the mother of a complicated, confused ten-year-old, but assuming his guardianship would be a start. A start for her and a start for Reza. They would learn about each other and work on their problems together. How to douse the fires in their souls. How to convert open sores into faint scars. How to find a path toward their futures that wouldn't circle them back to their pasts. And if they succeeded in doing all that? She would adopt him.

"What will happen to Reza while we wait to hear from the authorities?" she asked Mansur.

"He'll stay here."

"And be beaten for running away."

He smirked. "Crime and punishment, *khanom*. That's how our society works."

Mindful that many government employees in Iran, most of them underpaid, barter favors for *roshveh*—bribes—, she said, "I wish to become Reza's legal guardian. If I donate some money to you on behalf of this orphanage, will you spare his punishment and speed up the paperwork?"

This time he grinned. "How much of a donation did you have in mind?"

Paree unzipped a side pocket of her handbag and took out a wad of paper money. "How about two hundred tomans?"

"Hurrying up the process will involve much time and legwork."

After counting out double the amount, she placed the money on his desk. "Surely four hundred tomans is sufficient for your time and legwork."

His grin broadened. "Fill out the paperwork and within the next two or three days, I'll personally deliver it to Children's Welfare."

Paree sat down and filled out the four-page form while he chain-smoked and busied himself with other paperwork. When she was done, she handed him the form. After entering additional information on it, he tore out the carbon copies and gave them to her.

"When can I take Reza?" she asked, folding the copies into her handbag.

He examined the originals for a long moment. "Report here, next Thursday afternoon."

"Very well. In the meanwhile, you won't beat him?"

"I will not."

She left him her telephone number and walked out.

Four hundred tomans for mercy. Four hundred tomans for a child's life. So little for so much.

Chapter 21

Still trembling and wondering about the punishment Agha Mansur had in store for him, Reza stood at the door of the dining room and looked for his friend, Fereshteh. He saw her sitting at the corner of a table, staring at her plate of naan and cheese and yellow liquid in a bowl. The Proctor pushed him into the room. "No supper for you, boy. Find yourself a place to sit and just look at what everyone else is eating."

With the children's eyes riveted on him, Reza weaved his way around the tables and flopped down next to Fereshteh, half his rear dangling off the edge of the bench. He was stunned at seeing her up close. Her face was ashen, brow beaded with sweat, eyes sunken and listless, dark circles under them.

"You look really sick, Fereshteh." he whispered.

"I'm sick and I don't care," she whispered back.

"I'll tell The Proctor, and he'll take you to see a doctor."

"You will do no such thing because I *want* to be sick."

"You're mad, Fereshteh."

"No madder than you, running away and knowing you'd get caught. Who caught you, anyway?"

"A nice lady."

"She couldn't be so nice if she brought you back, could she?"

"Maybe not so nice if she doesn't take me out of here."

She pushed her plate of cheese and naan in front of him. "I don't want this."

He pushed back the plate. "You eat it. You need it much more than I do."

She had a coughing fit, and when it was over, she stared at him through eyes that had turned bloodshot and moist. "They caught you, and now they'll punish you."

He shrugged.

"Do you still have the ring I gave you?"

He showed her his index finger. "Do you want it back?"

"No. That ring is yours to remember me by forever and ever. And you promised me you'd wear it forever and ever."

"I'll keep my promise."

Her eyes drifted to the window. "What was it like? I mean running around on your own, outside *jahanam*—hell."

"Free. I was free, Fereshteh. I was almost on top of Mount Damavand."

Even though he was free only for a short time, the experience had been well worthwhile. He had tasted a bit of life again and he had tasted snow. Sure, he had faced more hatred and loneliness, and he had faced hardships and danger. But such were the conditions of freedom, the conditions of living as a lone bird, unprotected, always in danger of falling prey to predators like Agha Tabrizi. As for that woman, Paree, she *was* nice to him, but he couldn't trust her. After all, she had brought him back to *jahanam*. He didn't think people like Paree could ever relate to poor people from slums and orphanages, or to children whose mothers had been in prison.

"Are you sure you don't want my food, Reza?" Fereshteh asked.

He shook his head. Maybe he would starve, like she seemed to be doing. Then maybe peace would come to him as it had done when he was starving and thirsty while walking up Pahlavi Highway. He had collapsed under the shade of an elm, feeling even more at peace than he sometimes felt before they took Mama away. If the young man with the funny accent hadn't given him the cherry drink and chocolate ball, Reza might still be under that elm tree, his body rotting as the floating part drifted far, far away.

Yes, he would now deny himself food and water, and once his body died, he would join his good mama, wherever good mamas floated to after their bodies died.

He had first heard about Mama's death while he was at a temporary home for children without homes. It was a brick house in the desert just west of Tehran, and there were thirteen other boys and girls there, all waiting to be sent somewhere else to live until they were old enough to live on their own. The woman who ran the home was pleasant, but her husband became nasty when the children misbehaved. One morning, she woke Reza up and told him to wash his hands and face and put on clean clothes because he must be ready to go to another place.

That was when he spoke his first words since arriving at the house for children without homes. "Where's the new place, *khanom*?" he asked her.

"It's near Karaj," she replied. "Agha Mansur's home for children without parents."

Reza shook his head. "But I have my mama, and *she*'s a parent." The woman looked at him sadly, and her eyes grew moist. "I'm terribly sorry to tell you this, Reza, but your mama died a few days ago and…"

That was all he heard. He leapt off the mattress and started hitting her and kicking her and calling her a liar. She screamed. Her husband ran in, grabbed a fistful of Reza's hair, threw him into the bathroom, and locked the door. An hour later, two policemen took him away in their police car. To a house for children without parents.

Children without hope.

* * * *

Soon The Proctor returned and told everyone to go into the courtyard. Everyone except Reza. He took him up two flights of stairs and into a cubicle of a room with a tiny barred window, a small mattress against a wall, and a hole-in-the-floor toilet that stank. It was the *otagh-e zendan*—prison room—for misbehaving children. They were locked inside it alone once classes ended for the day, and they were kept there overnight without supper—after a thrashing.

"You'll stay here and rot for all anyone cares," he now heard The Proctor telling him.

"No beating, sir?"

"We shall see. Tomorrow, probably."

The Proctor walked out and slammed the door behind him. Reza lay on the mattress and stared at the ceiling, cobwebs around the edges, spiders living a life any way they chose. Happy lives, free to go wherever they wished. From ceiling to ceiling, window to window, tree to tree, mountain to mountain. He imagined himself as a spider living in the pine trees near the hotel where Paree had found him. He would drop down to the stream, find a floating leaf, hop on it, and drift away to a lake surrounded by a forest and mountains, where he'd live in the trees below or in the mountains above. He would eat snow for food, snow that tasted of roses and honey. The leaves of the forest would keep him warm, the snows of the mountains would keep him cool, and the waters of the lake would keep him refreshed.

Someday, Mama and Fereshteh would join him. Mother Spider, Girl Spider, Boy Spider, living together in their heaven, playing games or listening to Mama telling stories about the Third Garden. The good stories, never the sad or angry ones. *Once upon a time, there was a little boy who lived in a garden. He had a happy life.*

Except on Thursday nights.

For the moment, Reza couldn't think of any happy stories about himself.

An hour later, the door rattled, the handle turned, and The Proctor walked in. "Stand up at attention when you see me, boy." He had taught all the kids how to stand at attention because, according to him, "Before coming here, I was an important army sergeant defending my country. So you brats had better show me respect."

Reza stood at attention and at once saw the tray in The Proctor's hand. A tray with a skewer of kebab, slice of naan, and glass of *doogh*—a carbonated, sour drink made from yogurt.

The Proctor sniffed and sneered. "You can thank Agha Mansur and *Khanom* Windom for this."

"Who's *Khanom* Windom, sir?"

"The horrible woman who brought you back here."

"She's not horrible, sir."

"I say she is, so don't contradict me."

"What does contradict mean, sir?"

"Shut up!"

"Yes, sir. How long will you keep me in this room?"

"Just for tonight, as a punishment for running away. Tomorrow you may join the rest of the children, but we'll keep a close eye on you."

He handed Reza the tray, walked to the door, and spun around. "That woman is making a big mistake, boy."

"I don't understand, sir."

"A big mistake. She can't possibly manage you like we can."

"Manage me? How will she try to do that?"

"She's taking you to live with her—this Thursday."

His mind suddenly fogging with the news, Reza almost dropped the tray. He stood frozen for countless heartbeats, sorting through The Proctor's words. *Taking—you—to—live—with—her. Taking—you—to—live—with—her. Taking you to live with her!*

He sank to his knees.

"Stand up!"

He stood, feeling a little unsteady.

"Did you hear what I said, boy? You're leaving here on Thursday."

Reza stared at the glass of *doogh*, at the bubbles floating to the top, bubbles of fresh air from the depths of sourness, filling him with new life, new hope.

"Talk to me, boy."

But why Thursday? At the Third Garden, those were the worst days of all. "Did you say Thursday, sir?"

"I did."

"Could she come on Wednesday instead?"

"Shut up and eat your food, boy."

* * * *

Reza lay on the mattress in the prison room, wondering—and worrying—about Paree. He had misjudged her because she was coming back for him, so she could obviously get along with children of mothers who were thrown in prison. Paree was not Mama, but she was kind and gentle like her—and sad like her. He wondered why she always looked sad. Maybe she knew that someday the police would take her away, just as they had taken Mama away. If that happened, they would hand Reza back to Agha Mansur and The Proctor, but he would escape again and find another Paree. This time, a much happier Paree.

As his thoughts drifted to life with her outside *jahanam*, a tiny gray bird with a red chest landed on the outside ledge of the barred window. It hopped up and down between the glass and bars, now and then pecking at the glass. A few seconds later, it flew away. The little bird reminded him of a happy story from the Third Garden.

He had climbed a pomegranate tree and picked the juiciest fruit he had ever tasted. As he nibbled the pulp from the seeds, a bluebird hopped on the branch and looked at him sideways through one eye. Reza put a seed in the palm of his hand, and the bluebird turned its eye onto his palm. One sidestep at a time, it inched toward him, the one eye flicking between him and the seed. The bird stopped a fingerbreadth away to take another look at him, and he didn't move. It hopped onto his palm, picked the seed, flew away.

A day later, Reza climbed the same tree, sat on the same branch, gave the same bluebird another pomegranate seed. He did that three days in a row, and the bird started following him everywhere in the garden, flying above him when he walked, perching on a tree branch when he stopped. One day when he was walking along the creek, he looked up and whistled at the bird. It sang a tune, flew down, and landed on his shoulder.

He named it *Kucheek*—Little. It was the only pet he ever had, and they were never far apart when he was outside in daylight—he imagined that after dark it went to bed in its nest. Often while feeding it pomegranate seeds, he would talk to Kucheek, and it would respond by singing him a tune or fluffing up and shaking its feathers. It never followed him into the shack after the first time though, because Baba chased it out with a shoe. Reza now wondered what happened to Kucheek. The last time he saw it was the afternoon before Baba left to go out for That Night.

Maybe Paree would treat Reza as he had treated Kucheek. Someone to talk with, someone to feed and protect. A pet.

* * * *

The next morning, The Proctor let him out of the prison room and told him to join the other kids for breakfast. As soon as walking into the cafeteria, Reza sensed that the kids seemed more gloomy than usual. He looked for Fereshteh but couldn't see her, so he assumed she was sick and was kept in bed.

During morning recess, no one bothered him or made fun of him. Not even Abdullah, who usually taunted him because taunting Reza was the popular thing to do, and Abdullah liked being popular. At first, Reza thought maybe the kids had changed their attitude toward him because of his daring escape, but he soon found out it wasn't the reason.

He strolled to the woodshed and sat down, leaning against it and daydreaming about roaming Mount Damavand with Paree. Two girls, whose names he didn't know but who seemed the same age as Fereshteh, walked over and disappeared around the corner behind the woodshed.

Although he couldn't see them, he could hear their conversation.

"Poor Fereshteh."

"Poor, poor Fereshteh."

"Who found her dead?"

"The matron, when she came to wake us up."

"Why did Fereshteh die?"

"Because she was sick."

"How did she get sick?"

"She didn't eat, that's how."

"Why didn't she eat?"

"Because she *wanted* to get sick."

"Why?"

"Because she wanted to go to *behesht*—heaven."

"Is that how you get to heaven? By not eating?"

"I suppose so."

"But during class, Agha Mansur excused me to go and pee. That's when I saw two men in white jackets taking her away."

"So?"

"She was on a stretcher and covered with a white sheet, and that means she didn't go to heaven."

"They just took her *dead* body away, stupid. Not the *alive* part that goes to heaven. No one can take that part away."

"Not even Agha Mansur or The Proctor?"

"Not even."

Reza smiled to himself. *So Fereshteh got her wish and she floated away from her body.* He looked to the sky, hoping to see a sign of her floating over him, smiling down at him, waving goodbye on the way to heaven. All he saw were three circling hawks, and he was sure they wouldn't harm her because she was an angel on the way to heaven, smiling and waving.

He thought of his own body on the way to Shemiran, ready to die under a tree, when all pain disappeared from it and from his mind. For a brief moment he thought he was in the air, looking down at his dead body at peace. Men in white jackets would have come and taken it away, but without the part that floats because, like the girl said, no one can take that part away. Not even Agha Mansur or The Proctor.

And where would the part of him that floats have gone? To heaven?

Was that where Fereshteh would end up?

As he thought of the last moments he had spent with her, the tears started flowing because suddenly he wasn't so sure if she would find her way to heaven. Some children end up in hell, don't they? That's what Baba said when he was angry. One time after Reza had forgotten to clear the weeds out of a cantaloupe patch, Baba yelled, "You will go to *jahanam*!"

Reza asked him what *jahanam* was. Pointing at the ground, Baba replied, "It's the opposite of heaven—a cave deep down under the earth. It's always on fire, and it's where rotten bastards are sent to burn forever."

He then gave his definition of bastard: kids who don't look like their fathers.

Years later, when Reza learned the correct meaning of the word, he thought that if he was in fact a bastard and not Baba's son, he should be thankful.

After a long time, the tears stopped flowing as he decided that Fereshteh was a *good* girl. And good girls always ended up in heaven.

What about him? Would he go to *jahanam* because he didn't weed a cantaloupe patch? Would he go to *jahanam* because he couldn't stop the policemen with clubs from taking Mama away?

It was all so confusing

Chapter 22

Paree decided to forgo her stay at Hotel Damavand—the four hundred tomans spent for bribing Mansur made the decision easy. Instead, she spent the rest of her free days volunteering at the hospital for the poor, which she knew would be her last days there before Reza moved in with her. The many hours of sharing a life of misery with the wretched souls of Tehran would soon be over. It was time for change, for sharing a life of hope with a child.

On Saturday morning, she started work at the Anglo-Iranian Oil Company's Tehran headquarters as secretary to *Mister* Parviz Shappour. He was a demanding boss besieged with work, having taken on the additional load of his British superior who was transferred back to England. The uproar over nationalizing Iran's oil industry was reaching its peak, and rumors circulated that the Shah might be forced to abdicate if he didn't bow to the nationalistic fervor.

The daily demonstrations had grown noisier and angrier, and Paree had even heard a few death slogans aimed at the beleaguered monarch. None of it bothered her, because her mind was consumed with Reza coming to live in her home. The money Mike gave her had dwindled down to the equivalent of two hundred British pounds, which was plenty to pay for at least another month of room and board and to buy Reza necessities such as new clothes and shoes. At the end of the month, her income from the Oil Company would start flowing in, which would not only pay the rent, but leave enough for spending on additional needs and a little entertainment. Not a bad new beginning—for both of them.

Despite her excitement in assuming Reza's guardianship, she was as yet uncertain if she had done the right thing. After all, he was from a violent background and he might harbor a violent trait. *Vahshee*—wild, Mansur had called him, but she knew she couldn't leave the boy at the awful place that seemed more like a leper colony for children. Given time, she would learn much more about him. If violence was in his blood, she would find it out and try to control it. If she couldn't, she would hand him back to the orphanage, which was a clause in the contract: *Should either party be dissatisfied with the guardianship, The Ward must be returned to the Mansur Orphanage within a year of The Guardian signing The Contract.*

Within a year.

A year of probation and probing.

A year of hoping and praying for the best outcome: Paree and Reza, a family of two.

But first, she must make Reza feel at home. As luck would have it, when she arrived at her apartment from work that Saturday evening, the woman next door, a widow and former schoolteacher, invited her in for a farewell tea—and to see if Paree wanted any of the furnishings. "Next week I'm off to live in Toledo, America," the neighbor announced. "Iran belongs to the mobs, America belongs to the people. And best of all, women in America are not treated as slaves to men."

After viewing the furnishings, Paree chose a colorful Isfahan carpet and a single bed. With the neighbor's help, she laid the carpet on her living room floor, and it immediately added considerable warmth to the apartment. They moved in the single bed and placed it next to Paree's, with two feet of space in between. Hers was a double, which made the bedroom look a bit lopsided.

During tea, Paree talked about Reza, after which the neighbor sorted through a stack of books and gifted her one entitled *Reading and Writing Farsi for Beginners*. Paree had given Reza's education much thought, wondering how he would react to school—a public elementary school was only a few blocks away from the apartment. She decided she wouldn't send him there until he adjusted to his new way of life. In the meantime, she would assign him plenty of homework, which he must complete while she was at her job, and which would keep him busy in the freedom of his unfamiliar surroundings.

As soon as leaving work the next late afternoon, she drove to *Lale-Zar*, a busy shopping district in downtown Tehran. As additional warm touches to the living room, she purchased two potted Persian fritillary plants in glorious shades of lilac, four colorful throw cushions, and a vase of artificial roses woven from Shiraz silk. For Reza, she bought a new windbreaker, two shirts, underwear, socks, slacks, hairbrush, and a few comic books. Guessing his foot size, she bought him gym shoes from Mr. Baghdessarian, who once sold shoes to Mike and who spent countless hours engaging in the favored Iranian pastime: *chooneh*—haggling.

It annoyed Paree no end, but without *chooneh*, merchants would cheat their customers. She came away with the shoes for Reza at half the asking price, and with Mr. Baghdessarian whining that soon he wouldn't have enough money to feed his family thanks to customers like *Khanom* Windom, who cheated the merchants so they would end up like the beggar staring at them through the store window. To whom Paree gave five tomans before climbing into her Chevy.

Back at the apartment, she was about to pour herself a cup of tea—for some reason, she had lost her craving for vodka—when she heard from her husband for the second time since his departure to England. Through the crackling, hissing telephone line, Mike told her he had paid a deposit on a cottage in the Cotswold Hills and wished she were there. He then asked how she was faring without him.

After telling him about her job at the NIOC, Paree said, "By the way, soon I'll be the legal guardian of a ten-year-old orphan. His name is Reza."

For a few seconds, all she heard were crackles and buzzes. "Are you still there, Mike?"

"I'm still here. Why the dickens did you—"

"He's a wretched child in need of tender loving care. That's why."

"What do you know about him?"

"Not much."

"What happened to his parents?"

"They died."

Sigh. "Please don't be so glib, Paree. *Why* are they dead?"

"I don't know the details. All I know is that he's miserable at the orphanage."

"I hope you'll make each other happier, then." He sounded stiff, indifferent.

"We'll do our best."

"Do you need any help with finances?"

"I don't, but thanks for offering."

"Maybe one of these days, you—"

The line went dead.

Paree wondered if she could ever convince Mike to return and help her with bringing up Reza.

A mentally stable, nonviolent Reza.

Chapter 23

After lunch on Wednesday, The Proctor ordered the kids to clean the tables and gave Reza a broom to sweep the floor. When they were finished, The Proctor walked around, inspected the work, and told Reza to sweep the floor again and the kids to clean the tables again. Once he thought the place was clean enough, he gathered everyone in the courtyard and had them pick up the trash while Reza swept off the dirt and dust. He then made the kids form six straight columns and stand at attention. A moment later, Agha Mansur walked out of the building, stood in front of the columns, and looked grim while puffing the last of his oval cigarette.

After crushing the cigarette butt under his shoe, he said, "As you all know, early in the morning, Fereshteh Farhadi departed this earth because of an illness. We're told she had a terrible lung condition. Let us bow our heads for a moment of silence in her memory."

Reza hung his head and the tears flowed. A moment of silence. That was all Agha Mansur would give Reza's forever friend, the beautiful, loving, generous friend who had given Reza her most precious possession: a golden ring. Twirling it around his index finger now, he wished he could go back in time to when she had crept into his sleep room, when they had nestled against each other and whispered I love you and I love you too. Surely her memory deserved much more than a tiny moment of silence.

Fereshteh: Angel.

The moment ended within a few heartbeats, and Agha Mansur lit another cigarette. "Today we shall have a visit from Dr. Sadr, an official from the Health Ministry. He will question a few of you who knew Fereshteh well, and afterwards, he will talk to me and tell me everything you told him." He looked over the kids, and his eyes, radiating suspicion from behind the horn-rimmed glasses, settled on Reza. "What you children tell Dr. Sadr is your business of course, but it's also my business." He kept his eyes fixed on Reza. "And once the doctor leaves, I will deal with any of you who dared to misrepresent the Mansur Orphanage."

Someone asked, "What does misrepresent mean, sir?"

"It means to tell lies."

* * * *

Reza sat across from the man in the blue suit and red tie, a thin man with a rim of black hair around a shiny scalp. He seemed pleasant and introduced himself as Dr. Sadr. They were seated at one of the plastic covered tables in the dining room, which was otherwise vacant and the cleanest Reza had seen it since he first came to the orphanage.

Dr. Sadr smiled. "I understand that you and Fereshteh were the best of friends."

"Yes, sir."

"Did you think she had been ill for a long time?"

"Yes, sir. She was coughing as long as I knew her. Her spit often had a streak of red in it."

"Why do you think they didn't take her to see a doctor?"

"I don't know, sir."

He loosened his tie and leaned forward. "Tell me, Reza. How are you treated here?"

Reza shrugged.

"Please, tell me. You don't want any other children to die, do you?"

"No sir, I do not."

"Then answer my question please."

"I hate it here, sir."

"Why?"

"Because they beat us and give us very little food and the place is horrible and they put us in the prison room and we can't ever go outside the walls."

"What's the prison room?"

"A little toilet room on the top floor. They lock us up in it all alone when they think we are bad. They beat us and don't give us any supper."

"Are you *sure* they beat you?"

Reza showed him the palms of his hands. The doctor grimaced at seeing them and abruptly stood up.

"Thank you, Reza. You've been most helpful."

Reza stood also. "Will you tell Agha Mansur everything I said, sir?"

"I must, yes."

"Please don't, sir."

"I must, because I wish to improve the conditions in this orphanage. If I tell him you think this is a wonderful place, it will never improve, will it?"

Reza shook his head.

"And I'll instruct him not to punish you for speaking the truth."

The doctor led him out of the dining room and into the courtyard to join the other kids. He went back inside, leaving Reza to worry about what kind of punishment he would receive for daring to "misrepresent" the orphanage. He was certain Agha Mansur would ignore the doctor's instruction not to punish him.

But Reza didn't worry for long, because he knew that the next day Paree would come and take him away from *Jahanam*—simply thinking about freedom would be enough to offset the punishment. Besides, another beating and another night in the prison room were well worth telling the doctor the truth, because the truth might improve the conditions at Agha Mansur's orphanage. And maybe once the conditions improved, there wouldn't be another Fereshteh starving herself to death as the only way of escaping from *jahanam*.

And maybe then, the kids wouldn't be so full of hate.

* * * *

Just before supper, The Proctor took him to Agha Mansur's office. Reza stood before the desk, ready for another beating.

His eye whites pink and his face crimson, Mansur slapped a hand on the desktop. "You went ahead and misrepresented our orphanage to Dr. Sadr, didn't you?"

"I told him the truth, sir."

"None of the other children said untruthful things."

"I didn't tell lies, Agha Mansur."

"You did, and therefore you will be punished."

Agha Mansur put on his smile for grownup visitors, which was frightening just then because his eyes and face were furious, but his lips smiled. He reminded Reza of Baba on Thursday nights when he would laugh and look angry at the same time.

"How will I be punished, sir?" Reza asked.

"You'll find out in due course. It will be the severest punishment you've ever received or will ever receive."

Chapter 24

Paree's boss invited her to the Oil Club on Tuesday evening. She would be his companion to dine and entertain Mr. and Mrs. Reginald Staunch-Stewart, who were returning to England because Reginald—"please-call-me-Reggie"—had decided to retire from the Oil Company. Reggie told anyone who cared to listen that he wanted to get away from all those Iranians at company headquarters who stared at him through hateful Iranian eyes.

Just before seven p.m., Mr. Shappour picked Paree up at her apartment and drove them to the club. At five-foot three, he was two inches shorter than her and wore ankle-high boots with two-inch heels, which she was certain were made exclusively for him. She wore flats because she was aware that many Iranian men had a serious problem with appearing shorter than their female companions. Yet another Iranian male fetish.

With the early spring weather cooperating, they dined outside as a small band played Big Band music, some fast, some slow, and some without rhythm or melody once the players relapsed into their Middle-Eastern-music-ear ways. Shappour danced poorly, as did Paree, so they bumped into other dancers and tripped over each other's feet until they gave up and sat out the rest of the evening.

The courses of Caspian caviar, crayfish mousse, and roast duck were delicious; so was the dessert of peach flambé. Not feeling at all hungry, Paree ate only a few nibbles of each course. The conversation was about oil, and throughout the meal she said little, nodding her head while sipping a club soda and thinking about Reza. More than once, Shappour nudged her because the guests had asked her about Mike, whom they had known for many years.

She hadn't heard the questions though, because she was thinking about what to prepare Reza for his first meal at her apartment and what to buy him for his birthday, the date of which Mansur had entered on the guardianship contract. Maybe a clockwork toy, like a boat he could play with while bathing in the tub before his bedtime. Which reminded her that she must buy a few more towels, two pairs of pajamas in his size, a toothbrush, and a tube of toothpaste—the kind that tasted of spearmint chewing gum. And she mustn't forget to get him a bar of soap shaped like Mickey Mouse, which was popular among children and lured them into using soap while splashing around in the tub. Also, she would buy him a picture to hang over his bed. Perhaps a picture of Mount Damavand, with a small lamp by the bed to illuminate it and to keep him from being afraid—in case he was afraid of the dark when she was out of the room.

Since she had Thursdays and Fridays off, she would go shopping first thing on Thursday morning before picking up Reza from the orphanage.

"How's Mike surviving the downturn in oil production?" Reginald's words drifted into her ears, and she realized they were directed at her.

"I wouldn't know, Reggie," she replied, and he went on to talk about how Abadan's refinery output was not meeting the people's demands and how Iran would have trouble surviving financially without the British managing its oil industry.

She nodded politely while wondering if Reza would have preferred *giveh*—soft shoes made of cotton thread—over the gym shoes she had bought him at half the asking price. The *giveh* may have been more stylish, but they were useless for running, and maybe like all children, Reza ran around a lot.

"Have you talked to him recently, Paree?" she heard Shappour ask.

"Talked to whom?"

"Your husband. Mike. Remember him?"

"Talked to him about what, Mr. Shappour?"

"Never mind."

After parting from their guests, Shappour drove Paree home in his black Humber sedan. He drove in silence, eyes fixed on the road, lips pursed, brow knitted. The tension transmitted to Paree, and she sensed he would not drop her off at the apartment before venting his anger, which she was sure was the result of her admittedly weak social performance at the Oil Club. He pulled the car to the curb in front of her apartment building, switched off the engine and headlights, and sat there tapping his fingers on the steering wheel while grinding his jaws. She was used to Mike opening the door for her, so she waited a few seconds for Shappour to do just that. He didn't though, and she felt relieved because she was anxious to escape the tension.

Hoping he had decided to contain his anger, she was about to open the door when he suddenly reached over and grasped her arm. "Something is going on with you, Paree. You're distracted. It's quite evident at work, and it was very evident this evening. Now I wish to discuss your problem, whatever it might be."

She studied his hawk-like face, which was amber under the streetlight accentuating the worry frowns of his brow and the busy muscles of his jaws. Deciding she couldn't keep the news to herself any longer, Paree told him of the Mansur Orphanage, of Reza Ahmadi, of their trip to the foothills of Mount Damavand, and of the boy's wretched background. And she told him that the following afternoon she would officially become Reza's guardian.

He listened intently, and when she was done, he squeezed her arm—hard. "Think carefully before you take him on, Paree. Children without parents are troubled. Deeply troubled. Nothing good comes of them. In Iran, it's almost a foregone conclusion that most orphans of today will become the criminals or vagrants of tomorrow. Stop this foolishness, Paree. Stop trying to relive your motherhood."

She shook her head. "No, Mr. Shappour. I must take Reza out of that awful place, or he'll surely grow up to become one of the undesirables you just mentioned. I will *not* turn my back on the poor boy."

"You will *not*? Are you sure, Paree?"

"I'm sure, yes."

"You're making a serious mistake, and it will force me to take drastic action."

"What kind of action?"

He bore his hawk-like eyes into her. "Please understand, I cannot have a constantly distracted secretary at this critical point of my career. For the first time since joining the Oil Company, I feel my chances of reaching the top echelons are excellent. An efficient, attentive secretary will assure my success, as it will assure hers. Therefore, you either leave that boy at the orphanage, or I must look for your replacement." He squeezed her arm again—even harder this time. "Well, what's your decision?"

Paree didn't hesitate. "Mr. Shappour, as I said before, I cannot, *will* not turn my back on that poor boy."

"Then you leave me no alternative, sorry to say."

"I'm sorry too."

She opened the door, nodded a farewell, and walked away.

* * * *

Very little sleep for Paree that night. She fretted into the early morning hours, agonizing whether she should call Mike and ask him for money, but she decided against it. Too proud. She pondered whether she should call Roger Holmes and ask him to find her another job at the Oil Company, but she decided against it. Too proud. And begging Shappour to reconsider his decision was out of the question.

Of one thing, however, she was certain. Reza would be with her regardless of what line of work she pursued. Even if it meant working as a street sweeper or charwoman.

She spent much of the day rewriting her résumé in calligraphic-style Farsi using a reed pen, which at the time, most educated Iranians considered the ultimate style of formal writing. The next morning, after combing the newspaper classifieds for job openings, she would schedule interviews with selected employers. In the afternoon, she would pick Reza up from the orphanage, feed him, and settle him down at her apartment. Once gainfully employed, she would devote every moment of her free time to healing the frightened, confused orphan.

And in the process, healing herself.

Chapter 25

Paree returned to the apartment at midmorning on Thursday after buying the necessities for Reza as well as a framed photograph of the Alborz Mountains. She hung the picture over his bed.

Sitting at the kitchen table, she was searching the *Etel-a-at* classifieds for job openings when the telephone rang.

Mansur was on the line. "Mrs. Windom, I'm afraid there is a problem with your guardianship of Reza."

"What's the problem?"

"We believe he must stay here until his behavior is greatly modified. He's not ready for life outside a strictly controlled environment."

Despite the sudden tide of rage, Paree kept a calm tone. "Why didn't you tell me this before I signed the contract?"

"Because since then, we've had more time to think about him and his wild ways. If you wish, you could try the orphanage in Isfahan—it's severely overcrowded."

Certain that Mansur was trying to extort more money from her, she could no longer contain her anger. "I suppose you want another pile of tomans to change your mind."

"The decision is final, and donations are always welcome."

"You never intended to let me take Reza in the first place, did you? All you intended was to cheat me out of four hundred tomans. I'm coming to collect the entire amount at once, and then I'll—"

"There's nothing to collect. All the money was spent for food and clothing."

"Food and clothing for whom? Yourself?"

Paree slammed down the receiver, retrieved the carbon copy of their contract, and studied it. She found what she sought on the bottom of the fourth page. *Should the Guardian have issues with the Manager, he or she may talk in person with an official at the Children's Welfare Administration, 500 Mehdi Avenue, Tehran.*

* * * *

Paree drove to the Children's Welfare Administration, which she was told would be open until one in the afternoon before closing for the weekend. Since she didn't have an appointment, for over an hour she waited impatiently in the hot, crowded lobby that was rife with body odor. At last, a male clerk with a squeaky voice called out her name and ushered her into the office of Mr. Jabbar Sharzadeh, Assistant Superintendent of Orphanages, Tehran Province. He was in his mid sixties, she guessed, with kindly, tired eyes and a few strands of hair that were gray mixed with rust brown.

She couldn't see the top of his metal desk for all the strewn papers and folders. The floor was cracked linoleum, the walls cracked plaster in desperate need of paint. The only decorative item was a framed photograph hanging above him on the wall. The black-and-white snapshot was of a blissful looking bride and groom. She wore a light-colored wedding dress, and he was in a dark suit with a white—possibly yellow or pink—rose pinned to the lapel. Paree recalled that Mike had worn a pink rose when they were wedded.

After their honeymoon at a Caspian Sea resort, he dried and pressed the petals and tucked them inside the back cover of their wedding photograph's frame. "This way, we'll always smell of roses," he said through a grin.

She no longer had the wedding photograph because Mike took it back with him to England, and she didn't object because at the time she was furious at him for not retiring and staying in Iran. Maybe she should have kept it, she now thought, because Reza—if she could rescue him from Mansur's clutches—would see the happiness in the photograph scented with roses, and it might cheer him up a little. Paree, too.

Mr. Sharzadeh followed her gaze to the snapshot and smiled. "My son and his bride. A delightful couple who'll live forever in joy."

Paree sat on a metal chair in front of his metal desk and looked at him intently. "Joy for *your* family, yes, but what about joy for those children at the Mansur Orphanage who suffer without families, without love?"

"Are you here about Fereshteh?"

"Who?"

He puzzled for a moment. "You're not with the Health Ministry?"

"No."

"A reporter?"

"No. Who's Fereshteh?"

"I'm sorry. I shouldn't have mentioned the unfortunate girl's name."

"But you did, so please tell me about her."

"No, I had better not. The case is under investigation."

Paree waved the copy of her contract at him. "Mr. Sharzadeh, I'm here to inquire about assuming guardianship of another child at Mansur's orphanage. Any information about the place would help me better understand and take care of him."

After hesitating, Sharzadeh said, "Fereshteh was a ten-year-old who died there recently. The Health Ministry is investigating her death and the health-related policies of the orphanage. Apparently, she had been ill for quite a long time without receiving any medical attention whatsoever."

At once saddened by the girl's death, Paree seized the opportunity to speak up for the children of despair. "She probably died of malnutrition and maltreatment. While the Ministry is investigating the health policies of the orphanage, your agency should investigate the people who run that terrible place. They're cruel. They beat the children, and give them no more food than would satisfy a mouse. The place must be shut down, Mr. Sharzadeh. Shut down and fumigated. The children must be reassigned to people who care for them. They must be taken out of the clutches of people like Mansur, who pockets government funds while denying the orphans adequate nutrition—and, I might add, extorts money from people like me who want to adopt or look after them."

Sharzadeh stood up, revealing a frail body and a slight tremor of his head. "*Khanom*, you're making serious accusations. Are they based on fact?"

"He took four-hundred tomans from me, supposedly to expedite an orphan's release to my guardianship. This morning, he called to cancel the arrangement—and refused to return my money. I'd call that extortion, wouldn't you?"

"I must admit, it does sound suspicious. Any other facts?"

"Please go and see the place for yourself, but be sure to make it a surprise visit. Take the children aside and talk to them. See how filthy and emaciated they are. Listen to them telling you how unhappy they are. Those are the facts, sir, because I've been there and seen the suffering at the hands of Mansur and his surly thug, the so-called proctor."

He sat down and ran a hand over his thinning hair. "Yesterday, a physician from the Ministry visited the orphanage. We haven't received his report yet, but I'm sure it will address the conditions there."

"Was it a surprise visit?"

"I don't believe so, no."

"Has anyone except me complained about the place?"

"You're the third in as many months."

"Was anything done about those other complaints?"

He threw up his hands. "*Khanom*, we paid little attention because the other complainants didn't seem…should I say…entirely trustworthy."

"Why not?"

"Because they were suspect, although we couldn't prove anything."

"Suspect of what?"

"Of assuming guardianship of orphans and selling their…um…services."

"What do you mean?"

"I don't wish to give out the details, *khanom*, but I suggest you use your imagination."

He paused for a few seconds while Paree followed his suggestion. As soon as she had an inkling, she blanked her imagination. "Mr. Sharzadeh, as I said before, I want to take one of the orphans as my ward, but Mansur has now decided to get in my way. I want the boy out today, sir. Today, before they harm him anymore. Before he dies like that poor little girl."

"What's the boy's name?"

"Reza Ahmadi." She placed the copy of her contract on his desk.

He glanced at it then rummaged through stacks of other paperwork until he found the original contract. After reading a handwritten note clipped to the front page, he said, "My clerk informs me this contract was delivered a few days ago. Yesterday, Mansur called and nullified it. I wonder what happened."

"I don't know."

He skimmed through the first page of the contract. "You have a son, Mrs. Windom?"

She gripped the edges of the seat, waiting for the sudden commotion in her head to calm.

"*Khanom*? About your son?"

"We lost him to the second world war," she replied in a near whisper.

"I'm so sorry, and let's hope it was the *final* war. Where was he stationed?"

"In North Africa, but must we talk about him?"

"No, of course not."

She breathed a silent sigh of relief.

After studying the rest of the contract, he gazed at her—with some admiration, Paree thought. "You seem to have excellent credentials for a guardian, Mrs. Windom. I'm impressed that in your list of references, you name a hospital director as well as a prominent member of our parliament, Minister Azerghani."

Since returning to Iran, Paree and Mike had been invited several times to gala parties at the British Embassy. She had gone there only once though, because of her distaste for banquets and parties ever since World War II, ever since Little John left their home with a khaki kitbag slung over his shoulder. The one affair Paree did consent to attend—Mike actually *begged* her—resulted in a friendship with the politician's wife, Golicheh, who rarely left the house because of her mentally impaired eleven-year-old son afflicted with Down syndrome. Like Paree, Golicheh had essentially withdrawn from social life. She spent most awake moments tending to her son and crying for him because she knew he wouldn't survive beyond his teenage years.

Sharzadeh rested a hand on the telephone receiver. "Mrs. Windom, would you mind if I contacted Mr. Azerghani?"

"Go ahead, but you're better off talking to his wife, because she and I are good friends. I don't know him as well as I know her. I've written the telephone number on the contract."

He dialed the number and chatted for a few minutes. When the conversation ended, he replaced the receiver and smiled at Paree. "Mrs. Azerghani says you're a kind and wonderful person. She also says you have a wonderful husband. Why isn't he here with you?"

"Because he's in England."

"Will he return to Iran soon?"

"I don't believe so. The British aren't very popular here. At least not nowadays."

Sharzadeh furrowed his brow. "I understand. Do you think that you and he will be…permanently separated?"

"I certainly hope not, but it's a possibility, yes."

"So you might be Reza's legal guardian without a man to help you raise him."

Smiling, Paree leaned forward, locked eyes with him, and responded in a calm, even tone. "Mr. Sharzadeh, do you consider that a woman is incapable of raising a child without a man?"

He stared at her for a long moment. She held his stare. He broke out in a grin.

"In your case, Mrs. Windom, I believe you're perfectly capable."

After stamping the original and Paree's copy of the contract with the agency's seal, he signed and dated them. "These will put you in charge of Reza, *khanom*. If you wish, you may go to the orphanage immediately. If anyone there gives you any problems whatsoever, call me, either here or at home." He scribbled his office extension and home telephone numbers on the back of Paree's copy, which he handed to her. "I believe you'll be a superb guardian to Reza, Mrs. Windom, and also a superb mother—if you ever decide to adopt him."

She thanked him, and he walked her to the door. Grasping the handle, he said, "I promise you, we will thoroughly investigate the orphanage, starting early on Saturday morning. If we confirm what you and the others have reported to me, we'll replace the supervisor at once—no matter what the Health Ministry's findings are. Then our government and I will personally thank you for salvaging the lives of all those mistreated children."

Paree walked away feeling elated, feeling as if she had contributed, albeit a small fraction, to the welfare of Iran's orphans. She had protected innocent victims of sadists like Mansur and his thug, innocent victims of disgusting people who took them and rented them out for nefarious purposes. Once outside, she broke into a near sprint to her car.

To save Reza from Mansur and his thug before it was too late.

Chapter 26

Sitting cross-legged on the classroom floor that Thursday afternoon, Reza gazed out of the glass-paneled double doors that opened into the courtyard, waiting for Paree to set him free, fretting that at the last minute things could go wrong.

"What is six multiplied by four?"

But maybe Agha Mansur had decided not to release him—the punishment for daring to "misrepresent" the orphanage. Or maybe Paree had changed her mind because Agha Mansur told her Reza was a bed-wetter. In either case, he would stop eating like Fereshteh had done, and he would die like she had died. He thought about the part of the body that floats away when the other part dies. It must be as light as air, like the clouds. Someday, he and Fereshteh and Mama would float in the air together, holding hands, singing songs, telling stories, and…

"I asked you once and I won't ask you again. What is six multiplied by four?"

…and floating to the other side of the mountains, where there are no people except Reza and Fereshteh and Mama. Where there are no orphanages and high walls and deserts and…

Thwack! The stick hit the floor in front of him and he startled. "Sorry, Agha Mansur. Six multiplied by four is…is…I think it's eighteen, sir."

"Wrong! Try again."

Six plus six equals twelve. Twelve plus six equals eighteen. Eighteen plus six equals twenty-four. "Twenty-four, sir."

"Correct. If you daydream one more time, my stick will come down on your hands. Is that clear?"

"Yes, Agha Mansur."

Mansur walked away from him, and Reza looked out of the double doors. The Proctor stood at the gate in front of a woman whose face Reza couldn't see, but whose dress was yellow like the one Paree was wearing when they first met. A sudden gust of wind blew her hair into view, and he saw the glistening black with the strands of gray.

He wanted to jump up, throw his fists in the air, and shout out his freedom, but he held back, afraid Agha Mansur would get angry and stop him from leaving with Paree. He sat still, his heart thumping into his chest, his pulse whistling in his ears.

A moment later, The Proctor walked into the classroom. "That woman is here to talk with you about Reza Ahmadi, sir."

"As I told you earlier, I've already talked to her and she can't have him."

"She says you have no choice because she has a signed contract."

"Who signed it?"

"Mr. Sharzadeh, Assistant Superintendent of the Tehran Province. I believe you know him, sir."

Mansur scrunched up his eyebrows. "So she went over my head to a higher authority."

"She must have."

"Where is she?"

"In your office."

"Didn't I tell you not to let that woman inside the premises?"

"Yes, but she threatened to summon Mr. Sharzadeh."

Looking furious, Mansur handed his stick to The Proctor. "Take over the class. Simple multiplications."

He stomped away, and Reza's heart thumped louder, the whistling in his ears grew louder.

"What's five multiplied by five?"

He could imagine Paree standing in front of Agha Mansur's desk, smiling, telling him he had no choice but to hand over Reza because she had a signed contract. He could imagine him furious because she had gone to a higher authority. The scar on his forehead would turn red and his eye whites would turn pink, which is what they did when he was furious at one of the children for misbehaving, daydreaming during class, or not knowing how to multiply six by four. But none of that mattered, because he would have to leave his office and take Paree to the sleep room to fetch Reza's belongings. After all, he had no choice because she had a signed contract from a higher authority.

"What's five multiplied by five, boy?"

"Me, sir?"

"Yes, you."

Five plus five plus five plus five plus five. "Twenty-five, sir."

More questions to the other children, more answers, some right, some wrong. More thwacks of the stick, some on the stone floor, some on the hands.

What could Paree and Agha Mansur still be talking about? All she needed to do now was pick up his belongings and take him out of *jahanam*. Forever. Or was Mansur so furious that he was beating her mercilessly into the ground?

Reza shivered at the thought and quickly put it out of his mind. Imagining the scene of Mansur unleashing his fury at Paree had stirred a horrific feeling inside him, a feeling that in the past, he had witnessed a similar scene of a man beating a woman mercilessly into the ground. He couldn't remember where and when, or whether it had been real or a nightmare.

The class continued and seemed like it would never end. At last, The Proctor glanced at his watch and said to Reza, "Here's the last question before recess. What is six-hundred and sixty-six multiplied by zero?"

Reza looked out into the courtyard.

* * * *

Standing before Mansur's desk, Paree handed him the signed copy of the contract. "Mr. Sharzadeh stamped and signed it. See for yourself."

Mansur glanced at the document and frowned. "May I ask how you managed to convince him?"

Paree smiled. "I was pleasant and courteous."

He glared at her. "Kindly stop the frivolous attitude and answer me."

"I simply pointed out the conditions in this place and told him I could take far better care of Reza than you or the proctor ever could."

Mansur fidgeted for a while and stood up, the scar on his forehead red, his eye whites pink. "I find you both arrogant and abrasive, Mrs. Windom." He pointed to the door. "Please leave my office."

"I'm not leaving without Reza."

"Get out!"

Paree walked to the door and spun around. "Very well, I'll get out and wait by my car for fifteen minutes. If you haven't brought Reza out by then, I shall go straight to the authorities. I'll also charge you with criminal neglect for causing the death of a child by the name of Fereshteh."

* * * *

Thwack! The stick pounded the floor. "Answer me or the next time I'll smack your head."

"Would you repeat the question, sir?"

"Six-hundred and sixty-six multiplied by zero."

160

"Nothing, sir."

And Reza had heard nothing from Paree or Agha Mansur.

The Proctor dismissed the class, but Reza didn't move. He saw Paree crossing the courtyard, heading to the double gates. He saw The Proctor unlocking them to let her out, and it felt like his insides would blow out of him like the air out of his chest, leaving him without breath, without hope. Slumped forward, he thought of Fereshteh, of how clever she had been to separate herself from the part they *can* take away. He wondered where she had floated to, whether she was invisible. Maybe floating over him in that classroom at that moment.

He lifted his head and closed his eyes, hoping she would float down and give him a sign. Like a brush of her breath against his face, like a whisper in his ear. *I love you, Reza.*

But he felt nothing, heard nothing. Just emptiness, silence.

Chapter 27

"Get up and come with me, Reza. First, we must collect your belongings."

The words trickled into his ears. They stayed there for a long moment. Just a string of words. Soon they trickled into his head, one word at a time. First—we—must—collect—your—belongings. They circled in his mind and finally became a whole sentence like Agha Mansur tried to teach the kids. *First we must collect your belongings.* The subject is we, the verb is collect, the object is belongings, and the rest of the words don't matter. Nothing matters except leaving *jahanam.*

"I said get up and come with me, Reza."

Mansur hovered over him, glaring at him. Reza stood up in a daze and followed him to sleep room two in a daze. He picked up his gunnysack from the bottom shelf of a wobbly metal locker and crammed his belongings into the sack, still in a daze.

"Follow me," Agha Mansur said.

"Where are you taking me, sir?"

"To go with That Woman, but I'm sure you'll be back here very soon—when That Woman has had enough of you and you've had enough of her."

They walked across the courtyard past the staring children, past The Proctor, past the woodshed. They paused at the double gates, and Agha Mansur told him to wave at the kids. Reza waved and no one waved back.

They stepped into Freedom-land. She stood there smiling, her yellow dress flapping in the breeze like a yellow bird about to fly, her hair blowing about, covering her face and then uncovering it to reveal her comforting smile.

Mansur left and slammed the gates closed behind him, but not before Reza heard him growl, *Ajooz-e pedar sukhteh!*—Hag of a burned father! Reza had heard the curse words, *pedar sukhteh*, from Baba and occasionally from other gardeners, which he had never completely understood but thought they must have had something to do with burning in the cave of hell Baba once talked about.

Paree must have heard Agha Mansur curse too, because she ran up to the gates and shouted after him through the barred opening. *"Boro be jahanam!"* Go to hell!

Her face flushed with rage, she stomped back, opened the passenger door, and helped Reza climb into the silver car with only two doors and with velvety seats. It was the same car that she had driven when they went to Damavand, and inside it smelled of *yasmin*, which was her scent and aroused Reza's memories of better yesterdays. Jasmines grew near their shack in the Third Garden. Mama used to dry the petals, grind them, and sprinkle them inside the shack to get rid of the outhouse stench that occasionally drifted in from the hole-in-the-ground at the southeastern corner of the Third Garden. Maybe he was now returning to the world of jasmines, the world of better yesterdays but with the occasional stench that jasmines made tolerable.

They drove in silence for a while, because Reza thought Paree was still angry at Agha Mansur, and Mama said you should always avoid talking with angry people. They passed a caravan of donkeys heading to Tehran, trudging along by the roadside, carrying gunnysacks of tomatoes and eggplants, their master smacking them with a stick. No different from how the masters, Mansur and The Proctor, treated the orphans. Reza felt sorry for the donkeys, and he felt sorry for the orphans because they were still in *jahanam* while he was in Freedom-land.

He glanced at Paree, and she was frowning—not angry frowns now, worried frowns that concerned him. "Are you worried about me living with you, Paree?" he asked her.

She looked at him, the frowns disappeared, and she smiled. "The opposite, Reza. I look forward to having you with me."

"Then what's bothering you?"

"How do you know I'm bothered?"

"The lines on your forehead. Mama used to get them on Thursday nights."

"Only on those nights?"

"Yes, because Baba would go to Karaj with his friend and come back late acting…"

"Acting what?"

"Different."

"Different? Like what?"

Reza shrugged. "Not like him. He spoke funny, and he swayed a lot. He'd get angry at nothing and laugh at nothing. It was a weird laugh. His face was angry but he'd laugh at the same time."

Paree nodded. "I understand. Anyway, I'm bothered because they sacked me from my work, so I no longer have money coming in. But don't worry. I'll find another job."

"Why did they sack you? Did you do something wrong?"

"No. I did something right."

He didn't understand, and she seemed reluctant to talk about it. "Do you need lots of money, Paree?" he asked.

"Not lots, no. Just enough to pay the rent and to feed and clothe us."

"If I wasn't with you, you'd have much more money for yourself, wouldn't you?"

"Don't say that, Reza. I'm very happy to share everything with you."

He thought for a moment. "Do you have a garden?"

"There's a piece of land in the back of the apartment building, but it belongs to the landlord. Why do you ask?"

"I can grow cucumbers and eggplants and watermelons and cantaloupes. We'd have plenty to eat, and you wouldn't have to spend as much money."

She smiled. "Reza, keep thinking, and maybe between the two us we'll figure out how to live happily ever after."

Chapter 28

Reza stood before the six-story, brick apartment building, his gunnysack slung over a shoulder and packed with all his possessions: tattered, soiled clothes, a silver-speckled, purple rock he had found in the *Baghah-e Sabz* creek, and an apple-sized rubber ball Mama had bought him two years before as a *Now-Ruz*—New Year—present. Paree waved toward a pair of third-story windows on each side of a balcony. "Your home is up there," she said.

Squinting in that direction, he asked, "But isn't it *our* home?"

"You're absolutely right, Reza. It's *our* home."

They rode the elevator, which was beside the main staircase, to the third floor. After stepping out, they walked along a green-carpeted corridor and stopped in front of a door marked 3-B. Paree unlocked it, draped an arm around Reza's shoulders, and guided him inside. He held his breath at seeing their home for the first time. It was clean, inviting, without stenches and flies, without mattresses on the floor and gunnysacks along the walls and rat holes in the baseboards. He gazed in awe at the colorful flowers, the leather furniture, the stack of comic books on the coffee table, and the view of the street below from the balcony. The view of Freedom-land.

She took him into the bedroom, and he at once noticed the second, smaller bed covered with a midnight blue quilt. "You now have your very own bed," Paree said. Hanging on the wall above the bed was a framed picture of snow-topped mountains, and he thought it might bring him happier dreams.

He wondered if he would prefer sleeping with her, because he remembered how warm he felt whenever Mama lay down with him and when Fereshteh crept onto his mattress at the orphanage. So lying next to Paree might feel the same way—as it did for a moment when he woke up next to her at the Alborz Hotel and then rolled away because he wasn't sure he could trust her.

They walked into the kitchen, which had a little round table, two wicker chairs, an icebox, and stove. "It's a *gas* stove," Paree said. "A dangerous convenience you mustn't touch until you know how to use it, because gas explodes if you're not careful." Reza didn't touch it. The icebox was tiny compared with the one in the owner's house at *Bagh-e Aval*—the First Garden.

Reza had seen it when no one was in the house and Baba had snuck him in through an unlocked rear door. After tiptoeing about the place, they had crept into the enormous kitchen with a sink almost the size of a tub and an icebox almost the size of Agha Akbar's car. Baba opened the icebox, and as steam drifted out, he rummaged around until he found what he was looking for. He took out two brown bottles with rippled caps, tucked them under his shirt, and said, "If you dare mention this to anyone, including your mother, I'll give you the biggest thrashing of your life."

Paree poured Reza and herself each a glassful of chilled watermelon juice and they settled at the round table. In between sips, Reza said if he had a garden to work in, they would have plenty of watermelons and cantaloupes for juice and plenty of eggplants and cucumbers for *bademjooni* stew and *khiar* salad. When their glasses were empty, she steered him to the bathroom, filled the tub, and told him to wash away the filth of Agha Mansur's orphanage.

Once she left, he bathed for a long time and used the soap that smelled of roses and looked like a strange mouse wearing shorts and enormous shoes, which didn't look right to him because mice have tiny feet. After doing his business in the commode that was like the one at Hotel Alborz, he dressed in his new clothes: blue polo shirt, tan trousers, and white shoes with rubber soles. Paree said those were gym shoes, meant for running and exercising, but they were also great for walking.

When he was ready, she took him downstairs and out of a rear door into a square piece of land that was in desperate need of nurturing. A woodshed was in a corner, and the land was surrounded by tall, red brick walls. "This could be your garden," she said, "but I'll have to ask permission for you to use it."

He would grow for her the biggest fruits and vegetables. All he needed were seeds and a shovel and some fertilizer. He looked forward to doing all that for her, because she had kept her promise by taking him away from Agha Mansur, The Proctor, and *jahanam*.

* * * *

After a meal of lamb and potato stew over rice, she settled on the living room couch and studied a newspaper while the radio played songs of a woman called Delkash. Reza sat cross-legged on the floor, listening to the music and relishing his new home. They didn't have a radio in the Third Garden, but there was a portable one in the bus to Karaj that Reza occasionally rode with Mama, and the driver always played the radio loud. All he played was *namaz*—prayer—songs.

Reza watched Paree reading the newspaper, thinking how pretty she was, even though she seemed much older than Mama. He loved how her hair flopped over her brow and flowed over shoulders, how her eyebrows arched, how sometimes her lips smiled and made him feel like smiling too, which he hadn't done much since That Night. And how as she sat, he could see her legs up to the knees. They looked like the dainty pair of vases Mama treasured and Baba smashed on a Thursday night because he was angry at nothing, and after smashing them, he laughed at nothing.

Without thinking, Reza went to the couch and settled next to her, a fingerbreadth away. She put down her newspaper and pulled him into her, and they just sat there in silence. It was like when he and Mama sometimes sat together on his mattress before bedtime, just enjoying each other, enjoying the warmth passing between them. He wondered if Paree enjoyed him like Mama did. Probably not, he decided, because she wasn't his mama. His guardian, she said, his protector, which meant she didn't have to *love* him. All the same, at that moment she *acted* like Mama. Sharing a moment of warmth.

"You're almost ten years old, Reza," she said when the moment ended.

"I think so, yes."

"Your birthday is coming up next month."

"You mean the day I was born?"

"That's right. It's in the papers they gave me. I hope to have a job well before then, because I want to buy you a nice present. What would you like?"

"You'll give me a present because I was born that day?"

"Yes. It's a custom all over the world."

"It wasn't a custom at the gardens."

"Well, it is here. Tell me what you'd like."

"A wheelbarrow to load the fruits and vegetables in and bring them to you."

She squeezed him. "How thoughtful of you."

"When's *your* birthday, Paree?"

"I'll tell you after I find a job and can give you a weekly allowance."

"What's an allowance?"

"Spending money to buy anything you want. Once you have it, you can spend a little of it for my birthday. In the meantime, wish me luck for the day after tomorrow. I'm off to look for work."

"Will I be alone in the apartment?"

"Yes, until midday." Her eyes grew sad and she squeezed him again. "I'm so sorry to leave you alone so soon after you moved in, Reza, but I have no choice. We need the income and we must have it soon."

Reza's dark thoughts suddenly erupted at the idea of her leaving him alone just a day and a half after taking him out of the orphanage. Mama never left him completely alone. She was always by his side or nearby, helping him with gardening chores or with packing fruits and vegetables inside wooden crates and loading them into the owner's truck. She said mothers are there to protect their children. How can they do that while leaving their little ones alone?

But Paree wasn't Mama. He wondered why she had become his guardian instead of his mother. Fereshteh once told him orphans are sometimes adopted so they can have new mothers and fathers.

Leaning away from Paree, he squinted at her. "Could you have adopted me if you wanted to, Paree?"

She frowned. "I suppose so, yes."

"Then why didn't you?"

"Because…because I thought we should first get to know each other better."

So he was right about Paree. She didn't *love* him, and that was why she didn't want to be his new mother. She must *like* him though, otherwise she wouldn't have become his guardian and brought him out of the orphanage. And since she was only a guardian, she could leave him behind in the apartment any time she wanted. Alone.

Everything was so complicated, confusing.

Chapter 29

Friday was a good day. Paree took Reza to a puppet show on the roof of Cinema Homah. Then he had kabob lunch at Shamshiri Restaurant, honey ice cream in a vaulted bazaar, and best of all, the Ferris wheel ride at Shahanshahi Park. For Reza, it was day of wonders, of seeing and experiencing things for the first time in the world outside tall, clay walls.

That evening, Paree introduced him to Agha Rahemi, the landlord, who said he'd stop by the apartment while Paree was job-hunting, and he'd be in his office on the ground floor if Reza needed anything.

Saturday was not a good day.

Early that morning, Paree wore a gray dress and reminded Reza she was off to look for work and would be back by noon. He must stay inside the apartment, she said, and keep the door locked and not open it for anyone except her or the landlord. He could listen to the radio, especially later on when *real* music played instead of *akhouns*—preachers—droning *namaz*, and he could read comic books.

Not long after they arrived at the apartment, he had browsed through some of the comic books she had bought for him. There were stories about a bear with a funny name, Winnie-the-Pooh, and about a man who could leap over tall buildings, and a boy who rode around the jungle on an elephant, talking to animals. The comics were difficult to read because he wasn't very good at reading, but along with the pictures he could figure out the stories. Happy stories.

Not angry or sad ones like Baba would sometimes tell him on a good day about people killing people and fathers killing sons. Like the stories from *Shahnameh*, which Ferdowsi wrote and someone made a statue of him because everyone liked his stories and he saved the Persian language. He wrote about Rostam and Sohrab, a warrior father who unknowingly killed his warrior son. And he wrote about nations fighting other nations with swords, bows and arrows, and spears. Baba said bombs and guns later replaced the ancient weapons because they could kill many more people much more easily. He added that anybody with a gun would always win a fight against anybody without one.

Reza hated guns now, and he shivered at the mention of the word. His father had an old rifle, which he told Mama someone gave to him many years before. Mama asked him who gave it to him, and Baba told her to mind her own business. Then he said he actually found it, and anyway it wasn't any of her business. He polished and cleaned it almost every day, and he kept it loaded beside his mattress when he slept—in case of night bandits, he said. The rifle had a long black barrel and a wooden stock, which was cracked and chipped but polished to a shine with special oil he kept in a jar that no one was allowed to touch.

He killed birds and desert creatures with that rifle, and he boasted he could see and kill a tiny lizard from a hundred paces away. *Poor lizard*, Reza remembered thinking.

One Friday afternoon, Baba took him into the desert and showed him how the rifle worked and how to use it. After teaching him, he pointed to a little gray bird sitting on top of a cone-shaped rock, gave him the rifle, and told him to aim at that bird and kill it. Reza aimed at the bottom of the rock, the bullet smacked into it, and the little gray bird flew away.

"That was a terrible shot," Baba said, snatching back the rifle, and Reza said he was sorry. Baba wouldn't let him shoot again. "You just wasted a bullet, and bullets are expensive," he snapped.

Reza mumbled, "They kill animals and people."

"What did you say?"

"Nothing, Baba."

After Paree left the apartment, Reza stepped onto the tiny balcony overlooking the street and watched her climb into her silver car and drive off. He stayed there for a long time, watching the cars speeding by, donkeys pulling fruit and vegetable carts, and people walking fast and looking a little grim, as if they didn't like where they were going. If he stayed there long enough, maybe he would see the same people walking back, and not so grim.

An angry looking man in a brown suit and white shoes stood on the pavement across the street, leaning against a lamppost and eyeing every passerby as if he were expecting someone. A donkey pulling a cart piled with tomatoes stopped in front of him by the curb and did its business—both businesses. The angry man shook a fist in the air and yelled, "*Khar-e ahmagh!*" Stupid ass!

The donkey's master, an older man in rags, shouted back at him, "*Boro be jahanam!*" Go to hell!

A crowd gathered while the two of them cursed each other, much of which Reza didn't understand. As curses turned to threatening words and threatening fists, the donkey trotted away, the master ran after it, and the crowd scattered.

At hearing the curses, dark thoughts crept back into Reza's head. Dark thoughts that had been with him ever since the police took Mama away. Police could take anyone away they chose, he supposed, because they had guns and clubs and everyone was afraid of them. Would they also take Paree away because she had cursed at Agha Mansur? *Go to hell!* She had shouted the curse at him from the orphanage's main gate, and according to The Proctor, Agha Mansur was a very important person—even more important than himself, a former sergeant in the army.

Reza now wondered if Agha Mansur might order the police to take Paree away for cursing him, and they'd have to obey him because of his importance. And after taking Paree, Agha Mansur would order the police to drive Reza back to the orphanage since he no longer had a guardian. Again, the police would have to obey him.

Reza went into the living room and sat on the floor, every so often glancing at the door. After a while, the landlord, Agha Rahemi, unlocked the door, walked in, and asked if Reza needed anything. Reza shook his head and asked if Paree would be home soon. The landlord replied, "I don't know, but I'm sure Paree won't have any trouble finding a job quickly. She's a very clever woman."

Time went by as slowly as an old donkey, and Reza's glances at the door became more frequent. His heart thumped louder, his thoughts plummeted deeper and deeper into darkness. A car horn blasted, and he ran to the balcony, but the car had already sped past. He looked at the clock on the coffee table, a clock with the hours marked in a language called English, Paree had told him. "By the time the little hand and big hand are together and pointing straight up, I'll be back," she had said. The little hand and big hand were past straight up now. To the right of straight up.

So it was just as he thought. The police had taken her away, and now they would take him away. He wouldn't let that happen.

But what if Paree was late just because she was still looking for a job and hadn't found one?

Everything was so complicated, confusing.

* * * *

He waited and waited as the landlord stopped by once more and said Paree should be home soon, but the little hand of the clock kept creeping to the right and the big hand circled around one and a half times past straight up. Reza could wait no longer. Now he was certain the police had taken Paree away.

He hurried to the bedroom and opened the closet door. His gunnysack was folded neatly on the floor, his shirts folded neatly on a shelf. He picked up the gunnysack and stuffed the shirts in it. His underwear was in the bottom drawer of the dresser opposite Paree's bed. He opened the drawer, removed the underwear, and stuffed them in the gunnysack too. Dragging it behind him, he headed to the icebox. She had made salami sandwiches for their lunch, each inside a brown paper bag—with all the worries on his mind, he had forgotten to eat lunch.

After putting one of the bags in the sack, he walked to the front door, stayed still for a moment, and listened. No one was outside. He unlocked the door, opened it, and stepped into the carpeted corridor. All was quiet. He crept down the main staircase, tiptoed through the vacant lobby, and walked outside. The sun was hot as the desert sun, and the street was quiet as the desert night.

He turned left and started his journey toward Pahlavi Highway, Shemiran, and Mount Damavand.

Chapter 30

The first two jobs she had inquired about were disappointments. One was as secretary to the manager of a small, modestly priced hotel, the other as secretary to an assistant manager of a local bank. Although the would-be employers granted her interviews, they didn't act overly interested—Paree sensed they were looking for much younger women. She wasn't overly interested either, because the wages were pitifully low and the work didn't seem challenging: answering telephones, taking dictations, and, she imagined, serving tea and biscuits or anything else the all-male employers desired. Another Iranian secretary/maid at the male-dominated Iranian workplace.

The third inquiry was at a travel agency called *Khuneh-e Safar*—The Journey House, which was located on the east end of *Takht-e* Jamshid, the avenue where her apartment was located. After keeping her waiting for over an hour while he met with an elderly couple, the middle-aged, affable owner who spoke Farsi with an Indian accent and whose last name was Agrawal, showed her about the premises. There was a spacious conference room with hung, framed posters of exotic locations, a basement stock room crammed with travel books and brochures, and Agrawal's office adorned with three Kashmir rugs, an ornate teakwood armoire, and a massive painting of the Taj Mahal.

They settled on leather chairs in his office and he skimmed through her résumé, after which he nodded his head approvingly. "I am so pleased you're fluent in English," he said, "because most of our overseas telephone calls and correspondence are from English-speaking travel agents." He also told her that the job entailed far more than mere secretarial duties. Upon learning the system, she would reserve flights, book passages on liners, find the right hotels for customers based on affordability, and advise them about the best times to travel to their chosen vacation spots. "And you'll learn much about the most interesting regions of the world," he added. "If you accept the position, I want you to start work next Saturday morning, nine o'clock sharp."

She accepted at once, despite knowing that the salary was a third less than the amount she would have received from the Anglo-Iranian Oil Company. She and Reza would be forced to move into a smaller apartment in a less upscale part of Tehran. The realization depressed her a little, but such was the price of independence. The price of choosing Reza over Parviz Shappour and the Oil Company, and choosing an apartment in Tehran over a cottage in the Cotswold Hills of western England, where Mike now lived.

His cottage was not far from a village called Bourton-on-the-Water. She and Mike once lived in that village and strolled in the surrounding countryside, where they would watch Little John climbing the lone chestnut tree at the crest of a field near their home. He would swing from branch to branch, and Paree's heart would skip a few beats, worried he might fall, but he never did.

After his escapades in the tree, he would climb down to gather the strewn chestnuts on the ground, picking out the sturdiest ones, heat-drying them, and then readying them for his favorite game, conkers. He would bore a hole through each chestnut and pass a piece of string through the hole. After tying thick knots at one end of the string to prevent the chestnut from slipping off, he would challenge his friends in the village to a championship match of conkers. They would smash the nuts-on-strings against each other until all but one cracked, leaving the unscathed chestnut in the hands of the champion.

More often than not, Little John would win the local matches, and proudly he would tell Paree, "Someday, I'll be the conkers champion of the whole wide world."

Happy days, happy years.

Then along came WWII. Battling chestnuts turned into battling bombs, guns, tanks, and rockets. They turned into battling humans, many of whom would be killed or left with indelible scars—some visible, some hidden deep within their souls to become blights upon their existence.

* * * *

After signing countless employment papers at The Journey House, Paree sped back to the apartment, suddenly realizing that she was over an hour and a half late and Reza would probably be worried. She bounded up the flights of stairs to her flat. The door was ajar. Her pulse raced as she raced inside. No sign of Reza. Not in the living room, bathroom, kitchen, or bedroom. The closet door was open. The gunnysack was gone, as were his shirts. The bottom dresser drawer was open too, his underwear gone.

In a near panic, she bounded downstairs and rang the buzzer to the landlord's office, but no one answered. She checked the garden, but no one was there. She ran outside, looked up and down the avenue, and shouted out Reza's name. A young man in tattered clothes approached her and said his name was Reza. She took out three tomans from her handbag, gave him the money, and asked if he had seen a thin boy carrying a gunnysack and walking the streets alone. The young man waved toward the east end of the avenue. Paree rushed to her car, her mind giddy, overwhelmed with guilt.

Yet again she had failed as a protector. As a mother.

* * * *

She found him on *Koocheh* Farghan, a side street off *Takht-e* Jamshid Avenue. The gunnysack was slung over his shoulder, his eyes to the ground, his gait slow, tentative. From the back, he looked like a hunched over, old person shuffling along the pavement, like Little John looked when he would wander off alone after returning from North Africa.

She pulled the car to the curb next to him and jumped out. "Reza! *Why?*"

He turned around and at seeing her, his face lit up. "I thought you weren't coming back, Paree. I thought—"

"Reza, you must learn to have faith in me." She rushed over and hugged him. "I'll be with you always, Reza-*jan*. Always."

He smiled, and she loved it when he smiled because it transformed his usually sad face to a happy face. The happy face of a child with a home and family.

Chapter 31

Reza watched Paree fold his shirts back onto the closet shelf and his underwear into the dresser drawer. All the while, she didn't act angry at all, not like Agha Mansur or The Proctor would have acted at the orphanage if instead of Paree, they had caught him running away.

When she was done putting his clothes away, she grasped his hand and led him into the kitchen. The two of them settled at the table to eat a late lunch.

"Did you find a job, Paree?" he asked after swallowing the first mouthful of his salami sandwich.

She sighed. "Yes, but we'll have to move into a less expensive home. The money they'll pay me isn't quite enough to keep us here."

"Where will we go?"

"I'll start looking for another apartment in the morning. As soon as we've finished eating, I must tell Agha Rahemi about the plan and give him notice."

"I'll come with you."

After lunch, they rode the elevator down and knocked on the landlord's office door. He opened it and smiled broadly at seeing them. A medium-built, bearded man with a constant smile, Agha Rahemi patted Reza on the head. "Didn't I say Mrs. Windom would come back soon, Reza? And I'm sure she has found an excellent job."

Reza nodded.

Paree told Agha Rahemi that they would be leaving the apartment by the end of the month. Looking disappointed, he asked her why. "Because I can no longer afford it," she replied and explained why not. He shook his head sadly. "I'm so sorry to hear that. You haven't been here for long, but from the day we met, I sensed you would be a fantastic tenant and a dear friend."

They shook hands, and Paree led Reza out of the office. They stopped in front of the elevator. As she was about to open the gate, he tugged at her arm. "Could I please see the garden again, Paree?"

They walked to the end of the ground-floor corridor and stepped out into the garden surrounded by tall brick walls. The grass at the center of the garden was uncut and starting to brown, weeds sprouting everywhere. At opposite sides of the lawn were rosebushes teeming with dead or dying blossoms. Along the walls were shapeless privet hedges growing out of control like the hair of most gardeners at *Baghah-e Sabz*.

Reza walked slowly around the garden, inspecting the grass and hedges and roses. At the far end of the lawn to the side of a small woodshed, he stopped for a long moment before a square patch of dirt covered with weeds. It would be perfect for what he had in mind.

When he was done, he came to Paree's side. "Could we please see Agha Rahemi again?"

"Why?"

"I'd like to ask him something."

"What?"

He smiled and shrugged. "It's a surprise, Paree. Could I please talk to him?"

The landlord seemed puzzled to see them again so soon. "Is there a problem?"

Reza responded. "Sir, if I make your garden pretty and grow fruits and vegetables in it, will you give me money?"

Agha Rahemi blinked at him. "One of these days, I'll hire a professional gardener—the last one quit a few weeks ago because of old age. I'm afraid you're too young for the job."

"But, sir, I've lived in a garden all my life, and I know how to take care of one."

On his good days, Baba had taught him much about gardening. How to seed and weed, when to water and fertilize, and which plants need sun, which need shade. Throughout those days, Baba was his friend like the bluebird. Except for Mama and the bird and Baba on his good days, Reza had no close friends in *Baghah-e Sabz*. Although three children lived in the other two gardens, they were much older boys and stuck together and bullied Reza. As he grew tired of being at the losing end of defending himself, he decided to stay within the walls of the Third Garden because the boys didn't come after him there—probably afraid of Baba and his rifle and his bad days. So Reza spent most of his time within those walls, either working alone or alongside Baba and the other gardeners, and by the time Mama told him he was nine years old, he felt he had become as skillful as any of them.

He smiled at Agha Rahemi. "Give me a chance, please, sir? I want *Khanom* Paree to stay here. She loves her home."

The landlord looked at Paree. "How can anyone resist such a heartfelt request?"

"How can anyone indeed?"

"All right. I'll hire Reza for a hundred tomans a week, provided he also sweeps the corridors every other day. But if he doesn't do a good job, I'll be forced to hire a professional."

Reza tugged at Paree's sleeve. "Will the money keep us in the apartment?"

After squinting at the ceiling for a while, she squeezed him against her. "Yes, it will be just enough, Reza. You're such a fine boy."

He turned to the landlord. "I'll need clippers, a shovel, and a scythe to cut the grass, sir."

Agha Rahemi laughed. "Nowadays we cut grass with lawnmowers, *pessar.*"

* * * *

Paree watched him using a hoe to remove weeds from the grass and flowerbeds. She watched him pushing the human-powered lawnmower, which was almost his size. Despite his slight frame, he seemed strong enough to use it effectively. When he finished mowing, she helped him rake up the clippings and dump them inside a trash bin that he had brought out from the woodshed. Paree was impressed at how meticulous he was, how he went down on his hands and knees to pick up every last clipping. Next, he started on the privet hedges and rosebushes. He worked like an expert, she thought. Like an expert who sought perfection and took pride in his work. All the same, she realized that even though gardening was in his blood, the boy needed much more than gardening in his life. He needed an education.

Later that evening, she approached the topic as they sat at the kitchen table for a dinner of spaghetti and meatballs, which he had never tasted before and seemed to relish. "You must become proficient in reading and writing," she told him.

"But I can read, Paree."

"Really?"

"Yes, really."

She dashed into the living room and retrieved a brochure she had picked up at the travel agency. After placing it in front of him on the kitchen table, she pointed to the heading: *Come to the beauty of our glens and lochs and mountains. Come to the beauty of Scotland.*

"Read aloud what that says," she asked him.

"Come—come to…"

"Go on, Reza."

"Come to *g-h-a-s-h-a-n-g-i*—beauty…"

"You don't know how to read very well, do you?"

"What are you telling me, Paree?"

"During the daytime while I'm at work, I want you to attend a public school. You'll be there with children of your age."

He cringed. His face paled, his eyes grew wide with fear, and his body trembled. "*Man nemiram, khanom.*" I am not going, lady.

He swatted the brochure away and ran into the bedroom. She followed him in, and he had already flung himself on his bed, lain there facedown, and buried his face in the pillow. She sat next to him and gently stroked his hair. "You must be educated, Reza-*jan.*"

He turned away from her. "I don't want to be educated; I want to be a gardener."

"You're capable of much more."

"No, I'm not."

"It doesn't matter, Reza, because you're going to school."

He curled up in the fetal position, started sobbing. "Then I'll run away again."

Paree thought for a moment. He had run away twice before, once from the orphanage and once from her apartment. He would surely do so again. Back to the streets, the hunger, the cold. Scenes of him sleeping under the pine trees, where she first found him, resurfaced in her mind's eye. The wet, sobbing child, frightened and willing to die because it was the only way to rid himself of the torment of being.

No, never again would she let that happen.

She bent over and rested a cheek on his shoulder. "Supposing I become your teacher," she whispered. "Would you like that?

The sobs quieted. "You will teach me—*here*?"

"Yes, right here in this apartment."

He rolled over and she let her hair brush his face. He glided his fingers over it, like Little John used to do when she would bend over to kiss him goodnight. Reza smiled, wiped away his tears. "Thank you, Paree."

"You'll have homework, Reza-*jan*."

"I'll do it."

"And don't think I'm going to be soft on you."

"I'll learn, Paree, but you won't beat me if I don't do well in some of the lessons, will you?"

"Oh, my dear child, how could you even ask such a thing?"

He sat up and threw his arms around her. "*Madrasseh-e Khanom Windom*." Mrs. Windom's School.

Chapter 32

Often he was tempted to call her Mama but he didn't, afraid that police sometimes took mothers away, and then the mothers died and went to heaven without their children. She was Paree Windom, his friend and teacher. And his Guardian. He had been living with her for almost three months now. She no longer looked constantly sad, and *he* didn't feel constantly sad. He fell into a comfortable routine: gardening in the mornings, naan sandwich at twelve o'clock—Paree had taught him how to read the English clock, working on her assigned homework in the afternoons, talking with her or listening to the radio or reading in the evenings.

And not once during those three months did he wet his bed.

On Fridays, she showed him Tehran and took him to the cinema if the films were for children. They watched cartoons about a sailor who loved spinach, cats that chased mice and canaries, and chipmunks that got into mischief. They watched movies about two men, one fat and one thin, and movies about three men, one with a dust mop for hair, another with peach fuzz for hair, the third with almost no hair. All of them silly and funny, although he didn't like how the one with the dust mop kept hitting his two friends. She took him to bazaars and parks and to a museum that displayed wax models of famous people, some of whom looked evil and frightening. Paree said they were criminals who had murdered people.

"Why had they, Paree?" he asked her.

"Because they were killers," she replied. "Killing was in their blood."

He wanted to leave there at once, because some said Mama was a killer, and he didn't want to look at a wax model of Mama made to look evil and frightening, which she never did in real life. Besides, he didn't believe what anyone said about her because she couldn't have been a killer. She was gentle, her smile was soft and warm, her eyes were kind. Not like those wax men with cruel, thin lips and narrow eyes, the lids halfway down like the hooded eyes of hawks that often circled the Third Garden, looking for helpless little victims to snatch away in their claws.

He completed all the homework she assigned to him, and within a few weeks, he could get through a comic book twice as quickly and with a clearer understanding. She bought him a storybook with many pictures, a Farsi translation of an English writer by the name of Lewis Carroll. It was about the adventures of a girl called Alice. Once he started reading it, he couldn't put it down, often asking Paree for meanings of some words and phrases. The girl's escapades caught his imagination.

Alice grew into a giant and then shrank to the size of a mouse. She went to a mad tea party and spoke with animals. As he read about the party, he caught himself giggling. He hadn't giggled since Mama tickled him last, which she did when tucking him in his floor mattress every night.

Meanwhile, the garden blossomed. The grass grew greener thanks to the fertilizer the landlord bought, and thanks to all the weeds Reza pulled. The rosebushes also flourished after he trimmed them, fed them, and regularly watered them. The privet hedges now looked like a perfect row of green with rounded edges and flat tops, and seeds sprouted in his watermelon and eggplant patch. He showed them all to the landlord, who said Reza was as good as any professional he would have hired.

On the early evening of his birthday, June tenth, Paree took him to an enormous store that was four stories high and crammed with people. They went to the basement, which was crammed with children's toys. He was amazed at the displays. There were toy trains that raced around tracks, toy babies that squeaked mama, and toy puppies that barked woof. Paree told him to pick out something—anything that they could afford, no more than twenty tomans. He picked out a little bluebird made of tin with a key sticking out of its side. When he turned the key a few times, the bird hopped up and down and chirped.

Once they returned home, Paree disappeared in the kitchen for a few minutes and came out with a chocolate cake and ten tiny lit candles circling the top. She sang him an English song that she said was called *Happy Birthday*. He didn't understand the words of course, but he loved the tune. She then told him to blow out all the candles and make a silent wish. After blowing them out, he closed his eyes and wished Paree was his new mama instead of his guardian.

They were nibbling chocolate cake when the doorbell rang, and Paree opened it. The landlord stood behind a shiny, bright red wheelbarrow, a blue ribbon tied to one of the handles. Grinning, he waved at Reza. "Come and see your birthday present, dear boy."

It was Reza's happiest day since before That Night.

* * * *

Paree settled into her job. It was interesting as promised, and she learned much about faraway places like Bali and Tahiti and Maui. Her Indian—from Bombay—boss didn't treat her like many secretaries were treated at the typical Iranian workplace, where they were forced to act more as maids rather than as knowledgeable women who could correct all the grammatical errors in their bosses' dictated letters and recompose them to make them more readable.

Since she wanted to devote all her spare time to Reza, she no longer volunteered at the hospital for the poor. On the Saturday after he moved into her apartment, she had telephoned the hospital's director and informed him she was resigning and explained the reason. The director said he was extremely sorry to lose her, since all the patients and staff thought she was the kindest woman in all of Tehran, which made her feel a little better about herself.

Most of all, Paree looked forward to spending the evenings with Reza, to checking his homework and talking to him about the exotic, faraway lands she had learned about at the travel agency. She brought home brochures, and he seemed mesmerized by the photographs, especially those of the Swiss Alps and Scottish Highlands. He asked her if someday they would travel to those places, and she replied they would if they had the money.

"Didn't you once live in a faraway land, Paree?"

"I lived in England for over twenty years before the war."

"What war?"

"The Second World War, when half the world tried to destroy the other half. It lasted five years and ended only six years ago."

"Was it a bad war?"

"All wars are bad, Reza."

"Were many people killed by bombs and guns?"

"Millions of people were killed, and many others survived the bombs and guns only to..."

"Only to what, Paree?"

"Never mind."

"Please tell me more about England."

She described the green hills, the beautiful gardens, and the ancient castles where many legends were born. Legends of King Arthur, Sir Lancelot, Lady Guinevere, and Knights of the Round Table. She said some castles had ghosts. Reza asked her to tell him about ghosts, so she told him they were people leaving their bodies after they died, wandering about, waiting to go to heaven—she refused to talk about the other place. He asked her if the ghost is that part of a person that can float and is as light as air and no one can take it away.

After thinking about his question, she replied, "That's what many people believe, yes."

He said maybe someday Mama would visit him as a ghost, and she held back a sob, knowing that she fantasized the same about Little John. Sometimes in the twilight of sleep, she would open her eyes to find Little John, whole in body and soul, standing at the foot of her bed and gazing at her. She would blink a few times and he would disappear, leaving her with nothing but the misery of reality.

But now with Reza in her life, even without vodka—she hadn't consumed any alcohol in over three months—reality wasn't so miserable.

Chapter 33

On the first of July, Paree received a letter from Mike, the first since he returned to England. In the interval, they had spoken by telephone several times, the conversations a little awkward, a little stiff, and a little detached—more on her part than on Mike's because she wanted to sound strong. To convey to him that without his presence and support, she was managing perfectly well in Iran's male-dominated society. During the last chat, she told him more about her duties at the travel agency, after which she told him more about her life with Reza and how it was progressing. Mike seemed quite interested in the arrangement and again offered his financial assistance, which she again declined.

The letter was far different from the detached tone of the telephone conversations.

Dearest Paree:

I miss you terribly. Please come back to me. Don't you miss me even a little bit? My going to a lonely home after a long day at the office is quite depressing, especially since it is in desperate need of the woman's touch—YOUR touch. If you decide to come back, I will call it The Gay Paree House. Surely living with me in a land that is not torn apart by political upheaval and angry mobs is far better than working in Iran. You could at least come for a week or two and decide how you would fare living in England again. I love you more than ever.

Your loving husband, Mike.

She noticed he didn't mention Reza, and wondered why. Was he jealous because she had a new relationship in her life—one that brought joy into her gloom? She didn't think so. Mike was a little stiff and occasionally domineering in his relationships, but he was never jealous. A more likely explanation was that he thought her guardianship of Reza was ill-fated and wouldn't last. He therefore avoided the topic.

Paree supposed that without Reza to care for, she might well have been swayed by the plaintiff letter from the man with whom she had shared many joyous years. A good man who loved her and whom she had grown to love just as much, until the winter of '43, when the chestnut tree faded her affection, when his strength provoked her envy.

Sitting on the Persian rug in the living room, Reza looked up from his homework of parsing sentences and trying to find errors that Paree had deliberately inserted. *Seven blackbirds sits on a wall* or *Jack and Jill goes up a hill.* "Who's the letter from, Paree?"

"Mike, my husband."

"Is he nice?"

"Very nice, but now and then he can be a bit of a dictator."

"What's a dictator?"

"Someone who wants to control people—to have them obey his commands."

"So Agha Mansur is a dictator?"

"He *was* a dictator. He's no longer in charge of the orphanage." A week earlier, she had telephoned the Children's Welfare Administration, anxious to find out if they had investigated the place. She spoke with Mr. Sharzadeh, who informed her that Mansur was currently awaiting trial for corruption and child endangerment, and he was no longer managing the orphanage that he had so arrogantly named after himself. Mr. Sharzadeh then thanked her on behalf of his staff and the government and the people of Iran for helping to rescue the unfortunate, wretched children from the clutches of "that demon." After which he asked how young Reza Ahmadi was faring in his new home. She replied he was no longer unfortunate or wretched.

"Did Agha Mansur leave?" Reza now asked her.

"No, he was fired, and the orphanage's name was changed to the Red Rose Children's Home."

He squinted at her. "So Agha Red Rose is now in charge?"

She laughed. "No, the orphanage is named after the pretty flower, which some say is the national flower of Iran."

He rolled onto his back, smiled, and sat up. "What did Mike write?"

"He wants me back with him in England."

The smile faded, and he frowned while twirling a lock of his hair. "What will you do?"

"I'll stay here with you."

"Don't you miss him?"

"Yes, but I have you with me now, and that keeps me happy."

He thought for a moment. "But you can't be very happy being so far away from him. Sometimes you look so sad."

"There are many reasons for people to look sad at times, Reza."

"Could we go and visit him?"

His request surprised her for a moment, but she quickly realized that Reza had wanderlust in him. Wanderlust to escape the known and discover the unknown. To climb a mountain and see what is on the other side.

Why not? It would be good for Reza to experience a different culture, and it would be good for her to experience her husband again. Then, all at once, the very thought of traveling to England pulsed pangs of anxiety through her, the anxiety of knowing they would be near the scenes of her torment.

"You looked happy, and then suddenly you looked sad," Reza said. "Why, Paree?"

"It's hard to explain."

He gazed at her through pleading eyes. "Couldn't we visit Mike just for a few days? Please?"

She held his gaze for a long moment. A few days and no more, she at last decided—but Mike would have to finance the trip, and she'd have to stay away from Bourton-on-the-Water and the stump of that chestnut tree at the crest of that lonely field.

Before retiring for the night, she wrote back to her husband.

Dear Mike,

I miss you too, even though I have become quite busy between working at the travel agency and caring for Reza. He has settled down to a peaceful life with me, and I thoroughly enjoy raising and educating him. We both would love to visit you, but at this time my finances will not permit the travel expenses. Perhaps in a year or two, we could manage.

Love, Paree.

* * * *

His response came ten days later, in a telegram instead of a hard-to-hear long-distance telephone call:

Dearest Paree. Stop. Will pay all expenses for both. Stop. Come soon. Stop. Love Mike. Stop.

Chapter 34

On that September Monday, exactly five months after starting work at the travel agency, Paree sensed Reza's excitement as they walked across the tarmac toward Swissair's DC-3, its nose proudly pointing up in the air as if anxious to touch the sky. He talked almost without pausing for a breath. "I've seen airplanes flying high but never up close, and this airplane is bigger than I ever thought. Isn't it too heavy to fly, Paree, because birds are much lighter and this bird must be a thousand times heavier, so are you sure it'll fly, Paree?"

"I'm sure, Reza-*jan.*"

As they stepped inside the plane, the stewardess in the red uniform put a hand on his shoulder and asked him his name—in English. He didn't understand of course, and Paree decided that while they were in England for the twelve-day visit, she would teach him some simple sentences in English. They sat near the front, and he sat at the window seat. The overhead speakers came on, which startled him, and she explained it was the pilot speaking on his radio to the passengers, telling them they must be seated with their seatbelts buckled. She showed him how to fasten his seatbelt, and he asked what it was for. "To keep you from flying off your seat," she said.

"So if I unfasten it, will I fly like an airplane?"

"No, you'll only fly if the plane has to stop suddenly."

"That sounds like fun, Paree."

"Not if you bang your head or break an arm or a leg."

The airplane door closed, the engines roared to life, and Reza covered his ears. As they raced down the runway, his eyes bulged at the amazing speed they had gathered. Then ever so smoothly, the plane rose into the air, and Paree saw his face pressed against the window so hard that she worried he might hurt himself.

She had the same wanderlust as he did, Paree imagined, recalling her first voyage out of Iran. It was on a liner from Abadan to Southampton in 1921, when the Anglo-Persian Oil Company first transferred Mike back to England. At the time of the voyage, Little John was no more than a tiny fetus lodged inside Paree's womb. She was seasick almost the entire trip, but Little John somehow survived her retching, vomiting, and the waves. The seasickness, however, did little to dampen her excitement of traveling to a faraway land.

From Southampton, Mike traveled to Gloucester, where he would familiarize himself with his new position and investigate houses for sale. She journeyed on by train to Inverness, Scotland, and stayed with Mike's parents, who had relocated there after spending most of their lives near Oxford. She fell in love with the Scottish Highlands, which she roamed daily with the Windoms as they filled her with stories—fact laced with fiction—of the Scots' courageous battles to prevent their homeland from becoming an extension of England.

Meanwhile, Mike purchased a cottage in Bourton-on-the-Water, a village not far from where the southwestern regional headquarters of the Oil Company were located. He and Paree moved into the cottage, Little John was born, and for the next eighteen years, the three of them lived there in *relative* bliss because she had always thought that *total* bliss was the sole province of the mentally impaired.

Then along came WWII and North Africa and Tobruk.

* * * *

The Swissair plane flew over deserts and stopped in Beirut for refueling. It flew on over the azure waters of the Mediterranean and circled over Rome, where it would land for another refueling. As it circled, Paree pointed out the Coliseum to Reza, and he asked why the place looked like it had been destroyed. So she talked to him about the two thousand year-old ruins of Ancient Rome, and about the gladiators who fought in the Coliseum and similar arenas. He didn't seem enthralled with gladiators, because he grimaced when she told him they fought each other to the death.

"Did the people *like* to watch them killing each other, Paree?"

"I suppose so, yes."

"And they thought it was *fun*?"

"Those were different times, Reza."

"Why were they different?"

"Because the people weren't as…as civilized as they are now."

"What does civilized mean?"

Paree thought for a moment. "Being civilized means treating others the same way as you would like them to treat you. It means obeying the laws, most of which forbid you from harming one another."

Reza frowned. "Then why did we have wars *after* we were civilized? You know, like the Second World War you told me about. Didn't you say half the world tried to harm the other half?"

"Would you like some Swiss chocolate and a glass of orange juice?"

From Rome, they flew on to Geneva then on to London. She wondered if Reza would have a squashed face by the time they landed at Heathrow. He had spoken little during the last leg of the journey, as if in a trance of constant amazement at the sights below him, especially as they flew over the Swiss Alps. Every so often though, he thanked her—you must thank Mike, she corrected—for taking him with her.

As they were flying over France, the stewardess stopped at their row with the beverage cart, and Reza asked Paree, "Does Mike go out once a week at nights and come back home late?"

Surprised by the question, she gazed at him for a moment and replied, "He used to go out on weekend evenings, but I usually went with him. Why did you ask me that, Reza?"

He shrugged.

At last, they landed at Heathrow Airport, with a few heavy thuds, which made a few passengers turn ashen and made Reza grin because he said it was fun. They cleared immigration and customs and stepped out into the crowded but British-subdued terminal. Mike was leaning forward against the barricade, beaming. Thinking he was as handsome as she remembered him, Paree felt joy mixed with apprehension as she walked toward him in the land that she had once vowed never to visit again. She waved and pointed him out to Reza, who gripped her hand, and she noticed his hand was a little sweaty, a little shaky.

Something is bothering him, she supposed. Something about Mike. *Or is it about any man who might compete for my affections?*

"What's the matter, Reza?" she asked as they approached the barrier gate.

"Does Mike have a gun?"

Chapter 35

Everything around him became a blur except the grinning mouth. Mike's grinning mouth. Reza studied it, looking for the slight curl of the upper lip that Baba usually had, but it wasn't there. He focused on the eyes. They weren't buried deep in their sockets, like Baba's. They were out in the open, blue like the sea over which the plane had flown—Mediterranean Sea, Paree had told him. Not angry eyes. Just loving eyes that were held on Paree, like Mama's eyes when she greeted Reza as he walked into the shack after working or playing in the gardens.

The eyes now shifted to Reza, and they smiled at him, welcomed him to England. He looked at Mike's hands. They didn't carry a gun or a bottle. They carried a bouquet of roses, some pink, some red, some white. Did that mean Mike was nice? Baba sometimes acted nice on his good days. More than once, he had picked jasmine flowers from the garden and bundled them and given them to Mama. But he wasn't nice when he returned from his Thursday nights out, when he carried a bottle instead of flowers.

Thursdays were never good days.

They passed through the customs gate, and Mike wrapped Paree in his arms as if he wanted her to melt into him. They swayed as one for a long time. Watching them, Reza wondered if they would be glued together if they stayed like that much longer. Mike finally let her go and stepped in front of Reza.

He bent down and ruffled Reza's hair. *"Khosh amadi. Farsi-e man chetowr-e?"* Welcome. How is my Farsi?

"Khoob-e, agha." It is good, sir.

Not counting the terrible accent.

They walked out of the terminal after Mike took the suitcase from Paree, which surprised Reza because in *Baghah-e Sabz*, the women and donkeys did most of the carrying. Mike ushered them to an enormous parking lot and stopped in front of a shiny, maroon car. On the hood was perched a glittering metallic model of a leaping animal.

As Reza gazed at the emblem, Mike said in Farsi, "The make of my car is Jaguar, and it is named after that wild cat."

"Why is the car named after that wild cat?"

"Because it makes people think they're driving a strong and ferocious beast."

"Why do people want to drive a strong and ferocious beast?"

"It makes them feel like they're…you know, sort of powerful."

Paree winked and smiled at Reza. "It's a male fetish."

"What's a male fetish, Paree?"

"You'll understand when you're older."

Inside the Jaguar was roomy, the seats leather, the dashboard polished wood that reminded Reza of Baba's polished rifle stock. The three of them sat in the front seat, Reza in the middle. They drove on the left side of the road, which seemed strange but he didn't ask about it because they were in a different world, and everything was bound to be strange.

Soon they were driving through the countryside that was green, teeming with woods and cows and sheep. Reza was in awe of the green and of all the animals. There were a dozen donkeys at *Baghah-e Sabz*, but no other four-legged animals except the owner's dog, a wiry little creature called Yahu. One time when Yahu strayed into the Third Garden, Baba kicked it and chased it away. They didn't see much of the dog after that.

All the same, Reza loved Baba—especially during the good days—until That Night, but he couldn't understand why afterwards he had completely stopped loving him. He didn't feel right about not loving him anymore, because Baba was his father and he was dead, and dead fathers had to be loved, didn't they? The Proctor said Mama shot him in the head, but Reza knew she couldn't have done it because she didn't know how to shoot a gun. He was sure someone else shot Baba in the head. Maybe a night bandit.

Mike was pleasant and smiled a lot. He said he'd speak Farsi until Reza could understand English, but Reza didn't think he could learn that much English during the twelve-day visit. Mike told him that the first three English words he should learn were please and thank you, and he had Reza repeat them until the pronunciations were right.

After Reza said "Tank you" a few times, he stopped.

Mike said, "Put your tongue between your teeth and blow. That's how you pronounce *th*."

They drove on a twisty road with endless rows of hedges and stone walls on both sides, and sometimes the road snaked under tunnels of trees with big leaves—English oaks, Mike called them. As heavy rain started, they drove through a village of stone houses with roofs that seemed made of straw. At the far end of the village, they stopped for lunch at a white building with a picture of a sword and hammer sticking out above the entrance.

"The Sword and Hammer Tavern," Mike said and made Reza repeat the words after him.

Inside smelled the same as Baba's breath on Thursday nights. The ceilings had thick logs for beams, and the floor was covered with the same kind of dark wood. Music flowed out of an enormous silver and glass box with moving parts that Reza could see through the glass. Another strange object in a strange world.

The music was a lot different from that of Persian *tanburs* or *setars*. A man with a deep voice sang to the music. He didn't sing at all like the gardeners or preachers did, which was through their noses and sounded like they were whining or had bad colds.

"The singer's name is Bing Crosby," Mike said as Reza gazed at the music player, which Mike called a jukebox. "He isn't bad for an American," he added, laughing. A bit of British humor, he explained, which Reza didn't understand.

They sat at a corner table, Mike spoke in English to a waiter wearing a red jacket, and soon they all had drinks. Sweet, carbonated drinks tasting of ginger for Reza and Paree. A large glass filled with coffee-colored liquid for Mike. Floating on the liquid was white foam, which looked like cotton balls full of bubbles. Mike said he was drinking stout, and he made Reza pronounce stout and told him it was the name of the drink, not a word describing a fat person. He laughed, and again Reza didn't understand his humor. Then Mike made him pronounce Guinness.

A few minutes later, the waiter brought them their meals: meat, potatoes, and green vegetable balls that Reza had never seen before.

"How do you like England so far, Reza?" Mike asked.

"Very nice, agha."

"Mike."

"Very nice, Mike."

Reza stared at the sheets of rain pounding the windowpanes that were mosaics of countless amber and jade glass shards. The patterns were not unlike those he had seen on mosques' domes while he and Paree walked around Tehran.

"Does it rain very much here?" he asked Mike.

"Yes, but you get used to it."

Reza liked the rain, because everyone at the Third Garden knew that without rain in the north, the creek would dry up, the crops would die out, and the garden would become no different than the barren desert beyond the walls.

The food was delicious and he overate. The meat was mutton, which he had to repeat after Mike; the potatoes were mashed, which he had to repeat after Mike; and the vegetable balls were Brussels sprouts, which he had trouble repeating after Mike.

As soon as they finished the meal, Mike's face grew serious and he leaned toward Reza. "How old were you when your parents passed away?"

Reza didn't answer and fiddled with his fork. He didn't want to talk about Mama and Baba. The excitement of being in Farawayland and of being with Paree had for the time being taken his mind off them and off trying to remember what had happened on That Night. Mike asked the question again, and Reza stared at his plate and fiddled more with his fork. Paree spoke a few words of English to Mike, and he didn't ask the question again, but he asked him about other things.

"What do you want to be when you grow up, Reza?"

"A gardener, agha."

"Mike."

"A gardener, Mike."

"Not a bad profession, but do you realize you'll never get rich?"

"I don't care, Mike."

"Where do you want to live when you grow up?"

"In the mountains, Mike."

"Why the mountains?"

"Because t-they're beautiful and no one…"

"No one what?"

"No one bothers anyone."

Mike puffed up his chest. "I used to go hunting around Mount Damavand—hunting for mountain lions with my shotgun."

Reza cringed. Paree again said something to Mike in English, and he talked no more about hunting for mountain lions with his shotgun. Instead, he talked about his younger days and playing a sport called rugby, and he wondered if Reza had ever played a sport, like soccer. Reza said he sometimes kicked an unripe pomegranate around with Baba.

But he didn't say only on Baba's good days.

Chapter 36

Reza slept alone that night.

Paree and Mike took him into the attic bedroom with sloping ceilings, rattling windows, and flapping curtains. Against the far wall was a single bed, which sank in the middle and was covered with a quilt made up of square patches in different designs and colors. Looking at it sadly, Paree said she had sewn it many years before. Reza asked her why she didn't use it for her own bed in Iran. She hesitated a few seconds and replied, "Because I didn't need it and still don't."

After lightly kissing Reza on the forehead, she showed him how to switch on and off the overhead light by pulling a cord dangling from the fixture, took Mike's hand, and led him out of the room.

At the foot of the bed was an ancient looking wooden chest with brass trimmings. Curious what was inside, Reza opened it. A soft, pale blue blanket, the same width and length as the chest, lay at the top. He lifted the blanket. Underneath was a framed photograph of a young man in uniform, wearing a strange dark hat that tilted to one side and had no rims. His face looked half like Mike's and half like Paree's. The eyes were more like hers, though—not as dark but enormous and a bit curved up at the outer corners.

After replacing the photograph and closing the chest lid, Reza undressed, climbed into bed, and snuggled under the quilt. He didn't turn off the overhead light because the room was a little strange and scary.

At first he couldn't sleep, the wind outside reminding him of the winter desert wind that sounded like jackals howling deep inside a cave. A long while later, he fell asleep and dreamed he was in a cave with Mama, a silvery mama floating above him in the darkness. He reached out to her, but she floated away, the cave caught fire, and Baba stepped out of the flames. His face was bright red, and he carried a bottle in one hand and a rifle with a glimmering stock in the other. Reza screamed and tried to run away, but his legs were like cement and he couldn't escape.

He woke up to a wet mattress and underwear, the overhead light still on, the wind still howling outside. After taking off the quilt, which was slightly wet, he spread it on the floor to dry and lay down beside it.

Overcome with shame, he cried himself to sleep.

* * * *

"Why are you on the cold floor, Reza?" a woman's voice asked him, and he thought he was lying next to the creek near their shack on the morning after That Night.

"I don't know, *Khanom* Sahderi."

A soft hand gently stroked his forehead. "This is Paree. Wake up, Reza."

As her words seeped into him, he opened his eyes and looked about in a daze. "Where am I?"

"In Mike's house in England." Wearing a lavender bathrobe as soft as cotton wool, she was kneeling next to him, her hair tickling his face.

Suddenly he remembered the wet bed because he felt the dampness in his underwear. "I-I want to get dressed now. Please leave, Paree."

She walked to the window and drew back the curtains, and the sunshine poured in. He grasped a corner of the quilt, stood up, and dragged it to the bed. Sitting on the edge of the bed, he spread the quilt about him so Paree wouldn't notice the yellow stains.

On her way out, she pointed to a dresser and said his clean clothes were in the bottom drawer. The moment she left, he removed his damp underwear and shoved it under the bed, out of sight. But he soon realized Mike and Paree would know he had wetted the bed once they discovered the yellow-stained sheets. They would ridicule him and send him back to Iran to some orphanage no different from Agha Mansur's orphanage.

After removing his clean underwear from the drawer, he quickly dressed and crept downstairs. Paree and Mike were not in sight. He tiptoed into the living room with the low ceiling, wooden beams, and fireplace as big as the outhouse in the Third Garden. He opened one of the glass-paneled double doors and stepped outside into the downward sloping garden of tulips and roses and azaleas, the morning dew dripping off in glittering little flashes. Wondering if England had mountains, he looked to the horizon and all he saw were green hills and woodlands and sheep grazing in the fields. A white wooden gate was at the end of the garden. He climbed over it and ran across a damp field toward the woods, where he would stay for a while and think about what he should do next.

He dreaded facing Paree or Mike, listening to them telling him only babies wet themselves, talking to him mockingly like Agha Mansur and the Proctor and most of the older kids at the orphanage did. He couldn't bear to hear that all over again, especially from Paree.

She and Mike hated him now, because he was sure all grownups and older kids hate bed-wetters.

* * * *

Mike had started snoring two minutes after rolling off her, which reminded Paree of what recently-wedded, eighteen-year-old Minu, her best friend during the teenage years, once told her about husbands:

"They pound away and before you figure out what's happening, they roll over and fall asleep and snore."

That night's lovemaking was no more pleasurable for Paree than it had been since Little John left for North Africa. Mike made a valiant effort at foreplay, but all too quickly his passion took command, and foreplay yielded to clumsy penetration. Afterwards, he said, "Sorry about that, my dear. It's been too bloody long."

She had readily yielded to him because he loved her, and because it felt good to be loved, but her passion just wasn't there. It died many years before, on a drizzly Sunday when she saw her son off at the Gloucester train station. Mike was at a crucial conference in London to deal with the nation's petrol crisis. A khaki kitbag slung over his shoulder, an excited expression brightening his face, Little John leaned out of a window and said, "I'm off to war, Mummy; aren't you going to wish me luck?" As the troop train puffed and steamed forward to war, he yelled, "Don't worry about me, Mummy. I'll be all right because I'm a Windom, and nothing bad ever happens to a Windom." The last optimistic words she would hear from her son.

Words that would prove to be far from prophetic.

After the lovemaking, Paree had trouble falling asleep because of Mike's crescendo-decrescendo snoring, and because her thoughts soon drifted to Reza. Would he love her as a son loves his mother, or would he just look to her as a means of surviving? *But isn't that what a child's love is all about?* Trading love for protection, a simple arrangement between two people, from which both benefit.

As she thought more about the love that she and Little John shared before North Africa and Tobruk, she grew certain that it was far deeper than an arrangement born of convenience. It was the *pure* love of mother for child, of child for mother. Which was what she desperately wanted from Reza, but she wasn't sure if he would ever be capable of giving it because of his wretched past.

After a few hours of fitful sleep, Paree had awakened at daybreak, no longer hearing snores but distant sobs instead, which immediately resurrected her pitiful images of Reza asleep under a pine tree near Hotel Alborz. She climbed quietly out of bed without disturbing Mike, slipped on her bathrobe, and tiptoed up to the attic bedroom. Reza was asleep on the floor, twitching, sobbing. As soon as arousing him to ask why he was sleeping on the cold floor, she understood the reason. The smell of urine and the yellow wetness of his underwear were giveaways, but she didn't want him to know she knew. She was well aware that the recurrence of bedwetting in children was sometimes a manifestation of low self-esteem, and drawing Reza's attention to it would have served no useful purpose other than to further damage whatever was left of his ego.

Her heart filled with pity for the miserable child, Paree returned to the master bedroom as Mike's heavy snoring resumed, echoing around the walls, reminding her to use cotton earplugs if she were to sleep with him again. After splashing cold water on her face and brushing her teeth in the adjoining bathroom, she dressed and crept downstairs. Walking past the French doors of the living room, out of the corner of her eye she noticed some movement outside and looked in that direction. Although a fleeting glimpse, she was sure she recognized the back of Reza as he ran toward the oak tree woods beyond the field at the rear of the cottage. She rushed after him, but by the time she stepped outside, he was out of sight.

With visions of Little John's solution looming in her mind, she hurried into the woods and ran around from tree to tree, looking for Reza. Unable to find him, she stood still, listening for his sounds, a breath, a footstep, a snapped twig. She heard nothing, only leaves rustling, birds chirping, a distant train huffing. She called out his name, but he didn't respond. She listened in silence for a few more minutes until she heard a muffled cough and immediately pinpointed its origin.

She found him sitting cross-legged under a bush of hawthorn next to a creek, staring into nothingness. Heaving a sigh of relief at locating him, she approached, but he seemed not to notice her. "Come back to the cottage for breakfast, Reza."

He didn't move. She stood in front of him and placed a hand on his shoulder. "Please come with me, Reza. We'll have a good old English breakfast."

His eyes drifted up and he looked at her blankly. "I want to stay here," he mumbled.

"Why? Don't you like the cottage?"

No response.

"Answer me, Reza-*jan*. Don't you like the cottage?"

He cupped his face. "I like it, but last night, I…"

She grasped his hands, pulled them away from his face, and smiled at him. "Accidents happen to the best of us, Reza-*jan*."

His eyes suddenly radiated concern. "You know?"

"Yes, I know."

"And you still…"

"Still what?"

"*Like* me?"

"I like you very much, Reza-*jan*." She almost said I love you very much, but it was too soon in their relationship. He wasn't at all like Little John before North Africa, an uncomplicated, adored son who took in his parents' love as naturally as he returned it. No, he was more like post-North Africa Little John, complicated, withdrawn, unable or unwilling to express his feelings. Besides, Reza might recoil at hearing her say I love you very much because he had been deprived of love, perhaps now afraid that if it were given back to him, it might be taken away again.

He looked at her, fear creeping into his expression. "Will you tell *him*?"

"You mean Mike?"

"Yes."

"I won't tell him, Reza. This will be our little secret."

Chapter 37

While Reza stood at the doorway, Paree removed the linen from his bed and pulled the mattress onto the floor to dry in the sunshine, which still poured in through the window. She found his soiled undershirt and shorts under the bed, bundled them up, and said she would launder them.

He watched her throughout in silence, feeling ashamed, humiliated, thinking she was angry at him but didn't show it because she was a nice person and maybe didn't hate *all* bed-wetters.

She asked him if he would prefer sleeping with her that night.

"Wouldn't Mike be upset, Paree?"

"No, he'll understand."

"You won't tell him about the…accident?"

"No, I promised, didn't I?"

Paree had him bathe in the guest bathroom while she and Mike made breakfast. After bathing and dressing, he walked into the smoky kitchen, where on the pinewood table were three dishes of English breakfasts with fried everything: tomatoes, eggs, sausages, and bread. Seated next to Mike, he noticed an orange and brown cat lying on Mike's lap throughout breakfast. Reza tried to pet it once, but the cat hissed and bared its teeth, and Mike said, "Alphonse the Cat isn't friendly to people it doesn't know well." When he finished eating, Mike put it on the floor and whispered shoo. Only one quiet little shoo, and Alphonse the Cat disappeared.

After breakfast, Mike had to go into work and deal with a problem of petrol delivery, something to do with railroad workers threatening to stop working. Which Reza didn't understand because at the gardens, if the workers didn't work they would be fired, so Agha Akbar, the head gardener, kept telling everyone.

When Mike left, Paree took Reza for a walk in the woods, following a path that snaked between the oak trees and next to a stream. At one point, she said jokingly, "I hope we're not lost."

Reza shook his head. "Getting lost is fun," he said, "because you see stuff you've never seen before."

The woods ended at the edge of a cliff overlooking green fields and a village in the distance. "That's the village of Bourton-on-the-Water," she told Reza, "and we used to live in a cottage there before we lived in Iran." He thought her voice sounded a little quivery.

He gazed at the stone cottages and at the building with a pointed top like a giant needle reaching for the sky. He asked Paree about it, and she said it was a church.

"What's a church, Paree?"

"It's like a mosque for people who are Christian."

"What's Christian?"

"A religion. Some people are Muslims, some are Christians, some are Buddhists. There all sorts of religions in the world, Reza."

He scratched his forehead and said, "Baba once told me I'm a Muslim, and he said I didn't have to go to a mosque on Fridays because we didn't have a car to get us there. But I think he usually didn't feel well on Fridays, and that's why we didn't go to a mosque."

"Did your father often kneel before the Koran and talk to Allah?"

"You mean *namaz*?"

"Yes, *namaz*."

"No, because Baba said he used to pray five times a day, but it didn't get him out of our shack and into a big house with lush gardens. So he stopped praying five times a day. He said it didn't matter anyway, because Allah just takes care of greedy rich people—like the owner of *Baghah-e Sabz*."

They grew silent, standing there for a long time as Reza took in the beautiful view of green hills before them. He glanced at Paree now and then, only to see her staring at the village, her eyes moist and as sad as he had ever seen them. He wondered what she was thinking, why she had her sad face on, why a single tear trickled down from the corner of one eye.

"Why didn't you stay in England forever, Paree?" he asked her, thinking she was sad because now she wished she had.

She shook her head and blinked away a tear. "What did you say, Reza?"

He repeated the question.

"Because of Mike's work," she replied. "Besides, I was homesick for Iran."

"Will you live in England again someday?"

She shook her head. "I don't think so, Reza. And certainly not without you."

"You don't like England, then."

"It's not that, no."

"Then what is it, Paree?"

"Bad, sad memories."

"Tell me about them."

She looked at him, and he noticed wetness again seeping into her eyes. "I really don't want to discuss them, Reza-*jan*."

"Why not?"

"Everyone has their own private little secrets, don't they? As I'm sure you do."

"Do your secrets have anything to do with the picture of the young man in a uniform and a funny looking hat, who looks half like you and half like Mike?"

She gaped at him through moist eyes. "What picture?"

"It was inside the wooden box at the end of my bed. I left it there, Paree. Who is he?"

"Someone who lost his soul."

"Is a soul the same as a ghost?"

"It's a lot of things. Your character, your mind, your emotions, and your relationships with people. In other words, it's what makes you who you are."

"Why did he lose his soul?"

"Because he saw something terrible, and it…it changed him."

"How?"

"He built an invisible shell around him, hid his emotions, and pulled away from people." She stared at Reza intently. "Isn't that what you did?"

"I don't know."

"Did *you* once see something terrible, Reza?"

"I can't remember. What about you, Paree?"

She winced. "Yes I did, and I don't want to talk about it."

A sudden, strange feeling came over him, and for a moment he thought he understood Paree and the young man in the picture.

Chapter 38

A while before sundown, Reza was sprawled on the living room floor in front of the unlit fireplace, immersed in his homework assignment, the last part of which was finding errors in two sentences she had written on a notepad. *Yesterday, Paree sat on a chair and sings a song.* Nothing wrong that he could figure out at first glance. He thought more as he mouthed the sentence. Yesterday, Paree sat on a chair and… *I get it!* She sat on a chair and *sang* a song. Next sentence. *Tomorrow, Paree sits on a chair and sang a song.* Easy. Tomorrow, she *will* sit on a chair and *will* sing a song.

"Did you finish yet, Reza?" he heard her ask.

He looked up at Paree, who was on the sofa and flipping pages of a magazine with a cover picture of black children with swollen bellies. He stared at it and at the children's eyes, sunken into their sockets like the eyes of Fereshteh the last time he saw her, not long before they covered her body with a white sheet and took it away. He felt a lump swelling in his throat and tried to swallow it, but it stayed there.

"Answer me, Reza-*jan*."

He looked away from the magazine cover and rubbed his eyes as if to wipe the picture out of them. "Yes I finished, Paree."

"What's wrong with those two sentences?"

"They're mixed up about before and now and later. Am I right?"

"Very good. Past, present, and future tenses, Reza. What happened yesterday has happened and we should move on to today. What happens today is happening, and we should enjoy it.

What happens in the future will happen, and we can't do anything about it."

He thought about what she said, and he was sure she was trying to tell him a lot more than about verb tenses. *And we can't do anything about it.* She was wrong about that, because his future, his destiny, would have been at the Agha Mansur Orphanage if he hadn't done anything about it, if he hadn't run away. He had changed it just as Fereshteh had done.

So what could *happen in the future may not happen if you do something about it.*

Paree sat down on the floor next to him. "Reza, I've been meaning to ask you about the gold ring on your finger. Who gave it to you?"

"A friend. The best friend I ever had. She was at the orphanage."

"Where is she now?"

"She went away."

"Where to?"

"She went to—"

A clatter at the door distracted him. He looked up to see Mike walk into the living room, his raincoat dripping rain on the floor. "I'm home with the chardonnay," he announced.

He waved something in the air. Reza stared at it.

A bottle full of yellow liquid!

He froze.

His stare drifted from the bottle to Mike, who seemed transformed. Now he had black hair, a black mustache, and black deep-set eyes. He sneered, snarled, bared his teeth, and flared his nostrils. He raised the bottle over his head.

And then he advanced, slowly, menacingly.

Reza suddenly felt as if he couldn't breathe. Inside was without air. He must listen to Mama's voice, now shouting in his head. *Get out, Reza! Get out of this shack now!* He must run outside, into fresh air, away from the bottle, away from the rifle. He must lie down by the creek for a while, breathe deeply, blank the terrifying images, and think happy thoughts.

He dashed out of the living room, out of the house and into the sheets of rain, toward the dark woods beyond. Where was that creek? Deep inside the dark. He ran between the trees until he found it. Sitting on the soaked, muddy ground, he sank his head between his knees, rocked back and forth. Voices shouted all around him, but he ignored them.

Someone rubbed his back. Someone squatted next to him. "What's the matter, Reza?"

"What brought this on, my boy?"

"What frightens you, dear child?"

"Get up and come back inside."

"You'll get soaked out here, Reza-*jan*."

"Come, my boy, stand up."

Someone behind him, grabbing him by the armpits, lifting him. Reza resisting, kicking, screaming.

The hands released him, and he fell onto his stomach. Unable to breathe, he lifted his face out of the mud. The rain ran down his forehead and gathered on his chin and drip-drip-dripped into the mud.

Baba drawing nearer, one step at a time, his forehead scarlet, his eyebrows scarlet. "Talk, my boy. Tell us what is frightening you."

And now Mama, stepping between them, tears streaming her cheeks. "Reza-*jan*, please tell us what troubles you. Whatever it is, we will understand."

Frightened as much as he had ever been, he lay there with his head turned to the side, eyes riveted on Baba standing a few paces in front of him, snarling, foaming at the mouth, daring him to…

He smelled the mud under him, which smelled like the mud next to the creek of the Third Garden. Slowly he came to his knees, waiting to hear *Khanom* Sahderi telling him, *vaziat-e bad tamam shodeh*—the bad situation is over. But she wasn't there. He stood up as the rain bounced off the leaves and dripped onto him. His underwear felt wet, but not *cold* wet. *Warm* wet. He must have pissed on himself again, so he let the rain wash away his shame. He stood there motionless until he realized where he was, until a gentle arm wrapped around his shoulders and he leaned against the soft body by his side. "Please come inside now, Reza-*jan*. You mustn't be afraid."

Still leaning against Paree, he let her steer him out of the woods, back into the cottage and into the bathroom connected to Mike's bedroom. She filled the tub and left. A moment later, she came back, hung his pajamas on the towel rack, and left again. After removing his wet clothes, he sank into the tub of steaming water and floated down a stream on a leaf to a lake surrounded by mountains. Mama and Fereshteh stood on the shore, smiling, waving. Then they suddenly transformed into Paree and Mike. Instead of smiling they scowled, and instead of waving they shook their fists. Unable to blank them from his mind, he cried in silence, distressed at what they must think of him now, after the bedwetting, after the tantrum in the woods.

"We need to dispose of that horrible little boy," he imagined them telling each other, which was what the chief policeman had said That Night before driving him to the place for children without homes.

* * * *

Mike paced about the living room while Paree gazed out of the window into the darkness.

"Something is deeply troubling that boy, my dear," he said.

She turned to him. "I know, and he needs time alone to sort things out. I wonder what set him off tonight. He saw the bottle, and he seemed fixated by it. Then suddenly he looked terrified."

"A distant memory, I should think. A memory of a horrific event, which he must have stashed away in a corner of his brain. So when he saw the bottle of wine, it became the trigger unleashing his awful memory. I've seen the same kind of reaction in you, Paree. Do you remember a few years ago at the Oil Club gym when you saw the khaki kitbag swinging on a hook? You panicked, didn't you? Screaming, running off at full speed until I caught up with you and shook you back to your senses—and in front of all those people."

Paree remembered it well. One of the most humiliating events of her life.

She thought about Reza's reaction in the woods, a quivering child, his body in the mud, his soul in the mud. He was a ten-year-old unable to confront his fears, always running away from them. Yet, she was certain that by continuously reassuring him of her protection and affection, his phobias would at some point fade. Although so far those reassurances had failed, she was determined to persevere.

She must not, *would* not fail Reza as she had failed Little John.

"The boy needs help, Paree," Mike said. "Professional help."

"*I* will help him."

"You're not a professional."

She shook her head. "I have the experience, Mike, just as you have. But you've put our horrific event out of your mind, while—"

"How do you know I've put it out of my mind?"

"Because you act as if it never happened, that's how. Anyway, I've kept thinking about that event, trying to figure out where we went wrong. Where *I* went wrong. In the end, I learned much more than a professional could ever learn from a textbook, or in a classroom, or by listening to someone else's problems."

Mike threw his hands in the air. "Just this once, Paree, will you please do as I ask? Let's have a psychiatrist see Reza while you're here. If that doesn't help, at least we can say we tried."

She hesitated. "Do you know anyone in the area?"

"Dr. Mary Lawrence. She and her husband live a couple of miles down the road, and we've become jolly good friends. I'll invite them for tea tomorrow."

* * * *

"Are you still in the bathtub, *pessar-jan-e-man*?"

As Paree's words trickled into his ears, Reza's spirits gradually lifted at realizing she had called him *pessar-jan-e-man*—my dear boy, which meant she couldn't be so angry at him.

"I'll be right out, Paree."

He came out wearing his soft new pajamas, which were pale blue dotted with prints of different animals.

She was sitting at the edge of Mike's bed, waiting for him. "As I told you this morning, Reza-*jan*, you and I will sleep down here tonight. Mike will sleep in the attic."

"Are you sure he wants to sleep in the attic?"

"He's the one who suggested it."

So maybe Mike wasn't bad after all. Reza smiled, and the dark thoughts drew farther and farther away as the evening wore on. They became distant shadows during supper, when Mike talked about fun stuff like his bicycle stored in the garden shed. They vanished when Mike said in the next few days he would teach him how to ride the rusty bicycle, but he'd have to lower the seat first because it was much too high. Maybe the tires needed blowing up, he added, and he'd show him how to blow up bicycle tires.

At bedtime and without the dark thoughts, Reza had no trouble falling asleep. He woke up in the middle of the night and could hear Paree breathing softly next to him. He curled up against her.

It was a good night.

Chapter 39

They had just finished setting up the tea trolley on the patio when an enormous black cloud appeared out of nowhere and started shedding its tears. They took the trolley into the living room. While waiting for the guests, Mike complained to Reza about the BBC Radio's weather forecaster, who he said was as good as a blind man in an archery contest. Then he had to explain the meaning of archery contest, which Reza quickly grasped. One of the boys at *Baghah-e Sabz* had a bow and arrow and often tried shooting down pomegranates with it and often failed. Reza didn't know what became of the boy and his weapon after Baba warned the boy that if he ever came to the Third Garden with his bow and arrow, he'd face a rifle. He said rifles are much more accurate than bows and arrows. And much deadlier.

Everyone at the gardens feared Baba because they all knew he had a rifle and a violent temper. He wasn't particularly tall, but after all the years of manual labor, he had grown as muscular and strong as a weightlifter. One of the gardeners, who was much bigger than him, once made the mistake of cursing at him after Baba accidentally ran a loaded wheelbarrow over the man's foot. Baba bulldozed him to the ground and smashed the poor man's face into a bloody mess of welts and gashes. No one ever cursed Baba again, but his coworkers often referred to him as *Atesh-toop*—Fireball. After another of Baba's violent fits because he tripped on a watermelon peel and smacked his forehead against a fig tree, a gardener whispered to Reza, "Let's hope you don't grow up to be like your father."

Although Reza didn't respond, deep down he clung to the same hope.

The guests, Mr. and Dr. Lawrence, arrived at a little after four o'clock, and Mike served everyone tea and scones. Paree and Reza sat on a flowery sofa, the others on flowery armchairs facing them. Reza didn't like English tea as much as Persian tea, which had a bit of a peppermint flavor to it, but he liked the scone because it tasted of sweet naan.

Mama knew how to make sweet flatbread—*naan-e barbari*, she called it. Baba had built a small clay oven next to the shack. He would fire it with twigs and dried branches under wire mesh that he had "borrowed" from the owner's screen door and covered with little rocks from the desert. Mama would add some honey to dough, which she'd flatten and shape into a perfect circle. After smearing cornmeal all over the dough, she'd place it over the rocks until it was reddish brown. Once it was ready, she would seat Baba and Reza on the floor of the shack and serve them the flatbread while it was hot. Even Baba would smile when he ate it, and more than once he said it was the best naan he had ever tasted. He didn't often say nice things to Mama, like Mike said to Paree.

The evening before, as soon as Mike arrived home from work, Reza had seen him kissing Paree on the lips and heard him telling her in Farsi that she was the most beautiful woman in the world.

Paree's face turned red and she said, "No I'm not. Look at the wrinkles around my eyes."

Mike grinned and said, "They're beauty wrinkles, my dear, and you shouldn't be upset at them."

Reza wished Baba and Mama had acted and talked like that to each other. Maybe then, That Night wouldn't have happened and he would still be in the Third Garden, sitting on a pomegranate tree branch with his bluebird or watching his watermelons grow in the patch at the southwest corner of *Bagh-e Sevom.*

And he wouldn't have been the cause of That Night.

Mr. Nigel Lawrence was tall, bald, and talked constantly. Reza didn't understand him because he spoke only in English. His wife, Dr. Mary Lawrence, listened to everything everyone said without talking much. Reza liked the thin, snow-white woman, because she smiled all the time and had bright green eyes that stood out, not sank in. They were eyes that were watchful and seemed understanding. Every so often, they would settle on Reza intently, as if to say, "We know you must be bored sitting there while the grownups talk in a language you don't understand."

Absently he would nod, and one of the green eyes would wink at him.

After everyone finished the tea and scones, Mike cleared the coffee table and said something in English to Mr. Lawrence, who said something back. Mike went to the closet in the foyer and took out a box and a board with brown and yellow squares, which he set on the coffee table. Dr. Mary Lawrence came to Reza, rested a hand on his shoulder, and smiled at him. She said something in English, and Paree nodded and said to Reza in Farsi, "The rain has stopped, so please come for a walk with us ladies while the men play *shatranj*—chess." And then she had to explain that chess is a board game. "A boring game at that," she added, "which sometimes takes hours and hours to finish." She also explained that many people believe the modern form of chess originated in Iran when it was the Persian Empire, and therefore Reza should be proud of his heritage. He didn't understand why he should be proud of his heritage for inventing a boring game.

After walking into the garden under brightening skies, the three of them talked and Paree acted as the translator. Through Paree,

Dr. Lawrence asked Reza to call her Mary and to tell them about his childhood years in Iran. So through Paree, he talked about the Third Garden and that he was a very good gardener. Mary wondered if his parents were good gardeners too, and he said Baba was.

She asked him, "Who was the better gardener, you or Baba?"

He replied, "Baba was better on his good days."

"What do you mean by his good days?"

He shrugged.

"Your father must have had not-so-good days, then."

He shrugged again.

"Did you have many good days yourself, Reza?"

He nodded.

"How about not-so-good days?"

He cringed.

Paree spoke a few words in English, and Mary didn't ask him any more about his not-so-good days. They strolled about for a while, and Mary wanted to know about his home at the Third Garden. He said it was a wooden shack with two windows and no electricity, but the oil stove, when lit, made it cozy and warm during winter nights. She wondered if he preferred Mike's cottage to the shack, and he said the cottage was very nice, but...

"But what?" she asked him.

"But it isn't..."

"Isn't what?"

"Home."

Once they were back inside, Paree told him to go to the attic bedroom, where it was quiet and he could concentrate on his latest assignment—the English alphabet. A for apple, B for boy, C for cat, and so on with some other English words that she and Mike had spent the morning teaching him.

Reza questioned why they insisted on teaching him English. Were they planning for him and Paree to move to England and live with Mike? After thinking about the possibility, he wasn't sure he liked the idea. Mike would be there the whole time when he wasn't at work, and Paree would spend a lot of that time alone with *him*, wouldn't she?

As soon as walking into the attic, Reza opened the wooden chest and lifted the blue blanket. The picture of the uniformed young man with bright, turned-up eyes, the big jaw, the hole in his chin, and the tilted hat had disappeared. When Reza had mentioned to Paree that he had seen the picture, she had looked sad and a tear had trickled down her cheek. He was now certain the young man was her and Mike's son because he looked half like Paree and half like Mike. If Reza and Paree moved to England, maybe the son would move in with them and *he* would spend a lot of time alone with Paree.

And *she* wouldn't have any time for Reza.

The negative thoughts roamed around his head for a while, and soon he grew quite ashamed of the selfish feeling that he didn't want to share Paree with anyone else.

But he couldn't help how he felt.

Chapter 40

As the chess war gathered intensity, the two women strolled outside in the now cloudless and pleasantly cool late afternoon. They stopped at the edge of an escarpment just beyond the oak tree woods, gazing at the village of stone houses in the distance.

"We thoroughly enjoy your company," Paree said, "but we also had an ulterior motive for asking you to tea this afternoon."

Dr. Mary Lawrence smiled knowingly. "It's about Reza, isn't it?"

"Yes. I became his legal guardian and rescued him from a dreadful orphanage. I rescued a troubled child, Mary."

"A very troubled child, I can tell. You see it in his features, especially in his eyes. Much like the looks of a frightened fugitive. Perhaps a fugitive from his not-so-good days."

"Exactly."

"Tell me about him."

"I don't know many details. His mother apparently shot and killed his father after a terrible argument. She confessed, was thrown in prison, and died a week later after suffering a seizure."

"That's so dreadful, so sad. Has Reza discussed with you his life and feelings before he was orphaned?"

"A few snippets here and there about the gardens where he lived, not much more than you heard earlier. He doesn't talk of his feelings."

"Has he said anything about his parents?"

"I know he loved his mother deeply, but I don't think he had nearly as much love for his father."

"Tell me how you met him and how your relationship developed. Also, please describe any abnormalities in his behavior."

Paree did so. From Reza's daring escape out of the orphanage, to her finding him and assuming his guardianship, to the bed-wetting, to the fear of the bottle in Mike's hand. At the end of the account, she added, "But deep inside, he's a wonderful, caring child. If only I could somehow reach inside him and pluck out all his misery."

Tilting her head, Mary squinted at her. "What does he mean to you?"

Paree hesitated. "I…well, maybe I feel…you know, sympathetic."

"There's more to it than that, isn't there Paree? Mike has told me all about Little John and his problems because of the war. Do you think Reza is now the object of your transference?"

"I don't understand."

"Has he caused you to revive an emotion from the past? And have you transferred your emotional needs from the past to the present? From Little John to Reza?"

She felt her face flush. "It's possible, yes."

They were silent for a while, Paree deep in thought, feeling guilty that perhaps she was using Reza to gratify her own emotional needs. *Using* him rather than *loving* him.

"Is that bad, Mary?" she asked.

"Is what bad?"

"That I'm using Reza for…for self-gratification."

"Is the maternal instinct self-gratifying, Paree?"

"I suppose it is."

"And do you consider the maternal instinct to be bad?"

"Of course not."

"Then you've answered your own question, haven't you?" Mary rested a hand on Paree's arm. "You and Reza both have serious issues that you must resolve. I can't help either of you without intensive therapy. How long will you be in England?"

"Another eight days or so."

"That's not nearly long enough for me to delve into your problems and help you sort them out." She looked at Paree intently. "I can tell you this, though. For a sane person such as yourself, facing the problems head-on is the first step to therapy. It seems to me you and Reza can help each other."

"How?"

"Confront the scenes upsetting you the most and talk to each other about why they upset you. Even if you don't know or can't remember the details of what happened, keep going back to those scenes. In other words, overcome your inhibitions. Then at some point, something will click and you'll un-repress what you've repressed. You'll come to understand why you have nightmares, why you're depressed when you shouldn't be, why some sights and sounds and smells trigger the depression—and even worse, a severe case of panic. Have you tried to do all that for yourself with Mike as your sympathetic ear?"

"No. Mike isn't the sympathetic sort. He put Little John behind him long ago."

"All the more reason for you and Reza to develop meaningful dialogues. Let the innocence of a child reach you, guide you while you're trying to reach and guide him."

"I'll do my best."

"Remember this, Paree. Despite their naiveté, children live in a world of symbols. Those symbols could be anything, and they're usually trivial. For instance, depending on the past experiences of the child, a hardboiled egg could represent a happy family enjoying a happy family picnic in the countryside. To another child, it could represent death because he accidentally saw Grandma Gertrude dead in bed with only the whites of her eyes showing. The last example is true, by the way."

"A troubled child?"

"Very, but he's much improved now. Let's get back to Reza. To learn more about him, do a crude Rorschach test. Draw something on a piece of paper that could act as a symbol, and then ask him to tell or write you a story about it. The first story that comes to his mind."

"What do you suggest I draw?"

"Anything you think of that might take him back to his past."

"How about a bottle?"

"No. You've told me how he reacted to it, so I suspect it'll be too painful for him to give up its secrets. At least not before you make some headway with him. I suggest you start out gently. Draw something very ordinary, something he sees every day and everywhere he goes. Like a plain circle, which I've often used as a beginning point to understand a problem child. Untroubled children will make up a story about the sun or the moon or a beach ball. A happy, fun-filled story. On the other hand, you'd be amazed at the stories troubled children tell you. Stories that'll melt your heart and let you peer a little deeper into their souls."

"In which case, that'll be one of Reza's homework assignments. Writing a story about a plain circle."

They were about to head back to the house when Mary grasped Paree's arm. "Don't let this become one-sided, Paree. You must open up to Reza too. It'll not only encourage him to respond in kind, but it'll also help you." She waved toward the group of stone houses in the distance. "That's Bourton-on-the-Water, isn't it?"

"Yes."

"Mike told me you used to live there."

"That's right, we did."

"Take Reza there. Walk around the village. Show him your former home. Take him to the field where—"

Paree froze. "Please don't even mention it, Mary. I can't. I just can't."

Mary stood cross-armed before her, glaring at her. "Well then, that's that, isn't it?"

"What do you mean?"

"If you can't—or won't—help yourself, how in heaven's name do you think you can help Reza? Think about it, Paree. Think about it long and hard, because without both of you cleansing your souls of guilt and torment, your relationship will end up in disaster."

Chapter 41

As they had done the previous night, Paree and Reza slept on Mike's double bed while he took the attic bedroom. Mike didn't seem to mind. "If that will settle the boy down, then by Jove let him keep sleeping in my bed." After a moment's pause, he added, "You've taken on a load of bloody trouble, my dear. I hope he won't make your life miserable."

Paree sighed. *Any more miserable than it has been since Little John went off to war?*

She awakened in the morning feeling tightness in her chest, a bounding pulse, and knowing that this would be the day for her to jump over the tallest hurdle she had ever faced. And wondering if she was capable of jumping over it without falling on the other side, falling to her doom.

Reza was nestled into her, sleeping, twitching. She gently shook him awake. "Time to get up, Reza-*jan*. We'll have breakfast and go for a long walk."

He opened his eyes, smiled. "Where will we go?"

"To a village."

"Why, Paree?"

"I'll explain later."

They washed, dressed, and went into the kitchen, where Mike was sipping coffee and reading the *Manchester Guardian*. He stood up, hugged Paree, and ruffled Reza's hair. She thought Reza cast him a faint but genuine smile. While preparing omelets, Mike showed Reza how to crack the eggs without shell fragments ending up in the blend. He took him through all the steps of cooking pepper-and-onion omelets, after which he commented on how well Reza had done and that he was a fast learner.

Once they settled to eat at the kitchen table, Reza asked him, "Where did you learn how to cook, agha?"

"Mike."

"Sorry, Mike."

"I learned during the First World War, in the trenches."

"Why were you in trenches?"

"Because we could stay low and duck out of the enemy's bullets flying all over the place."

Paree noticed Reza's eyes widen, and she could see a trace of fear entering them. He asked Mike, "Did you kill anyone in the war?"

Paree softly kicked Mike's shin, and he shook his head and said, "I didn't kill anyone because I chose not to."

She didn't know if his answer was truthful, and she didn't *want* to know.

After breakfast, Paree announced that she and Reza were going for a walk. Mike offered to join them, but she declined. This was a day for just Reza and her. He said he understood, and she was thankful he had readily acquiesced rather than engaging her in a lengthy argument, which she sometimes thought he relished because he once told her that while attending Oxford University, he was on a debating team. Maybe now, age was softening him.

The walk started at the front gate on the single lane road lined with blackberry bushes and stinging nettles, which she warned Reza to avoid because they made the skin itch and blister. Carefully avoiding the nettles, she picked a handful of blackberries and gave it to him. After swallowing a few of the berries, he said they tasted kind of weird, sweet and sour at the same time, like happy and angry at the same time. They walked on, and Paree felt increasingly apprehensive as they neared the village of Bourton-on-the-Water.

They crossed a narrow stone bridge spanning a sluggish river of greenish water—the River Windrush. Reza stopped in the middle of the bridge to gaze at the water. Paree saw the faraway look creeping into his eyes as he followed the slow voyage of a floating dandelion. She led him away.

They walked along a street of stone cottages and shops as passersby waved and smiled and said good morning. She returned the greetings, and Reza said Paree must have many friends everywhere. She responded, "You don't have to be friends in order to greet each other pleasantly." He looked a little puzzled.

They stopped at a general store that had just opened, and she bought him a Cadbury's Mars Bar. He took one bite of the chocolate and caramel bar and said, "It's almost as delicious as the honey ice cream in Tajrish."

"I'm glad you like it, Reza. It was always the favorite treat of Little…" She didn't finish.

"Who is Little?"

"I'll tell you later."

They passed a walled enclosure, inside which, Paree said, was a miniature model of the village built with the same stone—Cotswold stone—as the real village's shops and homes. Perhaps they would tour the place on their way back.

After turning onto an unpaved side street lined with more stone cottages, they stopped in front of one with drawn curtains and a thatched roof.

"This was our cottage many years ago," she said, trying to wish away the sudden uproar in her chest and stomach…and failing.

"It's beautiful, Paree. Can we go inside?"

"No, it belongs to someone else now." She pointed to a window on the second level. "That was our bedroom." She pointed to another window jutting out of the gables. "And that was…"

"What, Paree?"

"That was…that was our son's room."

"Is he the young man in the picture I saw?"

"Yes."

"What's his name?"

"*Kucheek Jahan*—Little John."

"Is he little?"

"No, he was never little, except as a newborn, but that was the name we called him and it stuck." She looked at the lace curtains drawn closed behind the window. "I see they kept our lace curtains," she muttered, her eyes growing moist.

"I wish we could go inside, Paree."

"Well, we can't."

"Wouldn't the people living there let us in?"

"Possibly, but I don't *want* to go in."

"Why not?"

"Because I…because I'm just not in the mood, that's why."

They walked on to the end of the street. Paree felt her chest was about to explode, and she caught herself breathing fast, sucking in the air as if she were at the top of Mount Damavand.

Relax Paree, settle down. It'll soon be over.

They stopped before a white wooden gate leading to an upward-sloping field of uncut grass. The gate was latched closed; Paree unlatched and opened it. They had walked only a few paces over the tall grass when she became giddy and flopped onto the ground.

I can't go on with this.

"Why did you stop, Paree?"

"Because I need to rest," she replied, feeling the sudden onset of a headache. Stress headache, hammering her skull, clouding her mind more than it was already.

"Please, let's keep walking, Paree. I enjoy seeing where you once lived. Did Little John like to play in the fields when you lived here?"

"He loved climbing the chestnut tree," she blurted, and immediately regretted saying it. Reza would insist on finding the tree, and she didn't want to be anywhere near where it once stood.

"Which chestnut tree, Paree?"

She waved toward a crest at the top of the field. "It was up there, Reza, but there's nothing to see. It's been cut down."

"Why?" She shrugged, and he tugged at her sleeve. "Show me where it was."

"Not now, Reza."

"When?"

"I don't know. Let's go to the model village."

"But I want to see where the chestnut tree was. Please take me there, Paree."

He reached out his hands, helped her struggle to her feet, and headed up the incline toward the crest. Her pulse whooshing through her temples, thumping in her ears, she followed him reluctantly yet obsessively, knowing he was leading her to the darkest chapter of her life. Knowing the hour had arrived when she must confront it and confront her fear. She trudged through the uncut grass, each labored step bringing her closer to the stage that she had avoided for eight years, the stage that was the showcase for eight years of nightmares and torment.

A lone chestnut tree in a lonely field.

Reza was a few feet ahead of her, now almost at the crest. He suddenly ran forward. "It's here, Paree! I found it!"

It was there. The stump that held the tree that held the branch that held the…

The earth spun, her legs gave way, and she collapsed into the grass. She lay there for a moment, panting. Then all went blank.

Chapter 42

He knelt next to her, grasped her limp hand and shook it, but she didn't stir. He shouted at her to wake up, but she didn't stir. He kissed her on the cheek, remembering the story she once read to him about a princess who was poisoned and woke up when the prince kissed her, but Paree didn't stir.

Please don't die, Paree. Please don't.

She was still breathing, slower than she was breathing before, but much more deeply. He lay down next to her and draped an arm across her chest, to feel it, to make sure she would keep on breathing. Maybe she was just tired and had fallen asleep.

Please don't die, Paree. Please don't.

He rested his head on her shoulder, and he remembered a time when Mama had fallen the same way after a quarrel with Baba. She just rested until sometime later she woke up with a purple lump on her forehead the size of a hen's egg. Maybe Paree would do the same. Rest for a while and wake up with a purple lump on her forehead the size of a hen's egg.

He felt her suddenly shake, and he sat up. Her eyes were open, blinking.

"What happened?"

"You fell asleep, Paree."

"No, I must have fainted."

"Are you all right?"

"Yes, Reza, I'm all right…my body is, anyway."

She stood up slowly, swayed a little, and steadied herself. Her gaze settled on the tree stump, which was covered with moss and rotting bark. She stood there like a statue, her eyes half closed, and

Reza thought she was in a trance, under the magical *telesm*—spell—of the stump. Or maybe she was praying, because her lips were moving a little. Some of the workers at the gardens became that way when they spread a cloth in front of them on the ground, faced the east, and fell to their knees and mumbled their *namaz* to Allah and to Mohammed. He once tried talking to a gardener who was praying, but Mama was with him and she said he should never talk to anyone in the middle of *namaz*. So he didn't talk to Paree.

He waited and waited, but she stood still, just staring at the stump through half-closed eyes, mouthing something in English. Soon it was as if she were carrying on a conversation with an invisible person living inside the tree stump. He didn't think she was even aware he was standing by her side and holding her sweaty hand. Or maybe she was still praying to Allah, so he remained silent until her lips stopped moving and he thought she had finished her *namaz*.

"Were you praying, Paree?"

She didn't answer.

"Were you praying?"

"No, not praying."

"Who were you talking to?"

"To…to Little John."

"Where is he?"

"Why did you do it, Little John? *Why?*"

"Do what, Paree?"

"Why? Why? For God's sake why, Little John?"

The tears started flowing down her face in tiny streams. They flowed onto her nose and chin, and they dangled there for a few seconds like dewdrops on a rose petal. Then they dripped onto the grass, and fleetingly Reza wondered if tears would make grass greener, if tears would make Paree happier.

She covered her face and sobbed.

"Did I make you sad, Paree?"

She kept sobbing, and he became more and more certain that he was responsible for her misery, because he had urged her to walk up the field to the tree stump instead of going to the model village as she had asked. Now, he felt terrible for bringing Paree misery, just as he had brought Mama misery during That Night.

Perhaps Baba had been right after all. *Reza, you're a rotten bastard!*

Paree dropped to her knees, crossed her arms over her chest, and looked up at the sky, dark clouds gathering, winds quickening, hair blowing, tears flowing.

Reza fell to his knees too and crawled before her. He wedged himself between her and the tear-wetted grass. She uncrossed her arms, and he buried his face between her breasts as if he would dissolve into her, and he felt her arms wrapping around him.

"Why, Little John? Why? Why? Why?"

"I'm Reza, not Little John."

"Why, Little John?"

"Look at me, Paree. I'm Reza."

She rocked them back and forth for a long time, and he felt like he was her child. Her Little John who had come out of the tree stump to comfort her.

At last, she released him and softly held him away from her.

She gazed at him for a long moment through teary eyes. "Reza-*jan*, I'm terribly sorry."

"Why are you sorry?"

"For…for being so upset."

A clap of thunder, and the rain started, Reza unmindful of the sudden deluge of big drops smacking into his head. "Please, won't you tell me about Little John?"

"Let's find shelter, Reza."

"No, I don't care if we get wet. I want to know about Little John. Where is he now?"

"H-he died eight years ago."

"Why did he die?"

"Because he *wanted* to."

All at once, Reza again felt terrible for his earlier selfish thoughts. The selfish thoughts that he didn't want to share Paree with Mike and with the uniformed young man in the picture. Her dead son who must still live within her, sharing silent times at a chestnut tree in a field. Like Mama still lived within Reza, sharing silent times at the creek in the garden of his imagination.

And Little John had died because he *wanted* to die, just as Fereshteh did.

Sharing a loved one with another was very confusing, but wanting to die wasn't nearly as confusing.

Chapter 43

From where they stood, through the sheets of rain Paree could see the outline of the gray barn at the far end of the field. When Little John was a child, she used to take him on daily walks through the fields, and the barn was often their shelter from an unexpected downpour. They would sit cross-legged on a pile of hay, and to pass the time she would tell him stories, mostly those she remembered from her childhood. She told stories from *One Thousand and One Nights,* about Ali Baba and the Forty Thieves, the voyages of Sinbad the Sailor, and Aladdin's magic lamp. And she told ancient tales of lost children wandering around in the desert. Lost, like the psychologically wounded survivors of WWII, wandering around in a world they no longer understood or cared to understand.

Paree took Reza's hand and they dashed to the barn, which was now empty of hay but full of dirt and dust. They sat on the floor for a while, listening to the tattoo of rain strafing the roof and to the occasional rumble of distant thunder.

He kept his eyes fixed on her the whole time, and she knew she had to tell him all, to vent the misery within her soul.

She inhaled deeply and began the tale. "That afternoon was just like this. Black clouds, rain, thunder…"

* * * *

A few minutes past noon on December 22, 1942, Little John appeared at their doorstep without warning. He was unshaven, wore a crumpled army uniform, and held on to a khaki kitbag slung over his shoulder. Paree at first froze when she saw him, thinking he was a mirage because ever since he left for North

Africa, she had lived every waking moment dreading The Telegram.

Dear Mr. and Mrs. Windom. Stop. Our deepest sympathies for the loss of Corporal John M. Windom. Stop. He gave his life fighting for our beloved country. Stop. May God rest his brave soul. Stop.

As soon as she realized he was indeed Little John and no trick of her mind, Paree engulfed him in a long embrace as the rain pelted down about them. He reacted little to the embrace except with a mutter of "Hi, Mother," his eyes faraway, his body motionless, limp.

She led him into the kitchen, sat him down at the table, and telephoned Mike at the office, but he was out inspecting a newly constructed petrol repository at a Gloucester army base. While preparing Little John tea and a roast beef sandwich, she showered him with questions of how he felt and what had happened to him and if he was happy to be home. He responded in one- or two-word answers and staccato phrases, without passion, his eyes fixed blankly on the pinewood table and the drawings he had carved on it over the years.

There was a car with four wheels in a row, Humpty Dumpty on a wall, a square house with a sunflower popping out of the chimney, stick figures of a man and woman holding hands with a stick child.

Paree was dismayed that after he had spent two years away at the warfront, a vacant stare was the extent of his show of emotion at their reunion. A vacant stare that hid the horrors of where he had been and what he must have seen and suffered. She placed the tea and sandwich in front of him, but he didn't touch either, just continued staring at the carvings. A moment later, he suddenly jumped up and muttered he was off for a nap. He left. Left her speechless. He disappeared up the stairs to his attic bedroom, and all became quiet.

Deciding that he must have been too tired to hold a meaningful conversation, Paree let him alone to sleep and called Mike again, who was now back at the office. He dropped everything and rushed home. After she told him of their son's odd behavior, he bounded up to Little John's bedroom, Paree following. They found him lying in bed, his eyes wide open, unflinching, held to the ceiling. Eyes like glass.

Gently at first then with increasing force, Mike shook him by the shoulders until he sat up. Looking dazed, Little John rasped a detached "Hello, Father."

They asked him pointed questions, received vague answers and a curt request to leave him alone because he still wanted to nap. Concerned, Mike and Paree complied with the request and went downstairs. He poured himself a glass of sherry and paced around the living room while they discussed their son.

"He's tired, that's all," Mike said. "Just dashed tired."

Paree shook her head. "Tired or not, he acts like a stranger toward us. He has changed, Mike, changed drastically. Shouldn't we call someone at his regiment and find out what happened to him? I mean, he came home so unexpectedly, while the war is still raging in North Africa."

Mike frowned and gulped down his sherry. "You do have a valid point, my dear." After gazing at the empty glass for a moment, he suddenly flinched. "Good heavens, I hope…"

"What is it, Mike?"

"I hope he wasn't dishonorably discharged."

"Why would they do that to him?"

"Well, if—for instance—if he disobeyed a command or behaved like a-a…"

"For God's sake, Mike, spit it out."

"Like a coward."

"Please, call his regiment immediately, Mike. We *must* know."

Mike did as she asked. He telephoned the personnel headquarters of the Eighth Army in London. After he identified himself and stated the reason for calling, the operator put him on hold for a few minutes until an ATS—Auxiliary Territorial Service—woman with a low-pitched voice came on the line. She told him that Little John had performed his duties well and was sent home on furlough for a while.

Mike asked her, "Wasn't that a bit sudden? After all, why would they send him all the way back to England on furlough in the middle of a bloody war in bloody North Africa?"

"Because he was obviously suffering from battle fatigue, sir."

"Kindly explain 'battle fatigue,' madam."

"You'd have to ask a specialist about it."

"What kind of specialist?"

"Someone who deals with battle fatigue."

Mike slammed down the receiver.

The days passed, Christmas passed, and Little John showed little enthusiasm for doing anything beyond staying in his room, door shut, curtains drawn, eyes to the ceiling. He didn't even help them decorate the Christmas tree, which was a family ritual before North Africa. He didn't get up at dawn on Christmas morning, inspect the surprises awaiting him under the tree, and run into the bedroom to awaken Mummy and Daddy and thank them for the best presents he ever had. Another family ritual.

For that special Holiday-from-the-War Christmas, they had bought him a gramophone, which he unwrapped only with their encouragement, muttered a thank-you, and disappeared into his room.

A day after New Year, Mike traveled to the Eighth Army personnel HQ in bomb-riddled London. He discussed the situation with an officer in charge of Health and Welfare Section, a heavyset, middle-aged major with an artificial arm that seemed useless. The major pulled out a file from a khaki file cabinet and placed it on his khaki desk. After studying the file for over five minutes, he closed it and told Mike that Little John had suffered battle fatigue and was sent back to England because of it.

Mike pounded a fist on the desk and yelled *dammit to blithering hell!* The major jumped up, ready to throw him out of the office. Mike muttered an apology, the major sat back down. Mike asked him what had caused the so-called battle fatigue that made little sense to him.

"Dash it all, man, can't you explain it to me?" he huffed. "I mean, fatigue is fatigue, whether it's from working too hard or playing too hard or fighting the enemy too hard without rest. Everyone gets fatigued at one bloody time or another, wouldn't you say?"

The major fiddled with a brass button on his army blouse, frowning, apparently trying to decide if he should give out all the facts.

"Dammit, major, he's my *son!*" Mike shouted.

"Kindly don't raise your voice to me, sir."

"Sorry, but don't I at least have the right to learn the truth about my own son?"

The major sat silently for a moment, gazing at the hand of his artificial arm. He suddenly nodded his head and leaned forward. "You're absolutely right, Mr. Windom. Here are the details, and I'm afraid they're a bit gruesome."

He said Little John had been stationed with Montgomery's Eighth Army during a night of bloodshed near Tobruk, North

Africa. When the guns silenced and the smoke cleared, he and another member of his platoon were reported as missing. A patrol was dispatched to look for them. After searching in the trenches and behind the desert mounds, the patrol found them. Sprawled on his back by the side of a charred Cruiser Tank, Little John was covered in dust and caked in blood. Next to him was his closest friend in the platoon, whose lifeless body was riddled with shrapnel, and whose face was shattered to the point of being unrecognizable—only his ID tag identified him. Little John lay there dazed, talking to himself, holding on to his dead friend's leg, staring at the foot, apparently unaware that the leg was severed from the body.

The patrol soldiers placed the corpse, leg, and Little John in the back of their armored personnel carrier and sped them to the Eighth Army's tent hospital. A surgeon examined Little John and could find no physical problems. For three days and nights, he kept him sedated, after which he officially diagnosed Corporal John Windom as suffering from "post-concussion neurosis."

He then shipped Little John and his post-concussion neurosis back to England, along with thirty or more wounded and maimed soldiers. On the same day that the transport plane landed at Croydon Airfield, another physician at a London army hospital examined him. He declared that Corporal John Windom was suffering from "nothing more complicated than battle fatigue" and sent him home to Bourton-on-the-Water for a to-be-determined period of Rest and Recuperation.

"It is an increasingly recognized mental disturbance," the major said to Mike after the account. "The problem most commonly arises in soldiers who have served many days at the front lines. It can also suddenly arise in soldiers who witness a comrade-in-arms dying, especially a gruesome death involving a shattered face or detached extremity. Those are exactly what your son witnessed, Mr. Windom." He tapped his prosthetic arm. "I lost the real one during the last war. I lost it at the same time and on the same battlefield as my closest friend lost his life. For many months afterwards, I felt terribly guilty that he died and I lived. Maybe it's what your son now feels—the guilt that he, too, should have perished."

After leaving the major's office, Mike made an appointment for Little John to see a Harley Street psychiatrist who had temporarily relocated to Oxford in fear of the London Blitz.

The evening before his appointment in Oxford, Paree asked Little John to go for a walk with her through the fields because it was such a pleasant evening, the winter air clear and milder than usual. He said he'd rather not. Paree kept insisting, and after a while he shrugged, put on his duffle coat, and accompanied her outside. They walked up the unpaved street leading to the fields surrounding the northern borders of the village. They walked in silence until reaching a wooden gate that opened onto a grassy field with a lone chestnut tree at the top of an incline.

Paree waved toward the tree. "That was your favorite hiding place, Little John. Do you remember?"

He shrugged.

"You used to hide up there and not answer me when I called for you. But all along, I knew you were up there."

"So what, Mother?"

"I'd stand under the tree, and a chestnut or two would plop down on my head. And I'd shout and blame the rascally squirrels until you'd admit you dropped the chestnuts on me. Do you remember?"

"I suppose."

"A bundle of mischief, you were."

"Mother, is there a point to this conversation?"

Although frustrated at his aloofness, she remained calm, maintaining a light air to her tone. "The point is, Little John, that I'd love it if you were a rascal again. I'd love it if you occasionally smiled. I'd love it if you came out of your trance and rejoined your family and your friends and the world."

"I'm here, aren't I?"

"Here in body, not in soul."

"That's enough, Mother. I'm going home."

She grasped his arm. "Please don't, Little John. Let's walk up to the tree and look for chestnuts. We'll roast them tonight, like we used to roast them over the fireplace on many a cold winter's night."

She tugged on his arm, and he pulled it away. "All right, Mother, but I won't stay long."

As they started walking up the hill, she asked him, "Why are you in such a rush to go back home? Do you have something going on tonight?"

"No, nothing."

"Then why?"

"Because I want to be alone. I want to be *left* alone."

"To your thoughts, I imagine. Can't you tell me what's in those thoughts?"

"Nothing you'd be interested in, Mother."

They reached the tree, and she started gathering chestnuts off the ground, now and then glancing at him. He stood still, looking intently at the tree, his eyes fixed on a thick branch that was midway up the tree and sticking out beyond the other branches. After a moment or two, she saw him smile, a peaceful sort of a smile. He stood there a few more minutes, slowly nodding his head as if he had made a decision, and then his smile broadened. All at once, he fell to his knees and started collecting chestnuts and stuffing them into his pockets. Once his pockets and Paree's tiny handbag bulged, they walked home, and he seemed much more cheerful, although no more informative than before.

During supper, Little John refused to discuss the war, but instead limited his conversation to polite questions, which he asked in a most pleasant tone. "How is work going, Father? Do you still miss Tehran, Mother? Are you thinking of buying a new car, Father? Have you heard from your best friend in Iran, Mother?"

At the time, Paree didn't understand his sudden shift to a more cheerful mood, but the next morning she understood.

He had made the most critical decision of his life.

Not long after dawn the next morning, Paree went to Little John's bedroom to bring him a cup of tea. His appointment in Oxford was at 9 a.m., and Mike was anxious for an early start to arrive at the psychiatrist's office in plenty of time.

The bed had not been slept in, and Little John was not in the room. She ran outside into the heavy mist, noticed Mike's Wolseley sedan was still parked next to the cottage, and she was surprised that the trunk was not completely closed. Mike kept some long-distance traveling items in the trunk: a toolbox, first-aid kit, four flares, and a towing rope. She wondered why the trunk lid was ajar, because Mike was compulsive about locking the car up before parking it for the night.

She called out Little John's name. No response. She looked for him by the stream in the nearby woods, where he had often wandered alone since returning from North Africa. He wasn't there. She ran back to the cottage, found Mike shaving in the bathroom, and told him Little John hadn't slept in his bed during the night and was nowhere to be found. Mike washed off the lather, quickly dressed, and they hurried to the village's main street. They asked a sleepy, elderly man waiting at the bus stop if he had seen their son, and he had not. They decided to search in the fields and woodlands surrounding Bourton-on-the-Water. Mike searched the south side, Paree the north.

She headed to the outskirts of the village and trudged through the misty fields and woods. She looked behind trees and hawthorn and haystacks, but found no sign of Little John. After two hours of a fruitless search, she headed back toward the cottage, now in a near panic, thinking that something terrible had befallen her only son. Her only child.

She found him ten minutes later as she stepped onto a field near their home.

At the top of the field, a lone chestnut tree. From a bough of the tree, a rope. At the end of the rope, a body.

Little John's body, swaying, twisting in the wind.

Lifeless.

Chapter 44

By the time Paree finished telling Reza of Little John's death in words he could understand, her face and blouse were soaked in tears, her voice was hoarse, and her body shook uncontrollably. Reza nestled into her, wishing he could make her happy and stop crying. Wishing he could bring back Little John, bring back Mama and Fereshteh, and even bring back Baba on his good days. He sensed Paree blamed herself for Little John's death, just as he blamed himself for Mama's death.

"It wasn't your fault, Paree."

She didn't respond.

"You didn't kill him, Paree. Little John killed himself. You told me he *wanted* to die. So it wasn't your fault, Paree."

Resting his face on her chest, he could feel and hear the heartbeat pounding inside her. It seemed fast, hard, angry. He said nothing, understanding she needed quiet time to let the chaos in her head settle down. Like the quiet Reza needed when they took Mama away and he stopped speaking for days while he was at the home for children without homes. For the first few days after he arrived at the orphanage, he and Fereshteh didn't speak either. They would sit next to each other in the courtyard and stare into space, each knowing the other was there but didn't need to talk because quiet was all they needed from each other. Quiet comfort.

They didn't talk until Fereshteh said, "This place is *jaharam*—hell," and Reza said, "Hell is for bad people. Were you bad too?" She replied, "I must have been, but I'll find a way to heaven."

And now Paree thinks she was bad and must be searching for a way to heaven. He wished he could find a way to prove to her she was good, and then maybe she would stop searching, because he needed her in *his* world. He needed all of her as one, not in two separate parts, one that is taken away while the other floats away.

After a long time, he heard her say in a near whisper, "Perhaps it *was* my fault, Reza. Perhaps I wasn't such a good mother."

"No, Paree. You're a *good* mother."

"God, how I wish I had done much more to ease Little John's suffering, to make him happy again."

"But you couldn't, Paree. He was sad, and he didn't want his body to live any more. He was like Fereshteh."

Paree pulled away from him, gazed at him through red-rimmed eyes. "Was she the girl at the orphanage who…"

"Yes, she was the best friend I ever had. She wanted to go to a better place, so she didn't eat. Then she got sick and went to heaven. Sometimes I…" He looked away.

She squeezed him back into her. "Don't say it, Reza. Don't even *think* it."

They were silent again, gently rocking in each other's arms, Reza stroking her hair like he once stroked Mama's hair when she told him bedtime stories. Mama said she loved the way he touched her hair because his fingers felt like they were full of kindness, which poured into her hair and went all over her body and made her feel so warm, so joyful. Now, he wished Paree had the same feelings as he stroked her hair, as his fingers poured kindness into her. And while he did that, he would make her think warm, joyful thoughts and get rid of chestnut tree thoughts.

"Did you tell Little John bedtime stories?" he asked her.

"When he was a young boy like you, yes."

"What was his favorite story?"

"Aladdin and the Magic Lamp. It's a tale of a young man who rubs a magical oil lamp and a *jinn* pops out of it and grants him three wishes."

"What was Little John's favorite game?"

"Conkers. It's when you bang your chestnut against someone else's chestnut, and the person with the nut that doesn't crack is the winner."

"His favorite things to eat?"

"Cadbury's Mars bars, like the one I bought you this morning. Oh, and Walls chocolate ice cream sandwiches."

"Will you get me one sometime?"

"Of course I will."

"Who was his favorite parent?"

She smiled faintly. "Don't ever tell Mike, but I think it was me, although he never actually said so."

"How do you know, then?"

"The way he always came to me when he was sick, when he was hurt, or when he was in trouble. Boys adore their mamas." She wiped away a tear dangling on the tip of her nose. "I imagine your mama was your favorite parent too."

She was, and now Paree treated him just like Mama did. But Paree was still sad, and she needed more cheering up, so he had to keep cheering her up.

"Let's go to the model village, Paree. I bet Little John loved to go there."

"Yes, he did. Very much."

"Then let's go."

"But it's still raining."

"I don't care, because getting soaked in the rain is like sitting in a tub or floating in a creek. It washes away stuff you don't want."

They walked arm in arm to the model village, and by the time they arrived, the rain had stopped, the sun was out, steam rose off the pavements and the river, and they were drenched. The cashier behind the kiosk looked at them and asked if they wanted to go home and change into dry clothes then come back.

Paree said it was all right because their clothes would drip-dry and wash away stuff they didn't want. The cashier looked at them puzzled, Paree paid, and they spun through the turnstile. As they walked holding hands along the miniature streets, Paree talked about Little John's favorite models. A church with high-pitched voices coming from inside. A tiny bakery with a tiny chocolate cake inside the window. A tiny watermill that spun under a tiny waterfall. And tiny cars, all shiny and wet and glimmering in the sunlight.

"This must be how Alice felt," Reza said.

"What do you mean, Reza?"

"Alice in Wonderland, when she turned into a giant and everything around her became tiny."

Paree laughed, and for a few seconds the sad left her eyes and the happy took over.

As they continued walking around, Reza wanted to learn more about Little John, about his favorite toy: a clockwork racecar. His favorite friend: a chubby boy by name of Chesterton Fowler who was the most impolite child in the village and was always in trouble at school. His favorite comic book character: Popeye the Sailor. His favorite dream: he found a magic carpet and flew to the stars.

Reza noticed that while talking about her son now, Paree didn't seem quite as upset.

Chapter 45

That afternoon, Paree rummaged through the bedroom and found Little John's framed photograph buried under Mike's underwear, where he had hidden it after she told him Reza had discovered it. She wiped the saline stains off the glass and placed the photograph over the living room mantelpiece. Reza saw her putting it there. He smiled at her and said, "You must be feeling a little better, Paree." She thought that for a ten-year-old, he understood much more than she had given him credit for.

Mike came home—without a bottle—soon after six and announced they were all going out to a restaurant in Cheltenham. They dined at The White Swan on the Promenade, a wide thoroughfare lined with trees and shops and townhouses. During dinner, Mike noticed Reza's gold ring for the first time and asked him about it. Reza said it was a gift from his best friend at the orphanage. She gave it to him not long before she floated to heaven.

Paree noticed Mike's eyes growing a little misty. "Tell me more about her, my boy."

"Her name was Fereshteh," Reza replied. "She was as pretty as Mama and…and Paree."

Mike grinned. "Then she must have been one of the three prettiest girls in the world."

Reza nodded, and Paree felt her cheeks growing hot.

After their dinner of roast beef and Yorkshire pudding, they went to the cinema and watched *Cinderella*. Whispering in his ear, Paree translated some of the dialogue for Reza. Seemingly enthralled with the film, afterwards he said he would love to go back in and see it all over again, but Mike told him maybe another day. Paree asked Reza why he liked the film so much, and he said the fairy godmother reminded him of her because she was so nice. Feeling her cheeks grow hot again, she smiled and said she was delighted he didn't think of her as the wicked stepmother.

"I would *never* think that, Paree. *Never!*"

That night when it was Reza's bedtime, he said to her, "I want you to sleep with Mike, and I promise not to make an accident."

"Are you sure, Reza?"

"Yes Paree, *very* sure."

* * * *

After tucking Reza into bed, Paree went to the living room. Mike stood by a window, gazing into the distance and sipping sherry as the radio blasted a military march.

"You're daydreaming, Mike. Something you constantly accuse me of."

He turned to her. "Not daydreaming, just listening to a brass band."

He switched off the radio and squinted at her. She understood that look. They hadn't had a chance to discuss her day with Reza, and Mike must have been waiting to hear all about it.

"How was your jaunt this morning?" he asked.

She hesitated with the response. *Agonizing? Depressing? Uplifting?* "It was…interesting."

He smiled. "I assume it was much more than that. Where did you go?"

"I…we visited the chestnut tree."

His mouth gaped. "You did *what*?"

"I finally did it, Mike. I confronted my greatest fear."

For a long moment, he stood there motionless, staring at her. Then his lips stretched into a broad grin, and he put down the sherry glass. He rushed to her and folded her in his arms. "Oh, my dear. I'm so proud of you. That must have taken every ounce of courage you could muster."

"It did."

He leaned back, searched her eyes. "How do you feel now?"

"A little relieved, I think. Actually, more than a little."

"What possessed you to go there?"

"Mary Lawrence suggested it."

"She knows her business, doesn't she?" He squeezed her and said, "Maybe now you won't mind living in England permanently—right here, with me."

Too much, too soon. "I don't know, Mike. Today was just a start."

He nodded slowly, understandingly. "That's all right, Paree. I can wait."

* * * *

Later in bed, she watched him absently flipping the pages of a book titled *The History of Rugby Football*.

Paree tapped him on the chest. "Put that rubbish away and let's get some sleep."

"It's not rubbish. And I don't feel sleepy."

"Why not?"

He gazed at her. "Because I have this gorgeous woman lying next to me in bed."

She sighed, knowing he wanted her, wondering whether she would enjoy him as she did before Little John's solution. For some reason, that night she needed intimacy. Perhaps it was the relief of baring her soul to Reza. Or perhaps, it was Mike's continued devotion to her and, in his own way, his acceptance of the child she had welcomed into her life.

He put the magazine away and drew her into him, his breath tingling her face like a gentle sea breeze. He kissed her softly on the mouth. "I love you so much, Paree," he murmured, his fingers gliding over her face, tracing the contours then working their way down. They slid over her pajama top and fumbled about with the buttons. She helped him with the unbuttoning. He kissed her breasts, softly, delicately, each kiss increasingly arousing her to levels she hadn't reached in many years.

She slipped a hand under his pajamas…

* * * *

Creaking floorboards jolted Paree awake. She reached for Mike, but he wasn't in bed. She sat up. In the dimness, she could make out his silhouette pacing back and forth before the window, the curtains open to the glow of the three-quarter moon.

"All you all right, Mike?"

"Go back to sleep, my dear. It's the middle of the night."

"You're pacing."

"Still can't sleep."

"Why not this time?"

"Thinking about you. Thinking how much you were like your old self tonight. How you were so…"

"What?"

"So…affectionate."

"I was, wasn't I?"

"Why were you? Because you braved the chestnut tree?"

"That and opening up to Reza. I hope he'll do the same to me one of these days."

"He's breathing new life into you, isn't he?"

"Maybe."

He turned on the bedside lamp and stood over her. "Has he become a-a replacement?"

Paree all at once stiffened, glared at him. "No one can ever replace Little John. *No one!* So get that through your head, all right?"

"Our son died over eight years ago, Paree. Why can't you find peace after all this time?"

"For God's sake, how in hell can I find peace? I cry for him constantly, for his broken spirit and for his broken neck. Just *once*, Mike, just once why don't you cry for him too? Then maybe you'll understand why he'll live inside me forever."

"But all I said was—"

"You and your damned British stiff upper lip!"

He sighed, lay down next to her, and softly pulled her into him. "Paree, don't you think I grieve for him? Don't you think he's always on my mind? Don't you think I see his death face every time I close my eyes or walk in the woods or sit alone in this bloody house and stare at the bloody walls? Don't you think I'm bloody *human*?"

His eyes grow moist and his lower lip quivered. He turned his head away, but not before Paree glimpsed the tears trickling down his cheeks.

Stunned at his reaction, she suddenly realized how hard he must have struggled all those years to hide behind his valiant façade, all the while inwardly suffering the full brunt of their tragedy.

She nestled into him, turned his face toward her, kissed him.

"I love you, Mike."

Chapter 46

For Reza, the time spent in England passed as quickly as leaves floating by in the creek of the Third Garden. He had seen Freedom-land at its best, without hate and anger, teeming with lush gardens and green hills and valleys. He had learned how to cook omelets and how to ride a bicycle. And best of all, for the last few nights he had slept soundly, without any nightmares, without any accidents.

But when the hour of returning to Iran drew near, the old doubts reawakened and quickly gathered strength—they had fallen asleep one by one since he and Paree visited the chestnut tree stump and the model village. Now, the same old selfish thoughts about sharing a loved one with another had come back, and he couldn't get rid of them.

During that final morning of the visit to England, his stomach became queasier and queasier as he watched the way Mike fussed over Paree, how they looked at each other with love in their faces, how they disagreed about stuff without fire in their eyes or Mike clenching his fists. So different from how Baba and Mama treated each other, especially how Baba treated Mama. Seeing the love that Mike and Paree obviously shared, Reza grew worried that he would never become a forever part of their love, not only because they had each other, but because they shared each other with Little John living silently inside them.

Someday soon, Paree would go back to live with Mike—Reza sensed it. If she decided to do that, she would leave Reza in another orphanage in Iran, and he would have to start all over again. With another Agha Mansur and another mean proctor. And with another Fereshteh, starving herself so she could find her way to heaven and leave him behind to worry that she might end up in hell. To cry for her, to cry for himself.

Maybe that time would come not long after he and Paree got off the airplane in Tehran. He could imagine her one night sitting at the edge of his bed, holding his hand. "I am returning to England, Reza, to be with Mike, to be near Little John and Little John's ghost. I'm so sorry, Reza-*jan*. I wish it could be different."

And he could imagine his response. "No Paree, you don't wish it could be different, because you love Mike and you don't love me nearly as much as him. Only Mama and Fereshteh love me more than anyone else in the world, and they're in heaven waiting for me."

Waving at them as they headed out to the plane with the white cross on the red tail, Mike seemed terribly sad. So did Paree, constantly dabbing her teary eyes with a handkerchief. She waved back at him and yelled that they must see each other again really soon. Reza waved too, now almost certain he would never see him again.

That vinegary feeling in the pit of his stomach was more intense than ever. It had become a part of him during his days at Agha Mansur's orphanage, and after Paree, it had turned on and off depending on the situation, depending on his dark thoughts about her abandoning him. But now the vinegary feeling wasn't on and off.

It had been there since early morning and all throughout the four-hour journey to Heathrow Airport. It had been there as they stood in line, as Mike hugged and kissed Paree, as she and Reza walked onto the tarmac. It had been there as they climbed the staircase-on-wheels into the airplane and the woman in the red uniform smiled knowingly at him, because she knew this would be his last ride on an airplane.

* * * *

Paree sat in the aisle seat, Reza next to her, his face pressed into the window, his breath steaming it. For the past few days, Mike had repeatedly asked her to resume their married life in his English cottage. "And I'll treat Reza as our son," he had added at the end of each plea. Hampered by ambivalent feelings, she had muttered noncommittal responses.

Accepting his invitation sounded like the ideal solution to her financial worries, to the challenges of raising Reza, and to her rapidly rekindling love for Mike. Nonetheless, she couldn't acquiesce on two accounts. First, she was as yet unsure of how she would fare living for the rest of her life in Little John's environs with the constant reminders. Second, she was certain that Reza's ongoing problems would cause conflicts between her and Mike, and the poor boy didn't deserve to be part of another troubled family. Neither did Mike.

Plug on in Iran for now, she decided. Somehow, reach Reza's inner soul, bring his anguish out into the open as he had done for her. Perhaps at the right time, in the right setting, she would broach the topic of his parents and of the events that caused the tragic shooting at the Third Garden. If he opened up to her, if his hurt lessened, then she would approach him with the offer for the two of them to live in England with Mike.

From early that morning, Paree had sensed that Reza had again withdrawn inside his steely shell, and she couldn't understand why.

"Did you enjoy your stay in England?" she asked him as the plane reached altitude and the No Smoking signs were turned off.

"Yes, Paree," he replied, looking out of the window, staring down at the glistening waters of the English Channel below.

"Tell me why you like England."

"I don't know."

"Is it because England is so different from Iran?"

"I don't know."

"Which country would you prefer to live in?"

"I don't know."

"I suppose it doesn't matter, Reza, because the country you live in isn't as important as the home you live in."

He turned to her, his lips quivering, his eyes searching hers. "Will you take me to an orphanage once we're in Tehran?"

Asked so unexpectedly, the question slammed into Paree's ears like a clap of thunder, stunned that after so many good days in England, he had relapsed into the same old Reza. Distant, insecure, confused, frightened.

She hugged him, hugged him hard. "*Never!* You're done with orphanages. You'll be with me, forever."

* * * *

He didn't believe her. Mama once told him that grownups sometimes tell lies so children's feelings won't get hurt. Like the lie Mama told the first time he saw a purple bruise around her left eye, which was swollen shut. He saw it on a Friday morning, a night after Baba came home with a bottle. "I ran into a tree branch in the dark," she explained after he asked her about the bruise.

At the time, Reza believed her, but now he suspected that Baba had beaten her, because on a few Friday mornings after that, he noticed the same kind of bruises on her face. He didn't recall actually seeing the beatings though, since on some Thursday nights when she was more worried than usual, Mama made him sleep outside under the moon and stars. On the other hand, maybe he *had* seen the beatings and then blanked them out of his mind. Like That Night.

If Paree put him in an orphanage, he would run away again, but this time he would be better prepared. During mealtimes, he would save some of his food by hiding it under his windbreaker and then inside his gunnysack until he had enough to last him for two or three days. And once he escaped, he would earn money by working in people's gardens on the way to the mountains.

Then at last, he would climb to the top of Mount Damavand, where Mama and Fereshteh would be waiting for him at the peak or on the other side.

Chapter 47

The plane swerved and dipped and landed with a thud. The engines roared and it seemed as if the plane would never stop, but it did. "We're almost home," Paree said.

Reza shrugged.

Home? There were plenty of homes for him. Homes for kids without homes. Homes for kids without parents. Homes for kids to escape from. He didn't need Paree just as she didn't need him, because she had Mike and Little John's ghost.

Reza wondered if he should leave Paree soon after arriving at her apartment—maybe on the first day when she returned to work. He would leave before she had a chance to tell him how sad she felt about taking him back to an orphanage. Before she had a chance to talk more about her dead son's happy days as tears streamed her cheeks, all the while calling Reza Little John until he reminded her he was Reza.

They rode a taxi to the apartment building. Agha Rahemi, the landlord, met them in the lobby. He kissed Paree on the cheeks, patted Reza on top of the head, and said with a grin, "Welcome back, Reza. The hedges need trimming, the grass needs mowing, and the corridors need sweeping."

"Yes, agha."

"Did you like England?"

"Yes, agha."

"It's good to be home though, isn't it?"

"Yes, agha."

After helping Paree unpack, Reza went into the garden and inspected his eggplant and watermelon patches. The shoots seemed healthy, and most of them had sprouted newborns, the children of his labor. As he gazed with pride at his handiwork, a pair of arms gently wrapped around his neck, and he felt soft hair brushing his cheeks. Paree's hair.

"Your garden is beautiful, Reza-*jan*," she said. "I can hardly wait for everything to ripen. Then we will celebrate with a feast of eggplant *pellow* for the main course and watermelon for dessert."

She kissed him softly on the cheek. He leaned back against her, and suddenly he wanted to stay with her, to make sure that the children of his labor stayed healthy and grew up without the sores of neglect. He didn't want to abandon them as orphans in a square patch of dirt and weeds, to abandon Paree to a lonely apartment without anyone to comfort her when images of Little John's death sprang into her head. As he thought more about it, he became convinced that she was now less sad because of him, so if he left her, she'd be sad all over again, and it would be *his* fault.

That night in bed, he wondered about his confusion, his up and down thoughts and moods. One time run away, another time stay with Paree, run away again, stay with Paree again. Up and down, up and down. Would his thoughts and moods ever stay at one level?

Everything was so complicated, confusing.

* * * *

The next morning before leaving for work, Paree asked Reza if he would be all right without her, and he said yes.

"You won't run away again, will you?"

"No, Paree."

"Promise?"

"I promise."

She gave him his homework assignment for the day. After drawing something on a piece of paper, she folded the paper three times and put it on the coffee table. She told him to write a story about what she had drawn—the first story that came to his mind without pausing to think about it. It would be a test of his imagination, she said, but first he had to finish his chores for the landlord. And after he was done, he had to bathe to get all the grime of gardening off him.

As soon as she left, he gardened, bathed, sat at the coffee table, and unfolded the piece of paper. Paree had drawn a plain circle on it, and a story immediately came to him without giving it much thought. The circle meant only one thing. It was the dry well at the northeast corner of the Third Garden. Mama often warned him not to go too near it because he might fall in and never find his way out. So he didn't go *too* near it, only near enough to throw stones into it and listen for how long the stones took to land at the bottom. He never heard them land though, so he thought the well either had no bottom or it was so deep that the stones would take days to land.

His eyes an inch away from the notepad, he wrote:

A little boy stands next to a well. He bends down. He looks down. He trips. He falls and falls and falls. He falls for days. He smacks into water. He can not swim. The water is cold. He is cold. He can not feel his body. He sinks. His feet touch the bottom. He kicks. His head comes out of water. He is inside a cave. The cave is on fire. A beautiful lady floats over him. Her hair is black and shiny. Her eyes are big and brown. She says she will take him home. She says she will be with him forever. A man comes out of the fire. The lady vanishes. The man carries a bottle. His eyes are red. His forehead is red. His eyebrows are red. He laughs but he is angry. He says the boy can not go home. The boy must burn because he is a rotten bastard. The boy floats on the water. He floats away. He sees a hole. It has no fire. It has a light at the end. He goes inside the hole. He crawls to the light. He climbs out. The hole closes. He is in a courtyard. Walls surround the courtyard. The walls are big and high. He can not get out. He sits beside a shed. He waits for the beautiful lady. The lady does not come. The boy is sad. He cries and cries and cries.

Chapter 48

The tale riveted Paree, her eyes filling with tears as the boy waits for the beautiful lady and she doesn't come. Reza was indeed a troubled child, insecure, in fear. Was she, Paree, the beautiful lady who promised him she would be with him forever but deserted him? There was still that distance between them, wasn't there? The distrust that came with Reza's distrust of his former life. If only he would talk about it, reveal the secrets of life with his parents at the Third Garden, and the secrets of the events that ultimately orphaned him.

The next day during lunch break at work, she drove to the nearest police station on *Koocheh* Bandar. The place was dusty and barely furnished, with a row of wooden benches at one end, a kiosk at the other end, and a framed photograph of Prime Minister Mosaddeq hanging lopsidedly on one of the cinderblock walls. The only person in the place was a blue-uniformed, middle-aged man with hedgehog hair and a Hitler-style mustache. He sat behind the kiosk, his eyelids closed, his chin resting on his chest. She rapped her knuckles on the kiosk. The officer startled awake.

"What do you want?" he asked gruffly.

"I need information about the family of my ward, an orphan. His parents were Abbas and Khatimeh Ahmadi. Late last autumn, she shot and killed her husband, and a few days later she died in prison. I'd like to know the details." Paree fumbled in her handbag and retrieved the contract proving her guardianship.

He glanced at it. "We don't give out that kind of information, so why don't you ask the boy?"

"Because he won't talk about it."

"Then why should *I* talk about it?"

"Here's why." She fumbled again in her handbag, took out a ten-toman note, and waved it at him.

His features brightened, and he grinned. "That's not enough for me to dig up confidential information."

She took out another ten-toman note. "Will that be enough?"

"One more should do it."

"Sorry, that's all I have."

"Wait here while I call a friend in Central Records."

After taking the contract, the money, and a notepad, he disappeared behind a metal door to the side of the kiosk. He was back twenty minutes later.

"Here's the story," he said, handing back the contract. "The Ahmadi family lived and worked near Karaj at a fruit and vegetable farm called *Baghah-e Sabz*—Green Gardens. Late one night, Mr. and Mrs. Sahderi, a worker and his wife who lived close by, heard screams coming from the Ahmadi home—nothing more than a shack at the far end of the farm. The screaming wasn't unusual, so they didn't pay any attention until they heard a gunshot. They ran to the shack and found Abbas Ahmadi's dead body with a bullet hole in the forehead. His wife, Khatimeh, was sitting next to him with a gun—a twenty-two gauge rifle as old as Mosaddeq. They took the rifle away from her, and the barrel was still hot. Abbas had obviously beaten her, because there were bruises all over her face and body. She had broken teeth, a broken nose, and a bloody gash on the back of her head. While Mr. Sahderi guarded the wretched woman, his wife ran to the farm owner's home, which wasn't far from the scene. She told him what happened, and he phoned the police, who arrived thirty minutes later. Before they even questioned her, Khatimeh confessed to killing her husband."

Frowning, the officer ran a hand over his hedgehog hair. "Funny how she could have shot her husband while…"

"While what?"

"While he was beating her. I mean, if you're being beaten up, how do you get to a rifle, load it, aim it, and fire it?"

"Maybe she did all that *after* he beat her."

He reflected for a moment. "Maybe, but I'd think with all the beating she took, she wouldn't have been in any shape to… Anyway, as you know, they arrested her and a week later she died in prison."

"Died of what?"

"Pressure on the brain."

"What caused that?"

He glanced at his notepad. "The prison doctor was sure she died because of the aftereffects of a recent head injury. He had examined her the morning after she arrived at the prison. He found a gash in the back of her skull, which he thought was caused by a blow from a blunt object. During the next few days, she must have slowly bled inside her skull on account of that blow. The blood then put pressure on her brain—enough to kill her. It's all written in the doctor's report. If you like, I'll send you a carbon copy for another twenty tomans."

"No, thank you. Where was Reza when the shooting happened?"

"After the incident, Mrs. Sahderi found him lying down beside a creek near the Ahmadi hut."

"Did he say anything?"

"As the police officers were about to put his mother into the patrol car, he turned wild. He started screaming and kicking at them. They held him down and questioned him, but he said he couldn't remember anything. So they left him there with Mrs.

Sahderi and took his mother to jail. Then he stopped speaking. That happens sometimes."

"What does? Not speaking?"

"No, blanking the memory after witnessing a grisly scene, especially if it involves someone near and dear."

She held back a shudder, thanked him for the information, and walked back to her car.

A grisly scene—especially if it involves someone near and dear. A scene like Little John witnessing his best friend's shattered face, severed limb, lifeless body. A scene like Paree witnessing Little John's purple face, grotesquely misshapen neck, body dangling off the end of a rope, twisting slowly in the wind. A scene that she had repressed as best she could, yet it kept popping up in her sleep, during moments of solitude, and with certain triggers that jolted her memory. A piece of rope, a lone chestnut tree, a khaki kitbag, and eyes of despair, as Little John's eyes were before he hanged himself. As Reza's eyes must have been after witnessing the grisly events in the shack, then often staring into nothingness, waging a silent battle to erase the horrific images etched inside them.

Recounting Little John's death to Reza had helped her. While far from curative, the venting had been palliative.

And that was what Reza needed. Palliative care.

Chapter 49

On Friday morning, Paree rose at dawn without disturbing Reza, who was asleep and twitching. She dressed, made a pot of tea, and sat in the living room, thinking about how she should approach him about the tragedy at the Third Garden. Come right out with it and ask pointed questions? Or cast out subtle hints and see how he reacts. Subtlety was the better approach, she decided, subtlety combined with much show of affection.

Her pulse raced at the thought of digging deeply into his soul, helping him fling open the doors and windows to let out all the rancid air polluting his mind. She *must* help him open those doors and windows, otherwise the boy would never experience a decent life. He would never grow up inside the steely shell that his mind had constructed around him, unable to let time progress, let life progress. He would forever remain the little boy in his story, imprisoned within a courtyard surrounded by high walls, waiting for a beautiful lady to rescue him from loneliness and misery.

No point in venturing out of that shell alone into the real world of ogres and fiery caves. No point in doing anything but dreaming of heaven like his orphanage friend, Fereshteh, had done and then willed the dream to come true. Another sad case of battle fatigue. A battle fought in the mind, with a tragic outcome.

Reza wandered in an hour later, rubbing his eyes, yawning. "Good morning, Paree."

"How did you sleep, Reza?"

"I don't remember."

"Any dreams?"

"I don't remember."

"Do you often have dreams and don't remember them?"

"Yes, but…"

"But what?"

"I always know if they were good or bad."

"Which do you have most, good or bad dreams?"

He didn't respond, and she was sure he wouldn't discuss his nightmares, his fears. Not yet.

"Would you like an omelet for breakfast, Reza?"

His expression brightened. "Yes, please."

"Let's eat in the living room for a change."

She prepared two omelets while he washed and dressed. When she brought the tray of omelets and tea into the living room, he was seated on the sofa in front of the coffee table, flicking through the pages of the *Alice in Wonderland* story book. Paree had placed it on the table while he was still asleep, thinking that Alice's adventures would be an appropriate starting point to her incursion into his soul.

She put down the tray, sat next to him, and they consumed their breakfast in silence.

"Do you sometimes wish you could have adventures like Alice?" Paree asked him as he sipped the last of his tea.

"Yes."

"Today is Friday and I have the day off. Why don't we go on an adventure?"

"Where?"

"To where you once adventured. Where you once lived."

He stared at her, that familiar look of fear creeping into his face.

She opened the book to the first page, which displayed a picture of Alice standing before a rabbit hole. "Look, we'll wander about like Alice, and we'll find a little creature hole. We'll imagine we're tiny people who can crawl inside and explore it. Then we'll each make up a story about our adventures."

"I don't want to go."

Paree took the tea glass from him, placed it on the table, and cupped his hands in hers. "Do you know how much you've helped me, Reza?"

"How did I help you?"

"You urged me to visit the place where I once lived."

"Yes, and you cried from the minute we got there, and you didn't stop crying until the rain stopped."

"But you made me talk about Little John and what happened to him. And you know what, Reza? Ever since then, I've felt much better. Thanks to you."

"I'm not going to the gardens."

"You must, Reza."

"What if I don't?"

"I'll be sad and disappointed that you won't let me help you as you helped me."

"So you'll put me in an orphanage?"

She squeezed his hands. "No, no! Never."

"Sad and disappointed," he mumbled. "Sad and disappointed."

He pulled away from her, stood up, walked to the window. He stared out to the street, his body still, hands pressed to his sides, legs and feet squeezed together, as if standing in a tight, enclosed space.

Paree came to him. "If you show me where you lived, next Friday I'll drive you to the mountains and we'll adventure there."

"I don't want to."

Paree was frustrated and a little annoyed at him. Why didn't he yield? Why couldn't he trust her to do the right thing? Maybe the gentle approach had been all wrong.

She stood between him and the window. "All right, Reza. It's obvious you don't trust me or want me to help you feel better. You can go right on being miserable, then."

"I'm not miserable."

She was ready to burst. To shake him back to his senses. Even to slap him and wake him up from the land of nightmares and fantasies in which he lived. *Get the photograph,* a voice inside her head shouted. On the eve of their departure from England, with Mike's permission she had taken the photograph of Little John from the living room mantelpiece and tucked it inside her suitcase—not to display at her apartment, but to keep it close by. To look at it every so often and hold back her tears and feel that she had confronted her sorrow, which might keep on clearing the gruesome images out of her mind's eye and restoring order to her chaotic soul.

And now she would put the photograph to another good use.

She rushed into the bedroom, opened the top dresser drawer, and picked up the rediscovered treasure from under a blouse. When she returned to the living room, Reza was still at the window, hadn't moved since she left him.

She stood before him, holding Little John's image in front of his face. "Do you see how you helped me, Reza? I can now hold my dead son's picture without going to pieces. Believe me, you'll feel the same relief as I did, and the pain will get much less."

After squinting at her for awhile, he took the photograph from her and turned it around. He held it up to her face. "Look at him now, Paree. Let me see you look at him now."

Oh God, please don't let me cry.

Paree stared at Little John's strong features, the proud forehead, square chin with the deep cleft, determined eyes upturned at the outer corners. That was Little John before North

Africa and Tobruk, before witnessing his friend's mutilation. His strength then ebbed and his features grew weaker, at times delicate and sad, at times like a stone sculpture devoid of feeling.

Oh God, please don't let me cry. Think of something quick! Something funny like the time you and Little John watched Mike showing off his canoeing skills.

She caught herself smiling and saw Reza again squinting at her.

"You didn't cry, Paree. You smiled."

"That's right, because now I feel much better about my memories of Little John."

"Tell me about the memories, Paree."

She didn't hesitate. "One time, Little John and I were standing on a riverbank and watching Mike paddle a canoe. The Avon River, I think. He was showing off, trying to impress us how good he was at paddling the flimsy canoe. Then all of a sudden, it tipped over. Mike fell into the river and made a huge splash. Little John and I laughed and laughed until we could hardly breathe."

"Was Mike angry?"

"No, he ended up laughing with us."

"Tell me another memory."

She thought for a moment. "We were having a picnic in the Lake District, a really beautiful part of England. There were many bees around our picnic basket, and Little John and I were worried they'd sting us. Mike told us not to worry. He said bees don't bother you as long as you don't bother them. Little John pointed to a bee buzzing around Mike's nose. Mike looked at it cross-eyed and said, 'Never fear, it won't sting me.' That night, his nose looked like an enormous red light bulb."

Reza giggled. "A red light bulb? That must have been so funny."

"It was hilarious, although Mike didn't think so. He almost stayed away from work the next day because he was so embarrassed."

"Did Little John go to school?"

"Of course he did. Most children in England go to school." She smiled. "Want to hear a funny story about him at school?"

"Yes, please."

"When he was thirteen years old, he found a filthy old cowbell, covered in cow dung. The bell was really loud. He washed it and the next day took it to school with him—that and a spool of cotton thread from my sewing kit. Before his last class of the day, he hung the cowbell off a window and drew the curtain over it—just enough to hide it. When class started, he pulled on the cotton thread, which he had tied to the bell. It clanged loudly, and every so often he clanged it again. No one could figure out what made the noise until the teacher discovered the bell. Then she traced the thread to the spool in Little John's desk."

Reza laughed. "So he was a bit naughty?"

"He was, in a funny sort of way."

"Did the teacher beat him?"

"No. She made him stay after class and write a thousand-word story about a cow and a cowbell."

"Did Mike get angry?"

"Well, he tried, but he couldn't help laughing after I told him what Little John had done. Did your father often get angry at you, Reza?"

"Yes."

"Why did you make him angry?"

"I don't want to talk about it."

"Then let's talk about what made him laugh."

After thinking for a few seconds, Reza grinned. "The owner came to the Third Garden one day to check the fruits and vegetables. He did that once a week, and Baba hated him like he hated all rich people. The owner was standing under a fig tree, and a huge crow was on a branch just over his bald head. The crow plopped droppings all over his head, and he was furious. He ran to the creek to clean himself, but he tripped and fell in. Just as he got out, another crow plopped more droppings on him. He screamed and cursed and got into his car and drove away. Baba and I saw it all, and Baba laughed so hard his face turned purple and he couldn't stop coughing."

Paree laughed too, and then she looked at Reza with pleading eyes. "Will you now please take me to where you lived? We'll talk about funny, happy memories. *Your* funny, happy memories."

He gave her back the photograph. "And you think going there will help me feel…feel a little better?"

"A *lot* better."

"All right, but let's not stay there very long."

Chapter 50

A few kilometers before Karaj, they drove south off the highway onto an unpaved, pitted road. It took them across railroad tracks and into the desert, which was searing hot on that late-September noon, the heat rising from the rocks and sand, distorting whatever lay beyond. After ten minutes of a jarring ride, they approached a clay wall and a barred steel gate with an overhanging sign that read *Baghah-e Sabz*—The Green Gardens.

"This is only *Bagh-e Aval*—the First Garden," Reza said. "We must go around it, past the second garden, and then stop behind the third."

Paree glanced at him. His lips were pursed, his face a sheen of sweat, his knuckles white from gripping the edge of the seat. She drove on past another clay wall and another. The road right-angled at the end of the last wall, and now they were at the rear of the three gardens. After parking the car to the side of a tall wooden gate, she climbed out and walked to the passenger side. Reza was hunched over, eyes closed.

She opened the door, softly grasped his arm, and said, "I'm here for you, Reza-*jan*, don't be afraid."

He stared blankly ahead as she helped him out of the car, steered him to the gate, and tried the handle of the built-in door. It was unlocked. She took his hand and they stepped inside a five-acre oasis of pomegranate and fig trees, fruit and vegetable patches, and a creek of gently flowing waters that meandered down the middle of the gardens. Depending on the direction of the breezes, the air was rife with the odors of jasmine, eucalyptus, or outhouse.

To the immediate right of the gate was a wooden shack, freshly painted green and a rainbow of flowers planted along the base. As Reza stared at the shack, his body trembled, his hands fisted, his eyes telegraphed fear.

Paree draped an arm around his shoulders. "Relax, Reza. We're together."

He didn't respond.

She saw a shirtless young man, gaunt, weather-beaten, digging a trench a few paces from the stream.

She walked up to him. "We're visitors. Do you mind if we admire this beautiful garden for a little while?"

He looked at her and glanced at Reza. "Go ahead, but I don't want to catch you or that boy stealing any of the fruit or vegetables."

"We won't."

She and Reza walked along a footpath that paralleled the creek. He was silent and wasn't trembling as much now. Paree supposed that his initial fear at viewing the scene of tragedy had lessened as they distanced themselves from the shack. They continued on to the other end of the garden. In front of another shack stood a rosy-cheeked, middle-aged woman in a loose gray dress and green headscarf. She was sprinkling a bed of violets.

As Paree and Reza approached, the woman noticed them and her eyes suddenly gaped. "Reza Ahmadi, is that *you*?"

He nodded, smiling faintly.

She put down the watering can and hurried over. "I'm Mariam Sahderi," she said to Paree. "I've known Reza since the day a midwife helped him into this world." She bent down and kissed his cheeks. "You poor boy, how have you been?"

He didn't respond.

"As shy as ever, aren't you? Do you still live at the orphanage?"

"No, *khanom*."

After introducing herself, Paree said to Mariam, "I'm Reza's legal guardian now, and he lives with me. I'm sure he feels much better since he left that place." She glanced at him. "Isn't that right, Reza?"

He nodded.

Mariam folded him into her arms. "You must thank Allah that *khanom* is caring for you, and you must thank *khanom*, too." She released him and turned to Paree. "We heard terrible things about the orphanage."

"And they were probably all true." Resting a hand on Reza's shoulder, Paree asked him, "Would you mind if Mariam and I talk alone for a moment?"

He walked to the flowerbed, picked up the watering can, and resumed Mariam's task of sprinkling the violets.

"Such a helpful boy, Reza is," she said, gazing at him. "He always was and always will be. If only…" She looked into the distance.

"If only what?" Paree asked.

"If only he had had a decent father. His mother was an angel, and heaven knows why she put up with that monster of a husband for so long."

After they talked briefly about Reza's father and about life at the gardens, Paree said, "I understand you were the first to find Reza after the tragedy. Where was he?"

Mariam waved toward the other end of the path. "On a little mound beside the creek to the east of their shack. He was lying there, absolutely still. Not asleep, mind you, because his eyes were wide open. You could say he was in a trance."

"What did you do, once you found him?"

"I held him, stroked his hair, and told him the bad situation was over. He stared at me, as if he didn't know who I was or where he was. Then he suddenly looked terrified and did something really peculiar."

"What?"

"He squeezed his legs together and crossed his hands over his groin. I thought he needed to relieve himself, so I pulled him up and told him to pee. But he didn't."

"Then what happened?"

"He just stood there looking like a frightened little boy in a strange world. Miserable child. I wish I could have done more for him afterwards, but we're poor people and could do little." After a pause, she asked, "Why did you bring him back here?"

Paree explained why, they talked for five more minutes, and she called Reza over. Mariam hugged him and kissed him on both cheeks, told him he was always welcome at the gardens and in their humble home.

Looking at the two of them now, Paree imagined the scene at the creek where Mariam had found him after the shooting. Reza standing there terrified, squeezing his legs together, crossing his hands over his groin. If he didn't need to pee, there was only one other explanation for the posture, Paree thought.

Self protection.

* * * *

As Paree and Reza headed back down the path, she marveled at the desert paradise, hidden and protected behind its clay walls, oblivious to the barrenness beyond and the gruesomely tragic history of its former residents, the Ahmadi family. She waved at the shirtless young man as they walked on toward Reza's former home, the freshly painted green shack. Stopping in front of it, Paree linked arms with Reza.

"Tell me about the good times, Reza."

He said nothing.

"Tell me about your adventures in the Third Garden."

He said nothing.

"What about the creek? Did you wade in it? Splash in it?"

He said nothing.

She led him to the creek and quickly located the mound where Mariam said she had found him after the shooting. Squatting at the edge of the mound, Paree dipped a cupped hand into the creek and splashed the cool water into her face. Then she splashed Reza, who was standing beside her. He didn't move, so she grinned and splashed him again. After hesitating for a moment, he kneeled down and did the same to her, with a faint smile.

She sat, took her shoes off, and dipped her feet in the water. "Ooh that feels so cool, Reza."

He sat next to her and did as she did, his eyes intent on a leaf floating downstream.

She followed his gaze. "Where will that leaf go, Reza?"

"To a lake surrounded by mountains," he mumbled.

"Wouldn't it be fun if we were tiny people and could ride on that leaf and float to wherever it would take us?"

Another faint smile, and he looked at her wide-eyed. "That's funny, I used to imagine that too."

"You and your mama must have spent a lot of time by this creek, just cooling off and letting your imaginations run free."

"Yes, we did. One time, Mama…"

Paree looked at him expectantly, waiting for him to finish the sentence, but he had already drifted off into his inner space, gazing dreamily at the creek. She filled her cupped hands with water and splashed his face again.

Startled, he blinked and turned to her. "Why did you do that, Paree?"

"Because you started daydreaming. What were you about to tell me?"

He wiped the water off his face. "I don't remember."

"You said, 'One time, Mama…'"

"Oh, yes. One time, Mama told me she wished we lived by a lake in the mountains. She would buy us a little boat so we could go paddling and fishing. We'd have a garden by the lake, eat fish and fruits and vegetables, and play in the mountain snow. And we'd never need anything else. Just Mama and me."

Paree hesitated. Perhaps now was the time to probe deeper. "Didn't she want your father with you?"

"No."

"Why not?"

He shrugged.

"Please answer me, Reza."

His brow knitted, he lifted his feet out of the water and studied his wiggling toes. Paree gave him time to gather his thoughts.

After a few moments of silence, she asked him, "It sounds as if Mama didn't like your father. Is that right?"

"I don't think she did."

"Why didn't she like him?"

He gazed at his toes. "Because sometimes he was really mean to us."

"Did you do anything to upset him?"

"No, but Mama once told me when she married him, I was already in her tummy. A tiny seedling."

"And that made your father angry?"

"Mama said he wasn't sure if I was his son, and that made him angry. I asked her why he wasn't sure. She said Baba looked at me when I was born and yelled I didn't look anything like him, so maybe I didn't belong to him." Reza scratched his head, scrunched up his nose. "And right after that, Mama told me she had been with many other men besides Baba. I asked her what that had to with me. She said I was too young to understand. Do *you* know, Paree?"

Paree felt a choking sensation in her throat. "She was telling you that being with a man is how…how a woman becomes a mother."

He squinted at her. "Was *your* mother with many other men besides your father?"

"I don't know. Maybe before they were married."

"What's a *jendeh,* Paree?"

She could feel her eyes growing moist, and she had a good idea where Reza had heard the Farsi vernacular for whore. "Why do you ask, Reza?"

"Baba always called Mama a *jendeh* when he was angry at her. What does it mean?"

"It…it means a woman who goes out with men for money. It's not a word you should ever use, all right?" She wiped off a tear running down her cheek.

"Are you crying?"

"No, just something in my eye," she replied, and her face grew hot.

"What was your father like, Paree?"

"He died when I was very young, so I don't remember much about him. What about *your* father? Was he ever nice to you, even though he wasn't sure you were his son?"

"Baba was sometimes nice, but never on Thursday nights, when he came home from Karaj. And he always came home with…"

"With what?"

"A bottle in his hand."

So that's your fear of bottles. "What did he do to you and Mama on those nights?"

Reza didn't answer.

"Talk to me, Reza."

"I don't want to."

"Remember, we're here to make you feel better."

"I don't want to."

"On the night they took your mama away, Mrs. Sahderi found you here, lying on top of the mound. Do you remember what you did as soon as she woke you up?"

"No."

Paree stood up, crossed her hands over her groin, and pressed her knees together. "That's what you did. Why, Reza? Tell me, and you'll feel much better."

"Why will I feel better?"

She sat back down and nestled against him. "Because you're keeping the secret inside you, Reza. By sharing it with me, you'll let it out and get rid of the shame. Once you do that, you'll understand why you shouldn't have been the one to be ashamed. Maybe it should have been your father."

His head bowed, his lips quivered, his body pressed into her. "That Thursday night, he came home and found me and stared at me with his eyelids halfway down and…"

Chapter 51

As Reza's mind drifted to That Night, the details of how it all began became gradually, painfully clearer. Soon, those details became as clear as that moment, as clear as he was nestled against Paree by the creek of the Third Garden, his head resting on her shoulder.

He was standing on the banks of the creek when the evening started, the last of the sun peeking over the horizon. He watched Baba washing himself with his special soap that he bought in Tehran. No one else was allowed to use it because it was his *own* soap. It smelled of lavender, the same scent the owner's wife had when she came to the monthly feasts at the First Garden. Baba finished washing and drying himself and went into the shack, and Reza followed him in. Mama said to Baba, "I suppose you'll be back as late as you always are on Thursday nights."

"It's none of your business when I get back," he hissed. "This is my night away from you and from this shit hole."

Reza watched him put on his best clothes: a white shirt, gray shalvar, and black belt with a silver buckle. Then sitting on the floor, Baba spat on his black boots and rubbed them with a towel until he got rid of the dust and dirt, until the boots were shiny and the towel was filthy. He put on the boots and stood in front of the round mirror that hung on the wall over his gunnysack, which no one else was allowed to touch because it was his *own* gunnysack.

After spitting on his fingers and twisting up the ends of his mustache, he rummaged about in the sack and removed a white jar. He untwisted the lid, dipped a finger inside, and scooped out a blob of white cream and rubbed the blob all over his head. Using his comb with a few missing teeth, he combed his hair over and over until he was pleased with how it looked, even though a spike of hair stuck out from the back of his head, which he couldn't see and Reza didn't tell him about it because it was Baba's *own* hair.

A horn blasted outside the gate, the ugly sound from the car horn of Baba's friend. Reza recognized it because it sounded like an old man clearing his throat. Baba wiped his fingers on the rug, put the cream jar back into his gunnysack, and walked toward the door. *Khoda-hafez*—goodbye, Mama called after him. He spat on the floor and disappeared. Reza noticed big frown lines now crossing Mama's forehead, and he knew why. She dreaded Baba coming back because it was Thursday evening.

After he left, she and Reza sat on the floor and ate supper. *Ash-e lubia*—bean soup—and naan and slices of cantaloupe. "Let us pray this night is better than the other Thursday nights," Mama said, and Reza understood. He thought she seemed much more worried than on most other Thursday evenings, so he asked her why.

"Because this week, your father kept more money to himself than usual," she replied. "And that means he'll have more *mashroob*—alcohol—to drink than usual."

Soon, her feeling of dread passed on to Reza, and he caught himself frowning and his heart beating faster. "We could walk to the other end of the garden and visit your friend, *Khanom* Sahderi," he said. "And we could stay there until Baba comes back and falls asleep."

"That would be fine, Reza-*jan*, but your father usually comes back very late, and *Khanom* Sahderi goes to bed early. We'll just have to do our very best not to annoy him and to keep out of his way."

After supper, they went for a stroll up and down the Third Garden, and Mama didn't say much. Just held Reza's hand and he noticed hers was cold and clammy. They sat by the creek when they neared the shack again, and it still smelled of Baba's lavender soap. They dipped their feet in the water and Mama said, "I have a feeling something very bad will happen tonight, Reza."

"But doesn't something bad happen *every* Thursday night, Mama?"

"Never mind. Tonight, you'll sleep where you've often slept before, under the moon and stars. When you're ready for bed, we'll take a blanket there, I'll wrap it around you, and I'll kiss the top of your head, the tip of your nose, and your cheeks. Then you'll sleep like a baby."

They returned to the shack and stayed up for a while, and Reza tried to make her feel less worried, but he didn't think he did. He asked her to play hide-the-handkerchief, but she said she didn't feel like it. He talked about his pet, Koocheek the bluebird, and said he thought it had built a nest in the pomegranate tree and maybe soon there would be lots of baby bluebirds because they always come out of eggs in nests. Maybe that was why the bluebird hadn't visited him that evening—it was keeping the eggs warm.

Mama didn't seem to hear him, her eyes looking pained, fixed on the shack door.

Outside grew dark but brightened again as the full moon rose in the eastern sky. Mama picked up the blanket and walked Reza to his open-air sleeping place. Next to the creek and in a clearing of bushes, they stopped at a spot where the dirt was soft but was always dry because it was on higher ground. Mama placed the blanket down and had Reza lie in the middle of it. She wrapped it around him and cuddled him and told him, "I love you so much, *pessar-jan-e man*—my dear son." She paused for a few seconds. "Please remember that for ever and ever," she added as if she were going to a faraway place and never coming back and didn't want him to forget how much she loved him.

Reza asked her, "Are you going to a faraway place and never coming back?" She kissed him like she had told him she would, said *shab-bekheir*—goodnight, and left.

Reza lay awake for a long time, listening to tree branches groaning in the wind, jackals howling behind the walls, and water slapping at the creek's banks. He gazed at the full moon, and it didn't look like a plump, smiling face that a full moon usually looked like. That night, it looked like a frightened face, waiting for Baba to come home, dreading to see him stagger into the gardens and drink out of a bottle and curse his life in a shit hole.

Reza fell asleep and woke up to the sound of bushes rustling next to him. He sat up and saw Baba swaying over him, looking like a glowing monster in the moonlight, a bottle in his hand, a strange look on his face, a weird smile on his wet, glistening lips. And his eyelids halfway down.

He put the bottle on the ground and…

* * * *

Paree sat silently as Reza stopped talking, his gaze held to the distance. Giving him time to sort things out, she watched his expression change from worry to confusion to utter fright.

She laid her hand on his cheek, gently turned his face toward her. "Look at me, Reza. Please tell me what happened when your father found you. Tell me what he did to you."

After a long moment's hesitation, he said, "Baba…he…he put the bottle down and sat next to me and…and his h-hands, they…"

Paree had suspected as much. No need for the lurid details. "His hands fumbled around your private parts, didn't they?"

"Yes."

"And what did *you* do?"

"I screamed for Mama."

"Did she come to your rescue?"

"Yes."

"Then what happened?"

"I don't remember."

"You must try, Reza-*jan*."

"I don't want to."

"You made me tell you the most painful story of my life, Reza-*jan*. Now it's your turn. Try to remember. Try really hard."

His closed his eyes, a stream of tears oozing down from under the lids, his long eyelashes beaded with them. When he opened his eyes again, the faraway look had crept in, and he was silent. Paree wrapped both her arms around him and pulled him into her. They sat there for a few minutes, swaying side to side, rocking back and forth. She kissed him on top of his head, on the tip of his nose, on his cheeks. She squeezed him hard and kissed him again.

"I can imagine what happened when you screamed, Reza," she said in a near whisper. "Mama rushed outside, she and your father got into a terrible argument, and he beat her because he was drunk. Drunk with rage and with lust and with whatever he had drunk out of that bottle. She managed to escape from him, ran into the shack, and picked up the gun. When your father followed her inside, she—"

Reza buried his face in her chest. "That's not what happened."

"Then *you* tell me."

Chapter 52

Relentlessly, That Night's images of the events inside the shack poured into Reza's memory. He tried to stop their flow but couldn't. He tried to blank them out but couldn't. Soon, he found himself watching them as if he were outside looking in, as if he were standing on the banks of a stream and watching leaves float by. His body was one of the leaves.

And as he watched, he came to understand a little more of his nightmares, of his dark thoughts, of himself.

* * * *

Looking like a silver ghost in the moonlight, Mama rushes toward them. For a few heartbeats, she stares at Reza's shalvar. It is drawn down to his knees. She pulls him away from Baba and pulls his shalvar up. Baba sits there, rubbing himself. Mama grips Reza's hand and runs him to the shack. Once they are inside, she closes the door, leans a chair up against the handle. They sit huddled in a corner, and she stares at the ceiling and cries a prayer.

Allah-e Akbar *please, please won't you deliver us from that evil monster?*

Seconds later, Baba crashes the door open. The bottle is in his hand. She jumps up and stands in front of Reza, screams at Baba. *Pedar-sag*—son of a dog! *Khar-e divaneh*—crazy ass! *Borro be jahanam*—go to hell!

He calls her a *jendeh-e kessafat*—filthy whore, and Reza doesn't understand what he means.

Baba steps up to her and raises the bottle. Mama covers the top of her head with her hands. He spins her around and smashes the bottle into the back of her head. She cries out, falls to her knees, and hunches over, looking dizzy as blood flows down her neck and back. Seconds later, she collapses onto the rug. He starts kicking her. Kicking her everywhere. In the face, sides, legs. She doesn't do or say anything, just lies there.

Baba, please stop. Please, stop!

Baba keeps kicking her.

Don't hurt Mama any more. Please don't!

Baba keeps kicking her. His eyes are wild and dancing about, the eye whites bright red. His teeth are bared, foam trickles from a corner of his mouth.

And he keeps kicking her, cursing her.

Reza's mind is a mess, it isn't working right. It just tells him to stop Baba, stop him any way he can. And the only way to stop him is to kill him.

Kill him now, *Reza! Kill him!*

The rifle is leaning against a wall to Reza's right, and he can't reach it from where he sits. Baba uses it to kill birds and creatures of the desert, big or small, ugly or beautiful. He boasts he can kill any creature with that rifle. Even a tiny lizard at a hundred paces. He once showed Reza how to use the weapon, and Reza's mind now screams at him to use it. Quickly, he crawls to the rifle while Baba is hurting Mama and doesn't notice him crawling. Reza picks up the rifle, pulls back the partly open bolt, looks inside the chamber. He can see the silvery end of a bullet's casing. He snaps the bolt into firing position.

Baba startles at the loud snap and spins around. He takes a step toward Reza, his mouth twisted, his eyeballs fire red. *What are you doing, boy?*

Reza stands up, releases the safety catch. *Either you stop hurting Mama or I'll have to shoot.*

Baba's mouth twists more and he advances slowly, holding the bottle over his head, ready to smash Reza like he smashed Mama.

Reza raises the rifle and aims it at Baba's forehead, at the spot where the bushy eyebrows meet in the middle.

You wouldn't dare shoot me, filthy bastard!

Please stop, Baba, and I'll put the gun down.

Give it to me, bastard!

No, I won't.

Give it to me now or I'll hurt you like you've never been hurt before.

I won't give it to you unless you promise not to hurt Mama any more.

Baba is a few paces away now, and Reza's finger caresses the trigger. Baba takes one more step, and Reza squeezes the trigger.

There is a thunderous crack and the rifle's butt slams into Reza's shoulder. It hurts but he doesn't care.

The middle of Baba's forehead spouts blood from a hole in it. He stands dead still, and for a moment he is like a stone statue with a scarlet forehead and scarlet eyebrows. He stares at Reza as if he can't believe the boy shot him.

Sorry, Baba. I'm very, very sorry.

Baba keeps staring at him.

Please forgive me, Baba.

The legs give way and Baba crumples on the torn old rug, now splattered with his blood and Mama's blood. He falls to the side, but his eyes are still fixed on Reza. The eyes do not move, he does not move. And Reza just stands there looking at him, waiting for him to stand up too. But Baba does not move.

Mama crawls to Reza on her hands and knees, kneels at his feet, looks up, face bloody, eyes swollen, nose bent, teeth missing.

What have you done, my child?

He was hurting you, Mama, and I had to stop him.

She stares at Baba, stares for a long time. *Oh my God!* She stares at the rifle, still clutched in Reza's hands. *Forgive us, o merciful God!* She reaches for the muzzle, but he releases the weapon. It crashes to the floor beside her.

Get out, Reza! Get out of this shack now!

But—

Get out!

He runs outside. He hears people shouting. He lies down by the creek and curls into a ball.

And his mind goes blank.

* * * *

The ground is cold, and he knows something terrible has happened but can't remember what. *Khanom* Sahderi is squatting by his side, stroking his head. *Sleep, little boy, sleep. The bad situation is over.* As she keeps stroking his head, he suddenly remembers Baba's hand touching him. He swats her hand away, jumps up, and covers himself. She says something else, but he ignores her.

He looks toward the shack. It seems eerie in the moon glow and the light rays dancing in circles like giant blue moths. Parked in front of the shack is a green and black car with bright headlights and spinning blue lights on the roof. Three policemen are pulling Mama to the car. As they are about to push her inside, Reza shouts *Mama! Mama! Don't let them take you!* She looks at him over her shoulder and smiles even though her face is bloodied, her nose bent, her teeth broken.

You are a wonderful boy, Reza-jan. *Don't ever forget that.* He runs to the policemen and tries to pull Mama away from them, but they shove him into the dirt and shove her into the car.

Mama is gone. Gone forever.

Beyond the Third Garden

Chapter 53

He had not spoken for several minutes, all the while sobbing, squirming, thrashing his arms about. At last, he became still and Paree held him tight, as tight as she had ever held Little John, as if to absorb all his anguish, all his wretchedness.

"Talk to me, Reza-*jan*. Tell me what *really* happened that night."

His face buried in her chest, he blurted the answer in between sobs.

"I killed Baba. Mama didn't do it. She pulled me away from him and took me into the shack, but he came in after us and started hurting her. He hit her with the bottle and he kicked her and he kept kicking her all over the face and the body and he wouldn't stop. I begged him to stop but he didn't, so I picked up his gun and again begged him to stop because he was hurting her and I was afraid she would die. But he didn't stop, so I shot him with his own gun because he was hurting her and I was afraid she would die. I shot him, Paree. I shot him with his own gun."

He sobbed uncontrollably now as Paree swayed him gently in her arms, waiting for him to calm, for the gruesome images to flow out of him and float away down the waters of creek. She could imagine the dreadful scene in that shack, the deranged father out of control, the injured mother unable to protect herself, the desperate son doing whatever it took to stop the horror.

Then the blast of the gun, the death of evil, the birth of guilt.

And when it was all over, the mother took the blame. A noble mother and child, each performing a selfless act.

But at least Reza had confessed the facts of the tragedy, and Paree was certain that he would experience the same amount of relief as she had—with her continuing help and support.

"You did the right thing, Reza-*jan*," she whispered. "Good people always do the right things, and you are good people. Do you hear me Reza-*jan*? You are as good as your mama was."

"I killed…"

"Because you had no other choice. I would have done just as you did. Any good person would have done just as you did."

"I squeezed the trigger and…"

"You rid the world of an evil man."

"I squeezed the trigger and his forehead…"

"The world is a better place without him."

"His eyebrows turned scarlet, and he kept—"

"You are a hero, Reza-*jan*. A hero to me and to anyone who learns of your sad tale."

"And he kept looking at me with the blood pouring out of his forehead. He stood there and kept looking at me. And when he fell to the floor, he kept looking at me."

"Because he finally understood you for the brave, decent boy that you are. Maybe in those last moments of his life, his evil mind wanted you to forgive him for the terrible things he did to you and to your mother."

The waters of the creek rolled by, another leaf floated by. A creature howled from afar, a donkey brayed, and a gust of wind whistled through the trees. She and Reza sat there as one, clutching each other, blending their misery as if the mixture would be milder, more bearable.

"I killed him," he muttered after a long while.

"Because he killed Mama," Paree said.

"He didn't kill her. She died in prison."

"You're wrong, Reza. Do you know why?"

"No."

"The prison doctor said she died because your father smashed her head with a blunt object—probably his bottle. He smashed her so hard that it caused her brain to bleed. The bleeding put pressure on her brain and a week later killed her. So your father murdered Mama."

"How do you know this?"

"I made inquiries, Reza. I made them because I had to know everything that happened to you and your family so I could figure out how to help you."

She leaned back, brushed the hair off Reza's eyes, and took his face between her hands. "*He* killed her, Reza, and *he* was the evil one who caused the tragedy that night. You have nothing to be sorry about. If you hadn't killed him, the authorities would have done it for you. They would have hanged him, which is what he deserved. Don't you understand, Reza-*jan*? Can't you see that you did the right thing?"

He pressed himself into her, and she noticed he wasn't trembling quite as much.

She smiled to herself, because at last she was confident of their relationship. By sharing their stories, their secrets and torments, they had cemented their bond.

They were now inseparable.

Chapter 54

The two letters from Mike arrived on the same day at the same time. Sitting at the coffee table in the apartment living room, Paree opened one of the letters, convinced that it was more of the same. She was right. The opening lines were about how much he missed her, how he wished they were still living together. The bulk of the letter was about how his work was demanding and profits were diminishing and the competition was gaining. As if the opening lines were obligatory words, obligatory pleasantries that civility demanded before the meat of the letter complaining about the mundane struggles of everyday life, which could never match those of the troubled mind.

The second letter, dated a few days after the first, was far more appealing.

Dearest Paree: With all the problems at work that seem unsolvable, I am thinking of retiring in two months. And do what, Mike? *Please join me so that we can enjoy the last and best years of our lives.* I'd love to, Mike, but I'm too busy trying to heal Reza. *You can bring Reza, and I will do my utmost to steer him toward a productive future.* How will you do that? *I will send him to the top schools and have him counseled about whatever ails him.* He doesn't need a counselor, he needs me. *I am sure you are counseling him as best as you can, but a professional would do much better. Please come to me, Paree. I miss you and love you.* I miss you and love you too, Mike, but at this point in my life, Reza must come first.

Reza looked up from his homework spread before him on the floor. "What did Mike write, Paree?"

Absently, she folded the letter back into its envelope. "He's thinking of quitting work and retiring."

"Does he miss you?"

"That too, yes. Meanwhile, get on with your homework. What was wrong with the first sentence of the paragraph?"

He glanced at the notepad and the error-filled paragraph that she had assigned for him to correct. "I don't know, Paree."

"Read it aloud."

"The man walked into a tiny men's store and bought a red tie and suit."

"Adjectives, Reza. Adjectives used in an ambiguous way. A tiny men's store could mean a store for tiny men or a tiny store for men. A red tie and suit could mean both are red or just the tie is red."

"What does ambiguous mean?"

"Not clear, more than one meaning."

"So when you tell me you want to send me to school, are you being ambiguous?"

"What?"

"Do you mean you want me to go away? Or do you want me to learn more stuff?"

She laughed, sat on the floor next to him, and hugged him. "I want you with me, Reza-*jan*, but at the same time I want you to be educated in a proper school."

"Don't you want to be with Mike too?"

"Of course."

"Then you should go to him, Paree."

"Without you? *Never!*"

"You could take me with you—if he wants me."

Stunned, she stared at him. All this time, she had sensed that Reza was more than a little jealous of Mike. Something akin to the

Oedipus complex, which she knew a little about from a long-ago friend who was studying psychology and had lent her one of her textbooks.

Oedipus complex: a child's attraction to the parent of the opposite sex and resentment toward the parent of the same sex.

Now, two months after their visit to the Third Garden, Reza seemed much less neurotic, less troubled. He still had his moments, though. The pained expressions that suddenly appeared for no reason, brief periods when he stared into nothingness, occasional sobs when he slept, fright in his eyes when she mentioned school, which he seemed to equate with orphanages.

"Did you hear me, Paree?"

She refocused. "Are you serious, Reza? Do you *really* want to go to England and live with Mike and me?"

"Yes."

She smiled. "And the three of us will live together happily ever after."

He smiled too. "Surrounded by mountains."

"In a lovely cottage with an enormous fireplace."

"And a garden of flowers and fruits and vegetables in the back."

"A beautiful lake in front."

"Bluebirds in the trees."

"Fishes in the lake."

"Far away from the Third Garden."

"And from the chestnut tree."

"Far, far away."

* * * *

Dear Mike: Your last letter was heartfelt and touched me deeply. I will come with Reza, but am forced to ask you to honor our three wishes. If you can't, I will understand. First, we would like to live by a lake surrounded by mountains—somewhere in Scotland, I should think. Second, there will be no alcohol in our lives. And third, we must adopt Reza as our son.

I miss you too.

Love, Paree.

* * * *

Dear Paree and Reza. Stop. Looking forward to having you both in my life. Stop. Will meet all wishes. Stop. Love, Mike. Stop.

Afterword

February 15, 2011: Scotland.

I gaze at the upside-down images of An Teallach Mountain's snowcapped peaks dancing on the lake waters, beautiful images that have replaced many bad days with good days. Here in the isolation of the Scottish Highlands, I can almost sense Mama, Paree, and Fereshteh's presence, floating about their cherished surroundings, watching over me, comforting me when dark thoughts threaten to invade my peace.

My name is Reza Windom now and I am seventy years old, living alone in a cottage on the shores of Little Loch Broom, the same cottage that Mike bought for the three of us as soon as he retired. Although a little faded and chipped, the sign he painted on the gate still stands: *Welcome to the Gay Paree House.*

He died of a stroke in the spring of 1966, died without knowing that I had shot and killed Baba, because neither Paree nor I told him. It was our big secret, Paree said, and no one must ever know. But now I am driven to tell the world, to vent the rancid air that lingers deep within me. Visions of That Night still appear in my twilights of sleep, but not as often and not as vividly. Baba's face isn't clear any more, just scarlet. Mama's face is the before-That-Night face, beautiful and adoring. Triggers that sprout the horrific images in my waking hours are still there, like guns, police cars, men holding bottles. But now I know they are triggers, so whenever the images stir, I think of good days in the Third Garden and happy times at The Gay Paree House.

Nowadays, the experts would call my problem PTSD. Post-Traumatic Stress Disorder, but I could give a damn what they call it. As far as I'm concerned, it will be with me for as long as I live. Guilt is a part of me, and in a way it is my savior, constantly reminding me that a violent streak lies dormant deep within my soul and I must never arouse it.

Ten winters after Mike's death, on a cold February night, Paree simply petered out and passed away in her sleep. Her last words to me were: "Thanks for everything, Reza-*jan*. Thanks for letting me into your life."

I know I owe Paree many more thanks than she owed me.

As I was growing to adulthood in the cottage, she and I often talked of our horrifying experiences, each treating the other as a counselor, and each benefiting from the other's understanding, empathy. She refused to let Mike send me to any other psychiatrist except Dr. Mary Lawrence, whom we had met during my first trip to Britain and whom we all liked. But Mary lived in Gloucestershire, too far away from us. So Mike said he'd try to find me a psychiatrist in Inverness, the biggest city in the Scottish Highlands. To which Paree said, "No quack in Inverness will ever benefit Reza as much as we will, so you don't need to spend your money. But if you insist on spending it, how about a generous donation to the Scottish Orphans Fund?" So the Scottish Orphans Fund was enriched by three hundred pounds, and I was spared a quack in Inverness.

I often wonder what might have become of me if That Night had not happened. Perhaps I'd be a gardener in *Baghah-e Sabz*. Perhaps a head gardener, blissfully unaware of the world beyond the mud-and-straw walls, going about daily life and watching the plants and vegetables and fruit grow because of my skills, feeling pride in the children of my labor. After a while of pondering the what-might-have-beens though, I realize that as long as Baba, Mama, and I lived together in the shack, there would have been another That Night and I would have ended up at an orphanage with another Fereshteh starving herself into her imaginary heaven.

I still wear the gold—gold-plated, actually—ring Fereshteh gave me just before I escaped from the Agha Mansur Orphanage. It is as thin as a thread now because Paree had it stretched once it became too small for my growing fingers, and much of the gold plating has chipped off. I wear the ring on the fourth finger of my left hand, like a wedding band. When Fereshteh gave it to me, I vowed she would be a part of me forever, and I kept my promise. Her memento will go with me to my grave.

I don't have a partner in life because I live in constant dread of my partner abandoning me. Despite the fantastic home life that Paree and Mike provided, I still suffer from pangs of separation anxiety. Living alone and unattached is all right as long as the mind is occupied, and writing keeps my mind occupied. Thanks to Mike and Paree, I received an excellent education that culminated in a Masters Degree for English literature from the University of Edinburgh.

I chose writing as a career because over the years of living with Paree, she had brainwashed me into believing I have a boundless imagination akin to that of the great classical novelists. Along with Mike, she had managed to dispel my one-time interest in gardening as a profession.

"You're capable of so much more," she kept telling me.

"Bloody waste of a bloody good brain," Mike kept telling me.

To date, I've written twenty-two novels and countless short stories, the characters of which the critics have variously described as grim or woeful or wretched. Bordering on the macabre, one of them wrote. But the critics generally give my work good marks, and the royalties are enough to keep me clothed, fed, and under the cottage's slate roof.

Three days a week, I volunteer at a nursing home in Inverness and perform the same helpful, feel-good duties as Paree performed at the hospital for the poor in Tehran. I spend as much time as possible chatting with the residents, particularly with the hopeless, helpless elderly who have few or no visitors, abandoned by their families and waiting to die. Having experienced in childhood the loneliness that they now must experience in the twilight of their days, I sense that during the special moments we share at the bedside or while strolling about the grounds, my empathy diffuses into them, uplifting their spirits. Uplifting my spirits.

My best friend Briana—she changed it from the Gaelic Brianag—lives in Badrallach, a nearby village where I buy groceries. She's another writer who is as fearful of life partnerships as I am. She visited me late last evening, and for the umpteenth time we reminisced about our pasts, not too different because she is also an orphan. Her parents were killed in a boating accident, which Briana, seven years old at the time, somehow survived to relive the tragedy in recurring nightmares about the scene of devastation—and always wondering if she was responsible. After the accident, she was raised in one insensitive orphanage after another, and on more than one occasion she considered suicide.

As we stood by the lakeshore reminiscing, Briana and I absently clasped hands, a subconscious desire for warmth to pass between us. We stayed that way for a long moment, mesmerized by the moon's reflection that danced a thousand glittering shards over the windblown water. Soon, the tender union of our hands led to more tenderness, and to areas in which both of us must tread carefully. Intimate areas that might lead to commitment, to partnership, and to bitter quarrels that foreshadow the downfall of many a relationship. So per our unspoken agreement, we spent the night together and parted in the morning. It is a weekly, thoroughly enjoyable ritual that brings us a night of intimacy without obligation, without adding to a lifetime of guilt should our relationship sour, which I don't think it ever will.

A lifetime of guilt.

It still haunts me that I was the cause of That Night. I am convinced that had I not been there, Mama and Baba would have survived to old age. No amount of logic, no amount of rationalization will ever rid me of that guilt.

I sit on a foldaway chair at the lakeside, sipping hot cocoa and admiring the sunset behind distant clouds, pondering my next novel, which will be more truth than fiction. More memoir than tale. It will begin at the Third Garden and end here at Little Loch Broom, floating on a leaf over clear water, a bared soul visible to all those who would desire a glimpse of a childhood most extraordinary.

About the Author

Dr. Iraj Sarfeh, M.D.

After devoting thirty years to surgery, all of them at universities, I needed a rest and a change. Practicing medicine was gratifying, but it deprived me of life experiences outside hospitals and clinics and operating rooms. Write, my children said, because you're a great story maker-upper. So I made up stories and published them. The first six were medical fiction, in the thriller or mystery or suspense genre with emphasis on surgeons whose characters are shaped by their profession. The next two, which are yet to be published, are of the literary fiction genre, stories in which I drew on my experiences as not only a surgeon, but as a person from Iran who lived away from home most of his life and who as a youngster suffered the barbs of prejudice. Connect with Jim at his website: http://www.ijsarfeh.com/

Tell-Tale Publishing would like to thank you for your purchase. As an added bonus, please accept a sample chapter from 'From the Ashes of Strife', also by Iraj Sarfeh. If you would like to read more by this or other fine TT authors, please visit our website:

http://www.tell-talepublishing.com

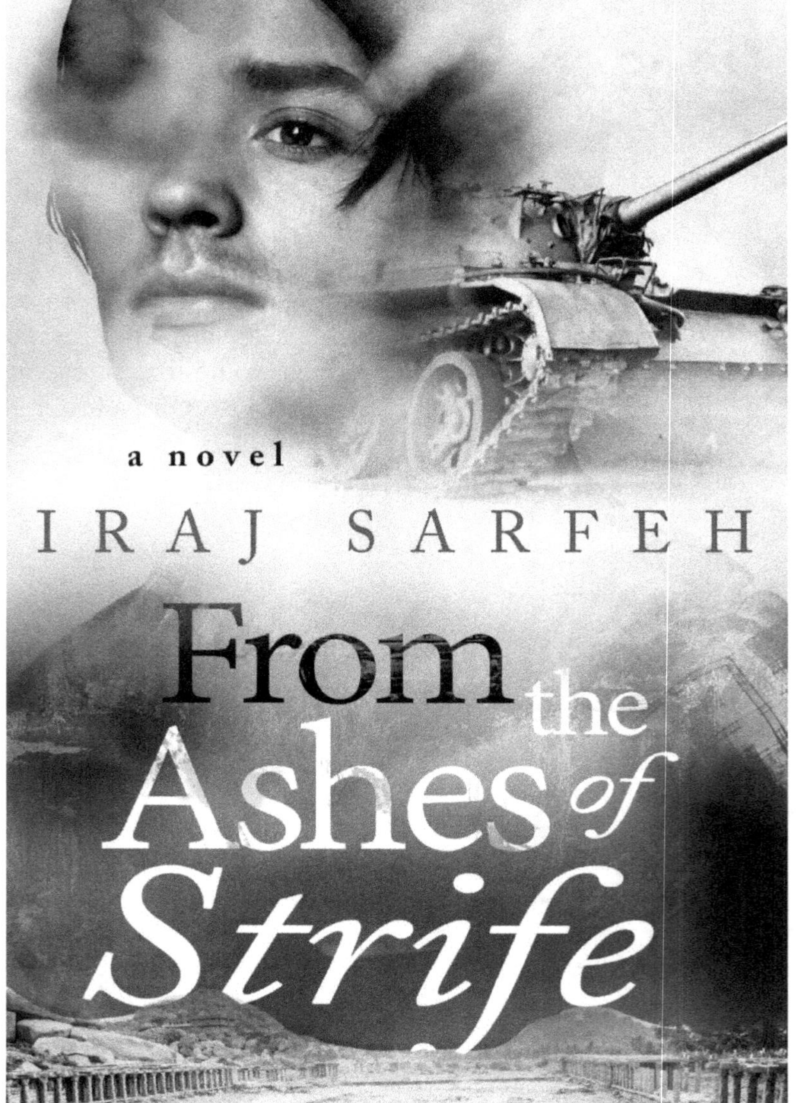
a novel
IRAJ SARFEH
From
the
Ashes of
Strife

From the Ashes of Strife

© 2015 From the Ashes of Strife, 2nd Edition

Swartz Creek, MI 48473

Cover design by Clarissa Yeo

Previously published by Musa Publishing, 2014.

Printed in United States of America

Deja Vu Imprint of TT

Praise for From the Ashes of Strife

Author Sarfeh has turned his formidable storytelling skills and many of his own experiences loose upon a riveting story of change, adaptation and eventual redemption. I will always find a special, enduring place in my memory for many of the memorable scenes in this novel. A young Iranian boy is torn from the secure home he knows into America, a place "Where everyone isn't angry all the time." His fight to adapt and thrive in a society he often finds hard to understand, is touching and educational, too. Often at odds with his father's military career mindset, the young man struggles to find his own way in a new world that will allow him to strive but also allow him to fail. The novel also explores the personal side of how the revolution in Iran dealt a heavy, cruel hand to an ancient, hospitable culture -- a culture that survives despite impossible conditions. Persian roots run very deep and very strong.

Sohrab is the ultimate outsider: turned away from his homeland, alienated from his own family, and not always at home in his new life. The author's use of shifting character points of view in alternating chapters, between the young man and from an observer following Sohrab's father's own turmoil and hidden demons, made it easy to absorb the feelings and motivations of both characters. The two are paired with ancient Persian stories of their namesakes. As the young man grows to adulthood and finds his calling, so does the battle-hardened soldier, in a uniquely Sarfeh-styled twist. In some ways, the characters in this book are tossed, incompletely prepared, into a maelstrom of conflicts that they all manage to muddle through. Fate is either kind, or it has a sense of humor. I found a close, personal connection with a young man, determined to prove nothing to no one, who finds that the pathway of mediocrity is not suitable for him. Just like his father always said. Loyalty can take many forms. Read this engaging story yourself and see if you don't end up cheering for everyone.

--Richard Sutton, Amazon Vine Voice

Foreword

I pledge allegiance to no flag, no nation, and no religion. Henceforth, my allegiance is to humanity.

Those are the final words of the last tea-stained page of Father's handwritten memoirs. They complete our story, which until now was a hodgepodge of mosaic pieces, without pattern or meaning. They tell much about Father, and therefore much about me. They tell of his strife-filled life, of the years spent in prison and mourning the decline of his cherished homeland, Iran.

And they tell of his feelings, conveyed in deeds and in words. The years of solitary confinement changed him. And as he changed, I changed. We traveled a circle in opposite directions, but we ended at the same place. Along the way, we encountered numerous obstacles forcing us onto detours—treacherous detours that in the end heightened the joy of our reunion.

Missing from the memoirs is an account of Father's seminal detour, one that he grudgingly related in his later years. It must have been too painful for him to commit to paper, except the single page with a heading and an unfinished sentence:

Tabriz, July 13, 1964:

Through the sheets of rain, I glimpsed the evil that…

CHAPTER 1

From the balcony, I couldn't see the pavement for the tops of heads. Most were covered with cloth—some white, some green, many red. Mother said white was for peace, green for Islam, red for anger. Between the heads, a forest of fists pumped in rhythm to shouts of *"Marg bar Shah!"* Death to the King! Throughout the month of June 1978, I had heard the same shouts almost every day on our street—angry shouts, frightening me.

That afternoon, a mullah in a black robe and turban led the mob. He stood on a wooden crate across the street, every so often flapping his arms like a raven about to fly, urging his followers to kill the Shah and anyone who opposed Islamic rule.

A soldier in fatigues strolled among the crowd, a rifle slung over his shoulder. When he was a few paces in front of the mullah, he stopped, slipped off the rifle, and held it across his chest, stroking the stock as if it were his cat. He fixed his black eyes on the mullah—steady, cruel eyes, as those of a hawk. Held under the mullah's spell, the people seemed oblivious to the menace of the soldier and his weapon.

Mother gripped my hand. "Let's go inside, Sohrab. I think something terrible is about to happen."

Glued to the unfolding scene, I stood motionless.

The soldier raised his rifle, and the mob didn't notice. He aimed it at the mullah's skull, and the mob didn't notice. Mother screamed, and the mob didn't notice.

The soldier fired his weapon. The mullah's forehead shattered. Blood gushed.

The crowd scattered as the body crumpled to the ground, eyes frozen wide in surprise and still as a pair of dead beetles. A yellow dog trotted over and licked the blood. The soldier grinned.

I felt dizzy, and everything went blank until I woke up in bed. Mother stood over me, damping my face with a cool washcloth. She said I fainted.

* * * *

We lived a kilometer south of the Shah's palace on *Koocheh* Kasram, a street with enormous houses surrounded by twelve foot tall brick walls. Ali, our housekeeper, said the mullahs often chose our street to hold demonstrations because many of the homeowners were the Shah's rich and powerful friends. He said being rich and powerful in Iran during those troubled times was a curse, which worried me because Father was rich and powerful.

Mother and I didn't watch the next afternoon's demonstrations. We never wanted to see another one. Sitting on the double swing chair at the terrace, we sipped watermelon juice as Ali swept the cement footpath. I loved racing my bicycle along that path, which snaked around the apple trees, privet hedges, reflecting pool, and under a wooden trellis covered with grape vines. It ended near the far end of the garden at Ali's wooden hut, where he and I read comic books and built model airplanes, and where he mouthed his *namaz*—prayers—while kneeling before the Koran.

The noise from the street grew louder. Ali disappeared inside his hut, came out a moment later, and ran to the terrace. He carried Father's pistol, black and as big as his forearm. "The general lent this to me in case of trouble, *Khanom* Vessali," he said to Mother.

The demonstrators wailed for the dead mullah as they smacked chains against their backs—a Moslem ritual of mourning, which Ali said was foolish because he didn't think Allah wanted mourners to harm themselves. Soon, the wails turned to shrieks and the mob wanted revenge. Three men wearing red bandanas scaled our brick wall. Waving a stiletto, one of them shouted at us. I couldn't hear the words, but he looked and sounded furious.

A gun blasted. On the wall below the three men, a puff of dust and debris burst into the air. The men vanished.

I looked at Ali. Grimfaced, he held Father's pistol in a trembling hand, smoke oozing out of the weapon's nozzle. Mother pulled me into her, smiled, and told me everything would be all right. Her eyes gaped; her body shook.

Seconds later, a jagged stone flew out of nowhere and hit Ali in the forehead. He fell to the ground as blood flowed from the gash. My stomach churned, my mouth filled with a sour fluid, and I wished the crimson would stop flowing out of Ali's head so he wouldn't die like the mullah. Mother pushed me down and knelt next to him. She told me to remove my T-shirt. I quickly did so, and she took it from me. After rolling it into a tight bundle, she put it over his wound and pressed hard.

"Will he get well, Mama?"

She nodded, and the blood stopped flowing. Before marrying Father, she was a nurse and could take care of our various ailments and injuries.

Ali was my best friend, a *real* friend who also treated me as his son, praising me, playing children's games with me, scolding me when I needed scolding. He had curly dark brown hair, and pockmarks covered his face. One time I made fun of them. Mother heard me, and she told me never to make fun of people's looks. She said Ali had a serious childhood illness that scarred him for life. Was that something to joke about?

Ali helped me build stuff, like the snowman we made two winters before. He stuck a potato in the middle of the snowman's face, broke two teeth from his black comb, and pierced them partway into the end of the potato. Grinning, he said, *"Moo-eh damagh."* Nose hair. We laughed and laughed until we could hardly breathe.

For *NowRuz*—New Year—he bought me a model airplane kit, a World War II Spitfire. It was missing a propeller. He wanted to exchange the kit for another, but I asked him not to. In our garage, I broke off a piece of wood from a crate of oil tins. Using his pocketknife, I carved out a propeller. Then I sandpapered it and painted it with the silver enamel that came with the airplane kit. When Ali saw what I had done, he put an arm around my shoulders and told me how clever I was with my hands. He said our hands are wonderful gifts from Allah. They can make things, and they can mend things. They can also destroy things.

* * * *

Outside was dark now, and *Koocheh* Kasram was deserted.

Mother tucked me in my rooftop bed and pulled the mosquito net over it. *"Shab bekheir,* Sohrab-*jan."* Goodnight, dear Sohrab.

Sleep was impossible because of the earlier excitement and because my trembling just wouldn't stop. Almost everyone at home was afraid. Mother, Ali, the cook. The gardener hadn't come that whole month. He said he quit because our neighborhood was no longer safe and belonged to angry mobs.

I wished Father were home because he never seemed afraid. Mother said he was the bravest, strongest, most fearless person she had ever known.

I crept to the edge of the roof and squinted below at the neighbors' terrace. Often at night, they sat at a bamboo table with a lit candle on top. Looking like two flickering ghosts, they listened to soft western music and sipped tea. Sometimes they stood and held each other tight and swayed with the music. But that night the terrace was dark, quiet.

I tiptoed downstairs into our living room. Mother lay on one of the four sofas arranged about an old oak chest. Like a waterfall, her black hair flowed over the edge of the sofa and touched the floor. She seemed dazed and didn't notice me.

I sat on the floor and stroked her hair. It was soft and smooth and warmed me all over.

"Aren't you feeling well, Mama?"

Startled, she sat up and looked at me through red-rimmed eyes. "I'm fine thank you. Why are you out of bed, my son?"

"Where is Baba?"

"Your father is still at the palace."

"Will they kill him?"

Mother slid off the sofa, pulled me into her, and squeezed me hard. "That was a terrible thing to ask, Sohrab. You must get rid of such awful thoughts."

"But Ali says the people want to kill all the Shah's friends."

"Don't worry yourself. Ali repeats gossip he hears on the streets, and most of the time it proves untrue."

"You promise Baba will be safe?"

"He knows how to defend himself."

"I wish he'd come with us."

"He will, if things don't improve here."

"But what if they improve?"

"We'll return and join him, of course."

"I don't want to come back, Mama."

"Why not, Sohrab-*jan*?"

"Ali says Iran is a bad country now."

"Think of our vacations at the Caspian Sea. Those will remind you how nice Iran was, and how nice it will be again."

The Caspian seaside was my favorite place. When I was four years old, Father bought us a cottage nestled in a small forest of plane trees along an isolated part of the shore. Ali and the cook always came with us when we stayed at the cottage. In the evenings, Father walked me along the beach and talked of brave warriors who had fought and died defending our land against invaders from across the sea. I was amazed that he only knew stories about warriors and invaders and death. Nothing like Mother's stories about princesses and puppies and life.

Ali and I often went on adventures in the forest. While we roamed about, he told me tales about Tarzan and the jungle where the apes raised him. Before becoming our housekeeper and my best friend, he had learned all about Tarzan from a picture book he found in a trashcan. I wondered what it would be like to grow up as Tarzan did. No school or homework. No angry mobs. No one telling me that someday I must become a famous soldier like my father, General Rostam Vessali, which seemed unlikely since I had never felt brave, strong, or fearless. At school one day, the biology teacher said a person's traits are inherited from the parents, so I thought most of my traits must have come from Mother: her hazel eyes, high cheekbones, slight build, and her anything-but-soldierly disposition. I had none of Father's fearsome traits: his Frankenstein size, stick-out brow, and anything-but-gentle disposition.

Mother ruffled my hair. "Now run off to bed, Sohrab-*jan*."

"But I want to stay with you, Mama."

"No. You must rest. Tomorrow our long journey begins."